THIRD ROCK FROM THE COWBOY

ROCKY ROAD RANCH
BOOK 4

LEXI POST

ACKNOWLEDGMENTS

For my husband, Bob Fabich, who told me about the ancient astronaut theory. I love that he is always open to possibilities.

Thank you to my sister, Paige Wood, for always pointing out the visual improvements needed in my writing. I love having an artist in the family!

I must say a special thank you to Tracy and Jason Warner for sharing their story about their dog Lola's tangle with a skunk...twice! I hope things are smelling much better now.

I'm so grateful to my Lexi's Legends for all their help with this book, especially Denise Hachicho, Patrica Way, Teresa Christianson, Teresa Fordice, Lenna Hendershott, Beverly Blank, Eileen McCall, Chris Jones, Marcia Bucktin, Roslynn Ernst, Rachael Bromley, Norah Warnock, Beckie Lowe, Deb Diem, Bette Read, Emily Kirkpatrick, Amy Hallmark, Katherine Horvath, and Beth Cotter.

Thank you as always to my loyal critique partner, Maire Patrick, who helps make my stories readable, and keeps in mind our wonderful editor Jill Stadler and our amazing publisher Tanya Anne Crosby, as she reads through my work in progress. I couldn't do it without her or them.

This story was inspired by a very old Greek play by Aristophanes titled *The Birds*. This play is a comedy where two older Athenians, tired of the constant bickering society of Athens, set out to find a better place to live. When they startle an enormous bird who accuses them of trying to capture him, they quickly tell him of their true quest. The bird fetches his master, a former king turned bird. The two Athenians convince the king and the birds from all over that they should build a city in the sky, rule over mankind, and oust the Olympian gods. There is much tomfoolery as this great project ensues, with many conniving Athenians wishing to take part, but all are sent away by the two main characters. In the end, not only is the great bird city built, but with the foreknowledge of Prometheus, the two Athenians receive the scepter of Zeus as his symbol of acceptance of their new leadership.

Though a comedy, there is much behind this play. Is there a better life than what humankind knows, and are there beings with far superior abilities? If there are such alien entities, could humankind change and adapt to their presence?

So if a cowboy, completely content in his own little town,

were to meet a woman who has traveled the world searching for proof that such entities exist beyond Earth, could he be open to both the concept and her? Is adaptation possible for him? And is she so alien to his world that assimilation is impossible? Are they doomed to exist forever in their separate worlds? Perhaps a great discovery will be the answer...one way or the other.

Reminder: This is a work of fiction. Though there are four mountains in Arizona called the Four Peaks, the town of Four Peaks doesn't exist, and therefore, the petroglyphs and other discoveries in this story are nothing more than the product of my overactive imagination.

CHAPTER 1

SILVER COLLINS, Ph.D., pulled on the reins as she'd been taught when their guide halted. Up ahead, there was a bit of commotion caused by what was clearly a bull and two cowboys. She didn't know anything about cows, or horses for that matter, but she was pretty sure the bull was not happy.

The larger of the two cowboys yelled something to the other before jumping down from his horse and opening a gate, which led out onto the ATV road where she and her colleagues were stopped. Immediately, the bull ran through, happy to escape. From her vantage point, she could see another bull head for the open gate too, or was its goal the cowboy? Unable to keep quiet, she yelled. "Watch out!"

The cowboy's head turned toward her, which was not what she'd intended. Luckily, he was quick on his feet, and he jumped onto the fence as the bull barreled over the spot where he'd stood.

Their riding teacher, a cowgirl named Vic, who was very petite but very knowledgeable, turned her horse around and scowled at her. "Never yell at a cowhand while he's working. You could get him killed."

Amber piped up next to her. "But if she hadn't yelled, he would've been hurt."

She and Jade loved how loyal Amber was to their team. They could always count on her.

Vic shook her head at all three of them, her black ponytail swishing while her hard blue gaze bored into them. "No. The shout drowned out the noise of the approaching hooves. It's a good thing Layne is still so quick, or you'd all be going home."

"Why would we go home?" Jade, the third of their research party asked before Silver could. Jade's mind was quick, plus she was a speed reader, which benefited them all.

Vic's nose twitched. "Because, ladies, Layne is going to be your guide for the rest of the month, and if he had been hurt, you'd have to leave."

Jade, as usual, didn't let it go. "I'm sure someone else could guide us."

Vic shook her head, and it looked as if she fought to keep from smiling. "Nope. No one else is available. You get the oldest ranch hand, who is not only a confirmed bachelor, but the ranch's foreman."

Even as they digested the new information, Silver eyed the first bull moving toward them, picking up his pace. She kept her mouth shut, hoping someone would notice because Vic's back was to the approaching animal.

When her horse Chestnut started to step to the side, she tried to control it, but Jade's horse backed into hers, and suddenly her seat started to tilt as Chestnut reared, neighing his displeasure. She dropped the reins and grabbed him about the neck, squeezing her knees as best she could to stay on, her own voice buried somewhere in the pit of her stomach.

Just as the animal came down, and she thought the worst was over, he took off in the opposite direction.

Shit. Without the reins, she could only hold on as Chestnut raced down the dirt lane.

A male shout sounded behind her, but she didn't dare look over her shoulder. What if her horse stepped in a divot and broke its leg or ran into a snake? Even as all kinds of worst-case scenarios ran through her mind, she heard hooves behind her. *Please don't let that be the bull. Please don't let it gore my horse. Please don't—*

"Grab the reins and pull!"

The shout not far behind her startled her, and she opened her eyes. When had she closed them? What she saw froze her in an instant. Chestnut was headed straight for the high fencing where the ATV road curved.

She was going to die.

Something brushed against her left leg before a shadow blocked the sun and her horse suddenly turned to the right, missing the fence and finally slowing. Still holding Chestnut's neck, she looked over at the man who had saved her life, and gratefulness filled her.

He wasn't just her hero. He was drop-dead gorgeous, at least in her opinion. He was a tall man, probably in his mid to late thirties, with broad shoulders, who sat his horse as if born to it. His black hair was long for a cowboy, just brushing the collar of his fleece-lined jean jacket. He had a bushy black mustache that she found oddly attractive, maybe because he had such a strong chin, and his eyes were intense, though shadowed as they were by his white cowboy hat. How did he manage to keep it on when her own hat was in the dust somewhere?

"Shit! Why didn't you pull on the reins?" He lifted her reins still in his hand.

His tone had her back stiffening, all gratefulness vanishing in an instant. Just what she needed—another man yelling at her.

Why did men think that was the best way to get women to understand them? "In case you hadn't noticed, I was busy trying not to fall off my horse and break my neck or get trampled by your angry bull." At her mention of the bull, she whipped her head around to look back the way they'd come and could see both Jade and Amber far from each other and the second bull between them. But each had a cowhand by their side. She turned toward her cowhand. "Where's the bull that came at me?"

He pointed ahead of them. "Old Glory's not stupid enough to run into a fence like Chestnut here." He held the reins of her horse out to her.

Reluctantly, she took them, not sure even where to go now, with a bull in front of her and another behind her.

The cowboy next to her turned his horse around, his back to Old Glory. "Vic, you and Nash get Hothead back inside the fence! Send the ladies down here!"

"Um, is that such a good idea?"

The man expertly backed his horse up a few feet to face her. "Miss..." He waited for her to fill in the blank.

"Silver Collins."

He lifted his hat and smiled at her. "Miss Silver, I'm Layne Dawson, head ranch hand of the Rocky Road Ranch. You can rest assured that I know what I'm doing."

His smile had her forgetting her objections completely. How did a man go from angry to charming in mere seconds? He was the one who would be their guide. That meant he was the one who had insisted they learn the basics of riding before starting their research. Jade had not been happy with that news when they'd arrived.

Silver, though, could appreciate it now.

"Silver, are you okay?" Amber rode up from behind her, but despite the concern in her voice, her gaze was focused on Layne Dawson.

That was so Amber, to be distracted by a handsome man, except when at a site. "I'm fine. Mr. Dawson kept Chestnut from running into the fence."

"Oh, then, Mr. Dawson, I must thank you for saving an important member of our team." Amber flipped her blonde hair over her shoulder, dislodging her cowboy hat. "Oops." She grabbed it before it fell.

Silver barely kept from rolling her eyes. Amber was an incurable flirt.

"Just part of my job, miss." The man lifted his hat an inch from his head and then set it back down. "I'm Layne Dawson, and I'll be your guide starting tomorrow."

"Now that's great news. It's a pleasure to meet you, Mr. Dawson. I'm Amber Morris. Please call me Amber. I'm the archeologist. I get to play in the dirt." She grinned.

Before Layne could respond, Jade rode up, obviously not happy. "I certainly hope the rest of our stay won't be so eventful. Silver, are you okay?" Jade's gaze swept over her thoroughly.

"Yes, I'm fine."

Amber piped in. "Mr. Layne Dawson here saved her. Wasn't that heroic?"

Silver stifled a groan, knowing exactly how Jade would react to that bit of news.

"Heroic?" Jade's voice rose. "To let two bulls out, who obviously despise each other, onto a road where three inexperienced riders are, is not how I define *heroic*."

Instead of taking umbrage at Jade's sharp tone, the cowboy somehow looked humble. "My pardon, miss. I was stopping a stampede from coming out onto the road, which I assure you would have been much more 'eventful.' My plan was to only allow one bull out so the herd would calm, but the second slipped past me before I could close the gate. I assure you, such an event will not happen again."

Jade knew, as they all did, the reason the second bull got out was because Silver had yelled. That he hadn't mentioned that particular point wasn't lost on their researcher. "Yes, well, I appreciate your assurance. I imagine dealing with two bulls is better than a herd of cattle. I do understand that they are much like lemmings, so I can appreciate your efforts. I'm Jade Lawerence, the researcher in our group. I have a bachelor's degree in history and a master's degree in library science with a specialization in ancient texts."

It was so like Jade to give her resume at the outset. Silver gave Layne another look as he smiled at her colleague. She'd never seen anyone, never mind a man, diffuse Jade's irritation so quickly. He must be part magician.

As if he felt her studying him, he turned toward her. "What is your job on the team?"

"I'm the anthropologist. I study human societies and cultures through time."

Layne's brows rose. "I imagine there are a lot of similarities from back then until now. After all, we're all human."

Amber nudged her horse forward a few steps before it balked at being so close to Layne's. "Maybe, maybe not. Silver is being humble. She's our resident ancient-astronaut theorist! You must have seen the documentaries, talk shows, articles? They're even talking about a movie. I can't decide who should play me."

But Layne had already moved his gaze back to Silver. "I haven't seen anything on ancient-astronaut theory. They don't play a lot of that on the television at The Stampede."

At least he hadn't made fun of the theory. She'd give him that.

"Stampede?" Jade lifted one sculpted eyebrow. "Is that a corral of some kind?"

Layne chuckled. "In a way." He moved his attention to Jade. "If corralling a bunch of cowboys around pool tables counts, though I believe that would be closer to a stockyard." He grinned, obviously enjoying the banter.

Hooves thundering behind her had them all turning to find Vic galloping toward them. Silver wasn't quite sure how the woman did it, but she managed to stop her horse between Amber and Layne. "Hothead is halfway to the south enclosure. Nash went after him. You want me to go with him, and you take the ladies back to the square?"

His charming demeanor changed in an instant, and he was all business...cowboy business. "No, you continue getting this team ready for tomorrow. I need to round up Old Glory. I'm sure he's headed toward the horse barn. Damn bull thinks he's a stud." He turned toward the three of them and lifted the front of his hat again. "Ladies, I will see you tomorrow."

Amber opened her mouth to speak, but Layne turned his horse on a dime and galloped away.

Silver watched him for a moment, not sure how she felt about him being their guide for the rest of the month.

"Silver, are you okay?"

She turned her head back toward Vic. "Yeah. I did everything you told us to do. I held Chestnut tight with my knees and grabbed hold of him, but he took off anyway."

Vic studied her for a moment. "You closed your eyes, didn't you?"

Surprised the woman had figured that out so fast, she nodded. "I didn't realize I had until I opened them, and then wished I hadn't."

Vic nodded. "You did good for your first runaway horse. My first one landed my backside in a pile of dirt, so pat yourself on the back." She addressed Jade and Amber. "Since Hothead headed west, we'll head east toward the new fences being put in. We've got a pretty good ATV road down there now, and I want to see you gallop."

"You mean my uncontrolled race after an old bull doesn't count?" She grimaced.

Vic smirked and shook her head. "Nope. It's the 'uncontrolled' part that doesn't work. You need to be in control of your mount at all times. As soon as your horse knows it has the lead, you could end up anywhere."

"Are you saying that if I'd been able to keep the reins while Chestnut reared, I could have kept her from running?"

Vic didn't answer immediately. "As a new rider, you could have slowed her down sooner. I did have to cut Hothead off from chasing Old Glory, which your horse didn't stay around long enough to see."

She didn't even want to know how Vic managed to turn around a charging bull.

"Come on, ladies. I want to be sure you know what you're doing before handing you over to Layne."

"Then we can hit the hot tub?" Amber put her hands together as if praying.

"Sure." Vic turned her horse eastward and set the pace at a walk.

Silver would rather go straight to the hot tub. She had a feeling she would be more sore tomorrow, but she'd be damned if she'd say anything. Hopefully, Layne would take it easy on them their first day.

After Amber and Jade brought their horses into single file behind Vic, she clicked her tongue to get Chestnut to follow. The horse acted as if nothing had occurred, though it had come seconds from getting caught up in a fence. She wished she had such a short memory. Unfortunately, her memory was stellar, photographic even. It came in very handy when studying petroglyphs and artifacts, but not so great when there was an episode in her life she wanted to forget, which included every interaction with her boss, Benedict Nagle.

She looked longingly at the hot tub next to the clubhouse of the Rocky Road dude ranch as they rode behind it, before they passed the fenced-in area behind the owners' house. She really shouldn't complain. That there even was a hot tub was a treat. They'd had much worse accommodations at other sites, since Benedict didn't like spending even one dime more than needed. The sleeping arrangements in Brazil had left a lot to be desired, and yet the ones in Portugal were rather lavish. The Rocky Road was definitely one of the better places.

Jade looked over her shoulder. "Come on, Silver. The sooner we get this done, the sooner we can get to the site."

"Right." And the sooner she could sink into that warm hot tub.

For the next two hours, Vic put them through their paces. Silver knew nothing they did was particularly skilled. As the cowgirl had said the day they arrived, she was just tasked with keeping them from breaking their necks. Did that mean Layne was going to expect them all to be experts? He'd expected her to reach down and grab her loose reins while racing toward a fence.

Even as she thought about his expectation, she bristled. Maybe if they showed they knew what they were doing, he wouldn't have to accompany them every day. She certainly wasn't excited to have him around. Or maybe Amber making googly eyes at him would keep him distracted from criticizing their riding technique.

Finally, they all rode back into the parking area in front of the Rocky Road ranch house, a sprawling adobe structure that looked as if it could withstand a tornado.

"Okay, ladies. You're free to go. Dinner's at six. Don't be late." Vic finished tying the reins of her horse Faithful to the corral fence before taking the reins from Jade and Amber. "Silver, just tie Chestnut up. I'll bring him in next."

She dismounted and secured Chestnut as Vic had taught them, and followed Jade and Amber toward the two-story log structure that was their home for the month. Maybe she'd get lucky and the petroglyphs they'd seen posted on social media were all there was, and they'd be onto their next site sooner rather than later. She'd prefer a short stay with Layne, their guide.

Amber sat on one of the couches in the open main room and started pulling off her cowboy boots. "I can't wait to get in that hot tub. My feet hurt."

Jade didn't resist the chance to chastise. "I told you not to buy new boots just to fit in. We're not here on vacation."

Silver walked into her room grinning. Amber and Jade never changed, and she appreciated that. Since they traveled so much and their living conditions always changed, it was nice to have one constant in her life. After changing into a black tank and bikini bottoms, she slipped back into her jeans, sweatshirt, and eschewed her old Chelsea boots for her tennis shoes. There may be a hot tub, but getting to it meant braving 40-degree temps. She grabbed a towel from her bathroom and walked back into the empty main room.

"You guys are slow."

Amber flip-flopped her way out of her bedroom wearing her bikini and a wrap about her hips. "Not that slow."

"You do know it's 42 degrees out there."

She pulled her parka off a hook by the door. "That's what this is for."

"Okay, I'm ready." Jade came out wearing the same sweater, jeans, and boots she'd had on earlier, her one-piece completely hidden.

After Silver and Jade grabbed their coats, they followed Amber to the pool and hot tub. Amber always scoped out the facilities even before unpacking. Within minutes they had undressed, their clothes piled on separate lounge chairs and they were sitting in the hot water.

"Oh, this feels so good on my feet."

Before Jade could scold again, Silver refocused her. "I hope there are artifacts around that rock or we may not be here long." She still searched for that one history-changing discovery, and the Rocky Road Ranch would be a pleasant place to make it, even if she wasn't sure about Layne. Their hostess, Amanda Dunn, was very accommodating and thrilled to have them.

"That would be a shame. I like this place. Have you noticed how good-looking all these cowboys are, especially Layne? And did you see the green eyes on Nash? Vic told me they are the only two single ranch hands, but that there are quite a few others in town, including all of Amanda's brothers." Amber wiggled her eyebrows.

Jade shook her head. "I doubt we'll get to town much, considering we don't have a car, and when I spoke to Amanda, she said Four Peaks doesn't have any private car services. Everyone around here relies on each other."

Silver swished her arms through the hot water. "I'm sure the ranch will get us into town when we need to go."

Jade shrugged, since she tended to prefer to order supplies she might need online. "I'm impressed with their Wi-Fi service. Remember when we were in the Andes and we couldn't get any Wi-Fi service at that boutique hotel halfway up the mountain?" Jade shook her head as if those were the worst accommodations they'd ever had.

"Yes, but Vic told me cell service is nonexistent on the mountains." She found it odd that with so many mountains, the conservation board hadn't approved at least one tower. Then again, maybe no company was interested in such a remote spot. That's how it had been in Egypt.

Amber slapped the water with her hand, spraying them all.

"Nothing was worse than that site in Mesopotamia. Those pathetic tents and the snakes and bugs." She gave a shiver. "Even that water was disgusting."

Jade gave a satisfied nod. "Yes, this place is definitely one of the better accommodations. We might as well enjoy it as long as it lasts."

"And the eye-candy is stellar here." Amber laughed, purposefully getting under Jade's skin.

Jade shook her head. "Here we have a solid roof over our heads, food, and that great room with the fireplace in our lodge is perfect for working. I'm sure we'll need a few items from town and from Dickhead."

At the mention of their boss, Silver swore. "Shit, I forgot to ask Vic about receiving packages." She rose, steam surrounding her even as the water sluiced downward.

Amber waved. "Do it tomorrow."

"We won't have her tomorrow. We'll have Layne." She stepped out of the hot tub and dried off quickly as the cold started to penetrate.

"I wish we could have him, if you know what I mean?"

"Really, Amber. The way you objectify men."

Silver didn't wait for Amber's response to Jade before quickly striding back the way they'd come. Her two team members would go back and forth in the same old bickering rut for a good fifteen minutes.

As she walked past their lodge, she noticed the ground appeared orange. She turned and looked up to find the sky turning a bright orange as the sun headed toward the valley between two peaks. The town nearby was called Four Peaks and, from what Amanda had said, all four peaks were part of conservation land. One of the peaks had the petroglyphs.

She turned back and jogged toward the corral, where Faithful and Chestnut still stood. The air, which had been quite pleasant during the day, was getting colder by the minute, but at least it was a bit warmer than the day they'd arrived. She zipped her fleece jacket up to her neck.

At the sound of voices, she slowed.

"I thought you said these horses were broke." Layne's voice floated out the open barn doors.

She stopped. Maybe now wasn't a good time.

"They are." Vic sounded pissed.

"Then why did that one bolt? We can't put newbies on skittish horses."

"Chestnut isn't skittish. He had a bull charging him, so he did what any other horse would do."

"Then why didn't the other two horses run?"

"For an old man who barely got his hide out of the way, you're not very observant. Old Glory charged Chestnut. I grabbed the reins of Amber's horse, and Jade's side-stepped into Nash, who controlled it. Silver did fine."

She raised her eyebrows. She did? It hadn't felt fine when she'd been heading for the fence.

"You call almost having to put down a horse and a guest getting hurt, *fine*?"

She had to agree with Layne on this one.

"Well, I'm not the one who let the bulls out. You could have asked for help."

Was that a growl? Did the cowboy actually growl?

"Vic, I didn't choose the time for two hardheaded bulls to fight. Nor did I choose for you to bring the scientists down the road at that time. In fact, I thought you'd still have them in the corral."

"What?"

At Vic's exclamation, Silver walked closer and stood just outside the open barn doors. Sure, she was eavesdropping, but they were talking about her, so it was fair.

Vic continued. "You wanted them to be able to ride to the north mountain by day four, but didn't expect them out on the ranch by day three? You asked for that, so that's what I got them ready for."

Silence met Vic's statement.

Silver forced herself to stay outside, even though she wished she could see their faces.

"You didn't actually expect them to be ready. Did you, Layne?"

There was more silence. Silver grinned. She wasn't even sure why, except that having Vic prove Layne wrong pleased her.

"Listen, old man, you give me a job and I get it done. It's as simple as that. If you didn't want them to be able to ride to the damn petroglyphs, then you should have assigned the training to Nash or Waylon. They'd be too polite to push too hard. But these women are smart. No, it's not their natural element, but they've ridden mules, even camels."

"Camels?"

At the surprise in Layne's voice, Silver nodded, pleased that he'd underestimated them.

"Yes, camels in Saudi Arabia. You do know where that is, right?"

"Don't be a wiseass."

"Then don't be a douchebag. You've got three scientists who will be ready to ride tomorrow whether you wanted to be their guide or not, so deal with it."

Oh, she just had to see the look on Layne's face now. Quickly, she stepped around the barn door and strode in as if just arriving.

Layne's brows were lowered, and his mustache moved as if he ground his teeth.

Vic noticed her first. "Hey, Silver. I thought you were headed to the hot tub."

"I was, but I had a question for you. Is now a bad time?" She purposefully looked at Layne.

"Not at all. You can help me bring in Chestnut and Faithful. Ever rub down a horse?" Vic started out of the barn.

Silver held back a smirk before turning and answering. "No, but if you show me how, I'm sure I can catch on. I'm pretty smart in that way." She grinned as she exited the barn, confident Layne couldn't see her. Maybe irritating their guide for the next month wasn't so smart, but it sure was fun.

CHAPTER 2

THE NEXT MORNING, Layne strode toward the barn on his way to the corral to meet up with the three women scientists he'd be escorting for the next month. He should be out moving cattle, helping put in the rest of the fencing on the new acreage, or getting the birthing enclosure ready. Instead, he was babysitting ranch guests. At least two of the three were easy to read, and as they were all women, and surprisingly attractive ones at that, there were worse chores.

Passing the barn, he grinned as he caught sight of the ladies. They were a far cry from what he'd envisioned as scientists. Each stood next to the horse Vic had chosen for them. Vic knew horses better than anyone. He should have known she'd do a good job of teaching the ladies to ride when he'd assigned her the task. He'd been dreading his assignment as guide since he first heard about it at the end of December, but now that he'd met them, he was far less opposed to the idea.

Vic caught sight of him first.

He brought his finger to his lips, wanting a minute to observe each woman. Amber, the one with long blonde hair pulled back in a ponytail, had her cowboy hat hanging around her neck and down the back of her blue parka. He'd guess her to be about 28. She had a round face with slightly chubby cheeks, and blue eyes if he remembered correctly. She was still fairly hesitant around her horse, but very friendly toward him.

Jade, the next woman after Amber, was a little taller and thinner and looked to be in her early thirties. While Amber had a slight tan, Jade looked as if she never ventured into the sun, which could be an issue in the desert. She had short, stylishly cut jet-black hair and dark brown eyes, both of which contrasted strongly against her skin. Her head was small and her face oval, but everything about her was petite except her height. She'd looped the cord of her hat over the pommel and seemed to be talking to the horse in a very serious way.

Silver was a bit harder to read. Beneath the cowboy hat she wore, her white hair fell to her shoulders, but she didn't seem old. She had no wrinkles around her green eyes that he'd noticed. Her face was shaped more like a heart, with a button nose that made her appear younger. If he had to guess, he'd say early thirties to mid-thirties, but he wouldn't put money down on it. She stroked the horse on the side of his face, her body language making it clear she'd been around animals before, if not a horse in particular.

Immediately, he categorized them as the newbie, the boss, and the unique. He was open to changing his mind about each, and looking forward to the month ahead. He stepped up to the corral and set one foot on the lower rail while he leaned his forearms on the upper one. "Howdy, ladies."

They turned as one to look at him.

He doffed his hat as was polite before resettling it on his head. "Today, I start my stint as your guide to the petroglyphs." He was about to continue when Amber spoke.

"Do we have to ride to get there? Wouldn't ATVs be faster? This ranch seems to have great ATV roads."

It wasn't what she asked so much as how she asked it, clearly looking for his attention. He certainly wasn't opposed to that. "Unfortunately, the ATV roads don't go far enough, and you'd have to walk a couple of miles just to reach the base of the north mountain."

Jade, who'd donned her hat and pulled the string tight, walked her horse a bit closer. "Is the petroglyph site at the base of the mountain?"

He shook his head and turned his attention to her. "It's about a third of the way up. Luckily, our land borders the conservation land where they are located, so we set up a shelter for the horses at the base of the mountain, in case the temperatures rise significantly."

"I see." Jade appeared to be in complete agreement.

He looked toward Silver, who had remained where she was. She gave him a nod, but didn't ask him anything. It was just as well. He climbed up onto the fence, and sat on the top rail. "Today, we will simply ride out to the site. It will take about two hours at a walk."

Amber smiled at that announcement, while Jade nodded, and Silver frowned, but still she didn't say anything.

"You all have food packed, so at the shelter we'll eat and then head up the mountain. It's imperative that you listen to any commands I make. This is the desert, and it's not unusual to come upon a rattlesnake, tarantula, or scorpion. Back in November, Brody Dunn even encountered a mountain lion on the south mountain. In addition to those dangers, we have coyotes desperate for food, ornery wild burros, and the occasional pack of javelinas."

"If I'm not mistaken, you also have quail, roadrunners, and jackrabbits. Correct?" Silver's statement surprised him. "Not everything in the desert is a danger."

He was revising his tag for her from *unique* to *trouble*. "No, not everything is dangerous. I'm explaining the dangers now, so that when I command you to do something, you understand why and I don't have to take critical seconds to explain later."

Amber smiled. "That makes sense. When do we leave?"

"Yes, I'm anxious to see these petroglyphs." Jade's tone made that obvious.

"You ladies mount up, and I'll be out in a minute." He jumped down from the fence and strode toward the barn, while Vic got the three settled. He had Honor saddled and ready in no time, then rode out of the barn to find the women waiting for him.

"They're all yours, Layne. I'm heading down to Hannah's place to help Tanner with the new fencing, unless you need anything else."

He shook his head at Vic. "I'll call you when we're back in range, unless you've shown them how to unsaddle their mounts and rub them down."

"Actually, I have. But call me anyway. I want to be sure everyone's fed and happy before I head home."

He touched his fingers to his hat brim before Vic headed out. Turning to face the three women, he smiled. "Okay, ladies. Let's get this adventure started." Clicking his tongue, he guided Honor onto the ATV road heading west.

Amber immediately brought her horse even with his. "Have you lived here all your life? Are you married? Have any children?"

"Yes, I have lived here all my life. Four Peaks suits me just fine. No, I'm not married and never will be. I have no children, but lots of nieces and nephews who I see regularly. Where are you from?"

He listened as Amber told him all about herself for the next hour. To be fair, he prompted her as they rode, since her life was far more interesting than his and so much of what she said included the other two women. When she'd finished explaining their different disciplines, he asked the question that had been on his mind since he'd heard they were arriving. "So you all make a real living doing this kind of thing?"

"Oh yes. We're considered experts. Our trips are funded by various people who are interested in history or aliens. Though, to be honest, we get paid more from the media exposure. I'm in charge of our social media. I'm proud to say that we have a lot of advertisers. I do play up the alien piece when I can. We get so much more engagement that way."

He was about to ask about that side of their work, when Jade rode up. "Amber, don't talk the man to death."

"Okay. Then you can tell him your version of where our funding comes from."

Clearly not happy to be ousted, Amber fell back to ride with Silver. There was plenty of room for the four of them to ride abreast between the fencing of the north and south enclosures, but since they were new to riding, he could understand their need for a bit of room.

"I apologize for Amber the chatterbox."

He looked over at Jade, who rode her horse as if she were in a dressage competition, back ramrod straight and both hands holding the reins, probably as Vic had taught them. "No need to apologize. A long ride is more enjoyable with conversation."

Jade lifted her chin at that. "Very well. If you are truly interested in how we are funded, I'd be happy to explain."

He gave the stiff woman his most charming smile. "I'm all ears."

A slight flush filled her cheeks before she spoke. "I won't bore you with the complicated details of all our investigations. However, this particular trip has been funded by the Sully Family Foundation here in Arizona. They say their mission is to better understand mankind's past to prepare for the future, but that's simply code for their hope to find proof aliens have visited Earth and will be back."

He started to chuckle, but made it a cough. "Do people really believe that?"

Jade sighed. "Indeed they do, and while I'm quite sure, based upon my research, aliens have not visited Earth, those who do believe they have are willing to pay well to find some kind of proof."

"So, if this foundation funded your trip, they are expecting some kind of alien connection?" He'd heard of Area 51 in Nevada, but the prospect of finding anything alien in Arizona was doomed to fail.

"Yes, but that's Silver's area of expertise. I just do the research to help her make any necessary connections. She's our resident Ancient Astronaut Theorist."

That's what Amber had mentioned the other day. He was going to have to look that up if he would be with the three women the whole month. "I had the impression you were the boss."

"Me? No. We work together as a team, though I'm probably the most organized. You have to be to do research. I use a very methodical approach...no book or manuscript is missed. Benedict Nagel, or Dick as he prefers, is our 'boss,' if you could call him that. He rarely comes to a site. He only cares about the money. He has absolutely no appreciation for the work we do. But since he's the one who finds us the places to go and secures the funding, we put up with him."

"So like an agent for a baseball player?"

Jade grimaced. "Unfortunately, no. Using your analogy, he's more like the owner of the whole team. We're just a very small team."

He had to admit the entire set-up was odd to him. Life was so much simpler when a person stayed in one place. Of course, with the dude ranch opening to the public in March, he could imagine the world coming to him. He rather liked that prospect, now that he thought on it.

"Is that where we're headed?" Jade pointed to the six-posted structure with a roof in the distance.

"That's the place. If you look up that mountain, you'll see a tree that looks like it's growing from a protruding rock."

Jade put her hand to the brim of her cowboy hat to find the spot he indicated then shook her head. "You obviously have great eyesight. I'll wait until we get closer. I do hope the carvings are worth the trip."

Since he had no idea what would make the petroglyphs worthy of study, he refrained from responding. They would know by the end of the day. "If they aren't, will you all leave early?"

"Probably, though even the smallest site usually requires at least three weeks of study."

"And if it's large?"

Jade waved her hand. "Oh, we could be here for months. But that would mean there's a lot more than what showed in the photographs we were sent."

Maybe he'd get lucky and there wouldn't be enough to study for more than three weeks and he could get back to herding cattle instead of herding women, though he'd never thought he'd think that. He usually enjoyed women, but the women he dated had jobs in fields he understood, like finances, insurance, retail, and the environment. Though there was that one lawyer he—

"Are you interested in history, Layne?"

He made his brain switch topics, but it wasn't easy. "Only the history of Four Peaks and cattle ranching. Though I did take astronomy as one of my science courses in college."

Jade's right brow lifted. "You went to college?"

Her surprise insulted him, but he took it as an opportunity to educate her. "Yes, I did. There's more to cattle ranching than riding a horse. Most of my sciences were in animal biology and behavior, but my senior year I had an elective, so I took astronomy."

The woman didn't seem to know what to make of the fact he was educated, as her mouth opened and closed multiple times before she final spoke. "Why astronomy? Were you interested in the Earth's relationship to the universe?"

He shrugged. "Not really. There's nothing we can do about that now, is there? No, I took it because before we had security cameras, I enjoyed looking up at the stars at night when out on the range. I thought if I was spending so much time looking at them, I should learn a bit about them."

"I suppose that makes sense."

He bit down on a grin, pleased he'd surprised the one he'd thought of as the "boss." Though now that he knew she wasn't, he needed a new tag. Maybe the "snob."

They rode the rest of the way with no further conversation, which suited him just fine. He stopped before the shelter, which wasn't needed this time of the year. Tanner Dunn, one of the family who owned the Rocky Road, had Waylon and Ernesto construct it. It was just a simple pole barn with six posts, a back wall on the west side, and a metal roof, but that roof was key to shade in the summer for the horses when the temperatures rose over 100 for months on end.

He halted Honor and jumped down. "This is where we'll tie our horses and have some lunch."

"It's only eleven." Silver spoke from Jade's other side.

He craned his neck to lock eyes with her. "Yes, and since I've been working since six this morning, I'm hungry."

Amber rode up. "Good point. Could you help me down?"

He was sure Vic showed them all how to dismount, but he

moved forward and assisted the newbie. Her hands definitely lingered on him longer than needed, specifically on his biceps. He smiled at her, changing her tag to 'flirt.'

"Thank you. Where should we tie our horses?"

Though he thought it was obvious, he showed her the rings in the posts. He'd also had Nash come out and fill the hay feeder. There was a bucket hanging off the side of that for when the small stream at the bottom of the mountain had water, which it did at this time of year. "Just make yourselves comfortable on a rock or something and enjoy your meal. When we're done, we'll hike up. I'll take the lead as there are parts with shale that could be dangerous." He frowned. "Where's Silver?"

The other two ladies shrugged as if her wandering off was normal, and continued pulling their lunches from their saddle-bags. All four horses were tied, but Silver wasn't under the structure with her horse. Spinning around, he scanned the desert and mountain before him. Where could she have disappeared to so quickly? She had to be nearby.

He walked around the structure to look behind it and stopped. "What are you doing?" Silver stood only five feet from a wild burro, holding out a partial carrot. He took three strides and grabbed her about the waist, lifting her out of harm's way. It only took seconds, but in that brief physical contact, his body came alive. He let her go as if she were a skunk that just sprayed.

"I was feeding the donkey. Look, you made me drop the carrot." She frowned and pointed to where the carrot lay in the dust.

"That's not a domesticated donkey you see at a petting zoo. That's a wild burro whose bite could send you to the hospital and whose kick could kill you. He's dangerous."

Silver cocked her head. "I don't think so."

The burro lowered its head and expertly pulled the carrot piece into his mouth.

"See, he likes it. He's friendly." She walked over to a prickly pear cactus where her box lunch sat precariously on top, and pulled out the other half of the carrot.

"And how do you know that?"

She stopped and studied the burro, who studied her right back, or rather the carrot in her hand. "He looks friendly."

"A wild rabbit looks friendly, but it can still bite you if it's scared."

"I don't think this donkey—this burro—is afraid of me. He likes me." She grinned at him.

He let out his breath, not sure how to get her to understand the situation. "Do you remember what I said just before we left to come out here. It's dangerous in the desert."

"Why are you being so uptight?"

At her words, he froze. Uptight? He was never uptight. He was laid back. He just went with the flow. It must be her. "I'm not uptight. I'm being protective. It's my job to make sure you and the others are safe while out here."

"If you're so protective, where's your gun?"

He hooked his thumb over his shoulder. "On my horse."

"Good thing Sweetie here isn't a rattlesnake." She lifted her chin as if daring him to counter her logic.

At the look in her eyes, he realized that was exactly what she was doing. She was irritating him like a stone in his boot. He crossed his arms and relaxed instead. "That's not a girl burro."

Silver blinked then looked at the burro again.

He followed her gaze to the animal. He'd noticed it was a male immediately, which is why he'd grabbed her out of the way. A fully intact male burro would be territorial. And this one was—he dropped his arms. "George."

"Excuse me?"

He hadn't meant to say the word out loud. But the fact that George was back surprised him. He'd been showing up at the ranch regularly and then disappeared for over a week. As much as Layne didn't want to admit it, he'd been concerned.

He walked around George, giving him a wide berth, but didn't see any wounds like he'd been in a fight.

"Are you saying this burro's name is George?"

As he finished his circle around George, who watched his every move, he stopped to look at Silver. "Yes. I named him George. It's not common for a burro to roam around by himself, but this one has been visiting the ranch regularly, alone."

She smiled triumphantly. "So he *is* friendly." She stepped forward with the carrot held out.

He jumped in front of her. "No. He's curious, maybe territorial, maybe has something wrong with him. It doesn't mean he's friendly. Trust me. I know this land better than you. You know petroglyphs better than me. We each have our expertise, right?"

"True. If you're sure?" She peered around him.

Layne took the opportunity to pull the carrot from her hand.

"Hey, that's my lunch."

He pointed with it. "Not anymore. Now go back under the shelter and eat the rest of it, or I'll be happy to eat yours as well as mine."

Her shoulders fell, and she walked to the cactus to retrieve her lunch. "Fine."

He lowered his hand and watched her walk back to the shelter, her hips swaying with her confident stride. "Definitely trouble."

A tug pulled on the carrot and he looked over his shoulder. "Well, I'll be damned." He kept his voice low and released the carrot as George gently pulled it from his hand. Slowly, he turned in place so as not to startle the burro.

George chewed happily, eventually swallowing it then looked him in the eye.

"I don't have anymore."

George nudged his hand.

He showed his empty palm.

As if satisfied there would be no more food coming, George turned south and meandered that way, stopping occasionally to munch on grass.

Layne finally moved. If George was headed for the south range, he'd find all he could eat. Right now, he had more pressing issues to deal with than a friendly burro. He had three women to get up a mountain and home again. Until their trips were made daily, the local wildlife could be an issue.

He just hoped George didn't show up again, or his own expertise on the land would appear to be nothing but a con to one woman in particular. His gut told him, Silver was not the kind to fall in line easily, and one misstep on his part, like touching her, could mess everything up.

CHAPTER 3

SILVER FOLLOWED behind Jade as they carefully made their way up the mountain between boulders, shrubs, and stubborn cactus. Now that they were almost to the site, her stomach tensed. She wanted it to be far more than what the tourists on vacation found. She wanted it to be invaluable. She wished more than anything to truly make a discovery that added something to the body of knowledge in her field. In four years, their trips had only added another example of what was already known. Yes, they had been in a new place which posed a few questions each time, but nothing significant.

She wanted significant. And she wanted it soon! She wanted to dig her teeth into a true discovery that lasted years, not months. Something that actually required her to rent an apartment and stay in one spot to delve deeply into what it meant for mankind. She was only 34, but she wanted to make her contribution in her prime, not when she was in her seventies and needed help getting off the ground.

Either that, or she hoped the site ahead was small, with nothing unusual and that it could be wrapped up in less than a month, so she could move on, have another chance. Their internet channel always brought in more advertising with new sites, and she shouldn't knock it. She made far more than the average professor of anthropology, but she was ready to be part of what was taught to students.

"Let's stop here for a moment."

At the sound of Layne's voice up ahead, she halted. "Why?"

There was a pause as she looked up the hill around her colleagues to see Layne staring down at her. He was just too easy to irritate.

"If you will give me a moment, I was about to explain." He smiled at her.

That was no fun. She waved to him to continue.

"There's a slide of shale about forty feet long. I'm going to lead each of you around it individually to be safe. That's how guests are brought to see the rock art."

Amber piped in. "That sounds smart."

Silver locked eyes with Jade before Jade turned forward to speak. "How much farther is it after this?"

Layne looked up the mountain then back at them. "Just another ten minutes or so. Okay, Amber. Take my hand."

Silver stepped on a rock next to Jade. "Do you think Layne will be disappointed when he ceases to exist the minute Amber lays eyes on the petroglyphs?"

Jade chuckled. "I doubt it. He probably gets a lot of female attention anyway."

"Good point." Though she still held a small grudge that he'd yelled at her because she couldn't grab the trailing reins while on a runaway horse, she did recognize that the man would be a hit with ladies, be they country, city, or otherwise. Maybe that was why she liked irritating him so much. He seemed too damned confident and...and happy.

Jade interrupted her thoughts. "My stomach always feels a little queasy before we see a new site. I don't know why?"

"It's the anticipation. I feel it, too, but it's more like my insides are turning to rock."

"Make that crushed rock and that's me. I just hope there's enough here to make the trip worth it."

Silver nodded as Layne approached.

"Jade, you ready?"

"Of course. Whatever needs to be done to get there."

Layne took Jade's hand. "Silver, don't wander off."

She rolled her eyes at him, but didn't promise anything. She wasn't usually so stubborn.

Jade and Layne started up around the shale.

She thought about simply following, but Layne did know the land, so this time she'd stay put. Instead, she turned to look at how far they'd come and caught her breath. Though they weren't even halfway up the mountain, the view was spectacular.

Sure, she'd been at the top of Mayan ruins and Sumerian temples, but the effect was not the same. There, the ground was covered by a lush canopy, the jungle ceiling close to the apex of the ruins. This was flat, brown, bare earth, spreading out for miles along the valley, the ranch the only sign of civilization, except for the town's main street in the distance, directly across from her.

What had the prehistoric indigenous people thought of this view. She imagined it was very similar, only with green vegetation and without the fences to keep the cattle in, though if she looked far enough to the east, she couldn't even make out the fencing. What kind of hunting was available? Then again, if they were the ancient Hunter-Gatherers, there would have been plants as well. She hoped the rock art harkened back to that long ago. A discovery dating back eleven thousand years would hold promise.

Sometimes she felt humans were much smarter back then,

needing little. But then again, they spent all their lives simply staying alive, even though evidence pointed to ceremonies and festivities. And what happened to the ones who lived here on or under the Four Peaks?

A piece of shale slid by her, startling her, and she whipped around to find Layne approaching.

"Are you ready?" He held out his hand.

"I am. I'm very curious about these ancient people." As she put her hand into his, she marveled at how small hers seemed, though they were equally rough. No wonder he rode his horse with only one hand on the reins. He didn't need two to control it.

He grasped hers firmly. "Be careful where you step. Though the shale is to my left and you're on my right, there's a lot of loose ground up here."

She kept her gaze on the ground, trying to ignore how warm her hand felt in his. "It makes you wonder why people would have come up here. Why did they climb the mountain and why only so far?"

He chuckled. "To be honest, as kids, we never thought about that. We just came up here once in a while for something to do or to make up stories."

Now that was interesting. "Stories? What kind of stories?"

"Nothing fancy. We'd look at the lines on the rock and pretend they stood for animals nearby or were different plants, trees, and even rivers. Then the next time we were fireside, we'd tell other kids what it all meant, like we were some kind of authority."

"When you say—" She grabbed onto his arm with her other hand as the dirt under her foot slid out, leaving her unsteady and in a lunge position.

He stopped immediately and pulled her up with one arm.

"The Four Peaks are beautiful, but not always friendly. Are you okay?"

It was a good thing she was limber or she would have had a sore groin come morning. "Yeah. Thanks." She let go of his arm, but continued to hold his hand, understanding more what he'd been talking about. "It seems that no matter how many places we investigate, we are never fully prepared. The world has so many different environments and cultures to learn about."

He shook his head even as he guided her forward. "I'm pretty happy with this small part of the world. In Four Peaks, everyone knows everyone. It keeps people honest and friendly, just the way I like it."

Honest and friendly sounded a lot like Layne Dawson. "You were talking about coming up here as a kid. Who did you come up with?" She could just imagine a dozen or so high schoolers climbing the mountain to get high, or competing to see who could scale it the fastest.

"Watch that scat over there." He pointed to a spot a couple feet in front of her. "That'll send you down the mountain quicker than a jack rabbit at a dog park."

She bit down on a smile at his expression and stepped around the small pile of scat. "What animal is that from?"

"Looks like fox. Coyote scat is usually larger."

"I didn't realize so many animals lived in this desert. I imagine you saw a lot of animals coming up here."

"I didn't come up that often, but when I did, it was usually with the Dunns, Tanner, and Jackson mostly. The Rocky Road has the only access to this petroglyph. Otherwise, you have to come in from the conservation land on the west side of town. By horse, it would take you half a day just to get here."

"So this wasn't a place that a lot of people visited."

He pulled her back to the left and let go of her hand. "No. Until we had special guests to test out the dude ranch in

November, there'd only been a handful who had been up here." He looked around. "Now where did those two go?"

She looked up just in time to see Jade's boot disappear behind a large rock. "There. Is that where we'll find the site?"

He let out a small sigh. "Yes. Trying to keep you all together is like herding cats."

She grinned. "I rather like cats."

"Yes, well, you better hope there's no mountain lion up there. Come on."

Layne started up the mountain at twice the speed they'd been climbing.

Though she was as anxious to see the site as her colleagues, she wasn't going to break her neck to get there.

She focused on where her feet were going as she climbed at her own pace. Finally, she made it to the large rock that was less an aimless boulder and more a part of the mountain. She stepped around the sharp edge of it where she'd seen Jade disappear, to find all of them standing six feet away from the surface. She joined them and looked at the rock face.

"This is well-preserved." Amber was in work mode now. "My guess is that's because this side of the rock faces the mountain which kept the elements from doing their worst."

Jade nodded. "You're probably right. This is obviously authentic. My guess just from looking at it would be it dates back to at least 6,000 BCE, but there's a good chance it's older."

Silver scanned the multitude of geometric shapes and yes, as Layne mentioned, squiggly lines. The rock surface was at least twenty feet high and thirty feet wide, yet the area of the petroglyphs was not more than six feet by ten feet. "Why is it so small?"

"And so it begins." Jade grinned. "Just one of many questions for us to answer."

Silver could think of a number of reasons, but the most

obvious was too depressing to think about. The people who had carved into the rock had not stayed in the area long. That meant there would be no significant find...again. The sooner they got started, the sooner they could move to the next possible discovery. "Let's get the preliminary pictures of the area, while Amber decides what patch of dirt she wants to claim. Jade, find us a place to work from, and I'll scout more of the area."

"More?" Layne's head snapped to her.

"Yes. You can come with me."

Amber and Jade immediately started moving around the space, which wasn't that large. From the mountain side to the rock face was barely fifteen feet, and it wasn't as long as thirty.

Silver walked past them to where Layne stood. "What do you know about the area to the east and west of this? What's farther up?"

"Farther up?" He looked up the mountain side. "We never went higher than this."

She gave him a smile. "Then this is your lucky day. Let's explore."

His hand came down on her shoulder. "Exactly how far do you plan to explore?"

She ducked underneath his touch and started walking. "Not far today, but in the next week, I'll explore quite a bit."

He stepped up behind her. "Then you should let me go first."

"Seriously? And how are you going to know where I want to walk?"

"You'll want to walk where it's safe." He stepped past her and continued toward the west side of the mountain.

She supposed he was right, but it would make it difficult to see, since he was a mountain unto himself. When they reached the end of the rock art, she switched her focus to the mountain.

Layne began ascending. She followed in his footsteps, scanning the area for any signs of other human work, no matter how small. They ascended another thirty feet or so when he stopped. "I think this is as far as we should go today. I didn't bring my hand gun, and I'm not in a hurry to disturb a rattlesnake without one."

"I forgot about the snakes."

His eyes widened.

She shrugged. "It happens to all three of us. We get so focused on discovering something else that we forget about our surroundings. Thank you. I agree. Let's go back down." She turned around, intending to return the way they came, when she noticed something on the top of the rock they'd come to study. "Look." She pointed to it.

Layne came to stand next to her. "What is that?"

She pulled her phone from the holster on her belt and zoomed in with her camera, then took a few pictures. Her heart started to race. She held her phone out so Layne could see it and zoomed in a little more. "What does that look like to you?"

"Those five squiggle lines with an arrow on top remind me of heat coming off the desert and being captured under a roof."

"I agree." Maybe the site was more than she'd first thought.

"So why is it on top of that rock?"

She hesitated to speak her thoughts, not wanting to be disappointed. "My guess, and it's only a guess, is that since the roof peak points toward the flat face of the rock with the petroglyphs, it could mean that rock is the roof of a cave."

"Really?" Layne took her phone and studied the picture.

"It's just a guess. We have yet to determine what the symbols mean on these archaic geocentric art sites. The going consensus is that the geometric images are simply from ancient ceremonies where they may have used a hallucinogen of some kind or went into a trance."

He handed her phone back. "Those etchings are what they saw?"

"That's the belief."

He frowned. "I thought people who hallucinate see pink monsters with green tongues who eat cars or something."

She raised her brows at the image he painted. "No. I'm guessing you've never been high."

"High on life." He grinned.

Of course. She should have expected that. "Okay, so try this. Close your eyes really hard."

"Why?"

"I'm making a point. Humor me."

He obediently closed his eyes, his straight nose wrinkling above his mustache. "Now what?"

"What do you see?"

His eyelids snapped open. "Very funny. You can't see anything with your eyes closed."

"No, I'm being serious. Close your eyes really tight and tell me what you see."

He just stared at her as if she'd asked him to fly off the mountain.

"Fine. You asked a question, and I was helping you understand the answer. Never mind."

She started to walk past him, but his hand on her arm stopped her. "I *do* want to know."

That surprised her. She was used to guides who thought they knew it all, or didn't care what she was doing as long as they were paid. She stepped back. "Then close your eyes hard and tell me what you see. And no, I'm not going to leave or play a trick on you."

His mustache twitched. "Promise?"

Now he was teasing. What planet was he from? She

smirked, since she was the ancient astronaut theorist and should be able to figure that out. She held up her three middle fingers. "Scouts honor."

His brows rose. "Were you in the Girl Scouts?"

"What? No. It was just a—stop stalling."

Layne obediently closed his eyes tight.

"Okay, now what do you see? It could appear white or bright?"

"I see...I see blotches!" He opened his eyes, his surprise real.

She couldn't help smiling. "That's great."

"It is? But I didn't see any squiggly lines like down there, though the blotches were kind of like squares with rounded corners. Should I do it again?"

She laid her hand on his forearm. It was hard beneath the lined jean jacket. "No. You won't see what they saw." She released his arm to point to the large rock below. "As I said, they were most likely in a trance, either from meditation or from a hallucinogen. Since we don't know what they used, we can't recreate it. But now you understand why this rock art is geometric."

He stroked his mustache on one side with his thumb. "I'd always wondered about the weird lines. I thought maybe a Native American tribe had some secret code, because there's no animals or stick figures like at the Grand Canyon."

Surprised he'd seen petroglyphs anywhere else, never mind remembered them, she gave him more credit than she originally had. "Yes, those are considered Grand Canyon Polychrome art. I haven't seen it in person, but it's well documented and I've seen many pictures, thanks to Jade and her research. Speaking of her, I should see if she's found a place for us to set up our tools and equipment."

"Then follow me. That way if you slip, I'll stop your fall."

It took her a moment to fully understand what he meant, but as they descended, it became very clear. He'd rather she fall into him than down the mountainside. Was it a cowboy thing to be so considerate, or was it Layne?

CHAPTER 4

LAYNE SLOWED Honor as he came up behind Jackson and Tanner Dunn, two of the three brothers who owned the Rocky Road along with their father. "Need some help?"

Tanner looked up, even as he held a fence post in place. "What are you doing here? I thought my wife had you escorting the scientists."

Jackson stomped down the dirt around the post before setting the shovel in front of him and resting a foot on the step of the blade. "Any pretty ones or are they all old enough to be your grandmother?"

He laughed before dismounting. "They're all pretty, and so is my grandmother."

Jackson rocked the shovel. "You are the luckiest cowboy I know."

"They're still scientists. They know a lot more shit than you do."

Tanner smirked. "That's not saying much."

Jackson, who would have told Tanner to fuck off a month ago, just shook his head. "Ignore him. He's just riding high because he got some this morning and was late getting out here."

That was no surprise. Tanner and Amanda were trying to get pregnant. Layne wished them luck. He wished everyone luck with kids. He liked kids, as long as they weren't his. "I'm crossing my fingers for you."

"Thanks." Tanner didn't stop grinning.

Layne knew well that morning-delight feeling. He'd enjoyed it himself a time or two. But too much of that meant a baby on the way, like his close friend had. He looked at Jackson. "And how's TJ? Has she shaken that cold yet?"

Jackson frowned. "No. Dani is taking her to the doc's today."

Layne may not have any children, but he had enough brothers and sisters and nieces and nephews to know a thing or two. "Put some of that menthol rub on her chest. Works every time."

"Really? Thanks. I'll tell Dani to pick some up while she's in town. You didn't answer Tanner's question, though. What are you doing out here? Did the scientists fire you, or did Amanda?"

Tanner looked hopeful.

"Neither. It turns out the ladies need to plan their approach to the site, given what they want to accomplish and the problematic terrain. In addition to tools and collection bags, they also have to get photography equipment up there and a canopy."

Jackson stared at him. "You sound like a scientist yourself."

He shrugged. "It's something new and different, so I'm learning a little."

"Uh-oh, Tanner. You're going to lose your foreman."

As if that would ever happen. "Wiseass. You know I'm not going anywhere...ever." He shook his head at Jackson. Still, it was good to see his friend throwing shit again. Jackson had come home from his last deployment a total mess, so having most of the old Jackson back was a relief. "So do you need any help out here? I figure I should earn my keep."

"About time, old man." Jackson grinned.

"Listen, I can still out-work you any day and put you to shame. You went all soft on me in the military."

Jackson let out a full-bodied laugh, something Layne had missed hearing. Before Layne could respond, Tanner stepped between them, his back to Jackson. "Okay, enough talking shit. I've got Jackson's muscle all day today and I don't want to waste it, so Layne, if you could run into town and pick up the fence hardware I need, that would be helpful."

"Sure thing. What do you need?"

"I left a list in the office. Whatever you do, don't ask Amanda for it or she'll decide you need to do something else. I may have let her have you for the month, but I'm not going turn my back on your offer to help."

Layne was pretty sure that when Tanner handed the reins of the dude ranch side of the operation to his wife, Amanda, he hadn't expected to have his right-hand man pulled out from under him in the first month. "Got it." He turned to his horse.

"Hey, wait up a sec." Jackson strode over, Tanner having already started for the trailer of fence posts.

Layne stopped. "Sure."

Jackson looked over his shoulder at his brother before turning back, his voice lower. "I was wondering if I could stop by your house one night this week. Now that the barn is up and Shotgun is settled in with Havoc and Dani's horse, I'd like you to take a look at the house plans before I show Dani what I'm thinking. I based it off your mother's house, because I always thought that was the perfect set-up for a family."

"You mean a big family. Are you planning on lots of kids?"

Jackson looked away. "I'm not sure. It really depends on my progress and Dani." He returned his gaze to look Layne straight in the eyes. "My psychiatrist says the medicine I'm on can cause memory loss, so I was hoping you could tell me how close I came in the design. I figure it'd be weird if I showed up on your mother's doorstep and asked to take a look around."

Layne set his hand on Jackson's overdeveloped shoulder. "Mom would be happy to see you, no matter the reason. She always said she'd ended up with eight kids though she only gave birth to seven." Beneath his hand, he felt Jackson tense. "But if you're not ready for a visit, no problem. I'm at the Stampede on Tuesdays, and I usually hit the Lucky Lasso Saloon or Boots n' Brew on Friday night, but any other night works."

"Thanks. I'll text you. I want to be sure Dani is home to watch TJ."

He chuckled, unable to help it. "Yup, you sound like my brother, who's a great dad." He lifted his hand and turned to Honor.

"I'm trying."

Layne mounted up. "That's all any man can do. Any man but me." Laughing, he turned his horse and headed back to the ranch house.

When he arrived, he tied the reins on the railing outside the porch of the one-story adobe home and walked in. Dropping his hat on the entry table out of habit, he started down the hallway toward the office, his rubber-heeled cowboy boots not making a sound on the travertine tiles. He slowed his step as he heard Amanda talking to Jeremiah, the patriarch of the family, who was still recovering from a massive stroke and was wheelchair bound. From the sounds of it, the man was being stubborn as she tried to get him to do his physical therapy exercises. Unfortunately, that trait came out in his sons every once in a while.

Continuing down the hall, Layne came to the office. He poked his head in to find it empty, so he moved to the desk. There were at least seven piles of papers neatly stacked in front of the computer. It was quite a different appearance from his own desk at home, which he liked to call an organized mess. It wasn't neat, but he knew where everything was, not that he had cattle and a dude ranch operation to oversee. And for that he was thankful. Way too much responsibility.

It didn't take long to find Tanner's hand-written list on the top of one of the piles. Layne picked it up and folded it before stuffing it into the front pocket of his jeans, then left the way he'd come, closing the front door quietly. No need to alert Amanda to his presence.

He turned around and walked right into Silver.

"Oh." She started to fall back.

He grabbed her to him. Immediately, the scent of cinnamon wafted up to him, filling his nose and causing him to feel as if he'd lost his balance, though both his feet were firmly planted on the porch. "Pardon me."

Her hands were pinned between her and his chest as she looked up at him. "You're like walking into a cave wall. Why were you sneaking out of the house?"

He ignored how good she felt in his arms and took half a step back, though he didn't let go. He jerked his head over his right shoulder. "I didn't want to interrupt the therapy session going on in there. Amanda has her hands full with Jeremiah."

Silver's curiosity immediately turned to uncertainty. "Oh, I didn't realize this was when she gave him therapy. I don't want to disturb her either, then." Her shoulders fell, obviously she was disappointed.

He'd always been a sucker for a damsel in distress. "Can I help?"

"I don't know. None of us have a car, but I need to go into town to pick up a few things. We never know what we'll need until we see the site, and we've already agreed on a few items, plus a few we forgot."

He smiled. "I can definitely help with that. I was just

headed to town myself to pick up some fencing hardware. You're welcome to come along."

"Excellent. Just let me get my wallet." She cocked her head. "But if I'm going to do that, you'll have to let go of me."

He dropped his hands as if he'd been burned. "Just making sure you're okay, and I didn't do any permanent damage." He let his gaze roam over her, telling himself he was just checking to be sure she was fine. That he noticed she had broader shoulders than normal for a woman, with the perfect size breasts, a slender waist and hips, and long legs was nothing...just him looking out for her.

She waved off his comment. "I'm made of stronger stuff than I look. I once had a camel step on my foot and break it, but I didn't know it was broken for almost two weeks."

He pulled back his head, finding that hard to believe. "How could you not know? Weren't you in pain?"

"I was, but I ignored it because it looked as if we'd found a connection between the site we were working and another in Utah, which would have been an amazing discovery. My focus was completely on that. It wasn't until we discovered there had been some vandalism at the site some fifty years earlier that I realized not only did we not have a new discovery but also the pain in my foot wasn't going away. That's when they got me to a doctor. But it's as good as new now." She raised up on her toes bringing the top of her head almost as high as his nose before returning her heels to the porch.

"I see that."

"I'll let the girls know I have a ride. I'll be right back." She turned toward the porch steps.

"No rush. I have to stable Honor first. You can meet me in the barn."

She had jogged down the steps, but at his comment, she stopped to look at him. "We are going by car, not horse, right?"

His lips twitched as he tried not to smile. "Yes."

"Okay, just checking." With that, she was off toward the guest square and her lodgings.

He moseyed down the stairs and untied his horse. "Sorry, Honor. It looks like you're getting a couple of hours off. I'll make it up to you tomorrow."

He walked his horse into the barn, unsaddled him, and gave him some oats, then stepped out of the stall. Since Silver wasn't back yet, he sat on a hay bale and waited. What would three scientists need? He hoped whatever it was that Four Peaks would have it. It wasn't a very big town. He just needed to go see Mr. Hardy at the Four Peaks hardware store. If they needed anything electronic, he'd have to call Sting, who didn't have a shop per se, but his barn was where everyone went to get tech help.

Layne pulled out his phone to be sure he had Sting's number, but the time on his phone caught his attention. It had already been a half hour. He rose, concern starting to edge its way into his brain. He headed for the open barn doors, just in case she forgot that's where they were going to meet. Stepping outside, he scanned the parking area, corral, and square of the guest quarters. Nothing moved.

She was probably just getting ready. Women liked to make sure they looked good for running errands. He was in no hurry. He walked over to the corral and put his foot on the lower rail. He was rarely in a hurry. Life had its own pace. He stood there watching the two-story log structure the ladies were staying in. It would be used for families next month.

Maybe they all decided to go and were getting ready. He envisioned the back seat of his pickup. If they all went, he'd have to do some quick rearranging. He had a harness he'd bought at a yard sale last month he'd been planning on fixing, and he'd never brought the air filter into the house after shopping last weekend. There was definitely a small bag of trash back there as well.

He pulled his foot from the rail, planning to clean out his backseat, then changed his mind. Why bother if he didn't need to? Best to just find out who would be coming. He strode to the steps and across the porch of the building where they were staying. Opening the door, he stopped.

Silver and Amber sat on a cushioned loveseat staring at something on a flip chart that Jade pointed to. At his entrance, Jade stopped speaking.

"Layne." Amber gave him a big smile.

He lifted his hat in greeting. "Ladies. I thought I'd check and see if you all were planning to go into town." He almost explained why and then thought better of it.

Silver jumped to her feet. "Shit, I'm sorry. I got caught up in the planning." She immediately walked toward him.

"Did you get your purse." Women didn't go anywhere without one.

"Crap. Hold on." She strode to the first room on the left, reached in, then held up a wallet. "Okay, I'm good to go." She stuck it in the back pocket of her jeans even as she stopped in front of him.

"Don't forget the list." Amber waved a piece of paper and started toward them.

She rolled her eyes. "I swear, if my head wasn't attached..."

"You'd forget it." He grinned at her surprised expression.

"Your grandmother tell you that, too?" She stood staring at him, her hand held out for the paper Amber brought to her.

"She did. But she said it more to my second sister than to me. That girl was into everything when she was growing up. I can't believe she remembered to grab her diploma from high school on her way to her wedding." He shook his head, pleasant memories of his sister floating through his head.

Silver took the paper from Amber, folded it, and put that in her pocket, too. "I'll be back later. If you think of anything else, text me."

"We will. Have fun, but not too much fun." Giving a wink, Amber flicked her hair back over her shoulder and headed back to where Jade stood waiting.

"Ready?"

He moved his gaze back to Silver. "I was born ready."

"Seriously? Let's go." She reached around him and opened the door.

Now she was in a hurry? He grabbed the edge of the door above her head. "After you."

She gave him an odd look before walking out.

He followed her down the steps, amused at her sudden rush.

She continued on ahead, past the corral and into the parking area in front of the house. She stopped in the middle of it and looked over her shoulder. "Which one is yours?"

"Mine's the truck." He walked toward her, stifling a grin as she scanned the area. There were five pickup trucks and one car.

Finally, she faced him, setting her hands on her hips. "Funny."

This time he did smile. "Thank you." He pointed to his truck. "It's the green one."

"I should have known." She started for his vehicle.

"Why? Do I look like the kind of man that drives a green truck?"

She stopped in front of the hood of his truck. "No, but you seem like a man who likes his space, and this is the largest truck parked here."

Impressed by her observation, he walked past her and

opened the passenger door. "You're right. I do like my space. I even special-ordered a bench seat for this truck."

She climbed inside. "I didn't know they made these anymore."

"They don't." He closed the door and walked back to the driver's side. He jumped in and started the truck. "You better buckle up. I wouldn't want you to hit your head on the ceiling."

She frowned at first before she quickly belted herself in. "I'd almost forgot this driveway is what gave the ranch its name."

"You may want to hold on to that handle as well." He waited until she had a good grip, then eased the truck down the Rocky Road Ranch driveway. Though he knew it like the back of his hand, there was no getting around the bumps or even a few potholes he likened to craters.

Silver didn't say a word the entire way down. But as they turned onto Mesquite Road, a much better dirt road, she let go of the handle. "And you drive down that every day?"

"I do. You get used to it after a while."

"I've been on mule trails smoother than that driveway."

Her odd experiences were interesting. "Where?"

"In the Andes. We were investigating rock art up there, like you have here, but it had actual figures. It was an area that had been lived in for generations."

"You go to a lot of unusual places in your work, don't you?"

She chuckled. "I never thought about it, but you're right—they are unusual for the average person who wants a vacation. Some are better than others."

"I guess there's not a call for your kind of work in the city."

"Actually, there are ruins found in cities almost every year. Someone takes down a building and needs to dig deeper for the new one and suddenly they discover a whole town. Or there's some treasure hunter diving in the ocean or a lake and he or she comes upon a giant statue, column, or vase. Next thing you know, everyone in the city is checking things out."

"That really happens?"

"Absolutely. It's a small world when it comes to ancient antiquities. News like that spreads like wildfire in this field, and everyone clamors to get the permits and permissions to be the first to excavate."

He didn't like the idea of a bunch of people converging on Four Peaks, though he was quite sure the town manager would love it. "Could that happen here if that rock is above a cave?" He slowed to a stop at the paved road before turning right into town.

"That all depends. There could be a cave, but then there may be nothing in it. Or there could be a vast system of tunnels with a culture's greatest artifacts. You never know. I'm trying not to get my hopes up."

"Is that because you'd be famous?"

When she didn't answer right away, he glanced over at her. She stared at him as if he'd turned into a rooster.

"Of course not. If I wanted to be more famous, all I would have to do is make wild postulations about aliens having lived here. No, I would be excited because I've always wanted to find a new site that could add to our body of knowledge about our ancient ancestors."

He wanted to ask why, but traded that question out for another, less weighty one. "You're pretty passionate about this stuff. Did you always want to be an anthropologist?"

She laughed. It wasn't a full-bodied all out laugh, but more of a soft, sensual laugh. "Hardly. I wanted to be a vet. I always loved animals, but except for a bunch of cats and a couple of dogs and some fish, we didn't own anything unusual, though we had a bunch of wildlife. I even got bit by a chipmunk once, trying to keep my cat from eating him."

"And did you save the critter?"

"I did, and my thank-you was a trip to the doctor's for a tetanus shot." She smirked.

"If you wanted to be a vet, then how did you come to this career?" He pulled into Hardy's Hardware, the hub of Four Peaks and parked the truck across the parking lot, so it faced Main Street.

She unbuckled her seat belt and turned toward him. "You could say it was the perfect storm. Two of my required courses, sociology and history, happened in the same semester. Added to that was a work-study opportunity on an 18th century archeological site. Suddenly, past people became so much more interesting than animals. In a way, it's similar, in that you have to figure things out without anyone telling you what happened."

That sounded pretty complicated. "So you like a mystery then."

She grinned. "Yes. That's it exactly. But it's so much more. It's figuring out what made people tick back then, what they valued, what skills they had, and how they lived. These are people who lived, loved, worshipped, and died before we came along. They are why we are who we are today." Even as she spoke, her cheeks became flushed with her excitement.

He smiled at her, enjoying her enthusiasm. "You really get into what you do."

Again she let out a soft laugh that floated over him like a caress. "I do. Sorry if I'm boring you. I know not everyone finds it as interesting as me."

"No need to apologize. I think it's interesting. I don't remember ever being so excited about a job."

Her brows furrowed. "What about your work as a cowboy? Doesn't that excite you? You must be good because you're the foreman at the Rocky Road Ranch."

"I wouldn't say it excites me. It's more that it's comfortable. I enjoy going to work."

"What do you mean? Didn't you have to train to be a cowboy? Go to school or apprentice with someone? I'm afraid I know very little about what goes into being a cowboy."

He unbuckled his own seatbelt and turned off the truck. No need to leave it running when the weather was so cool. "Everything I needed to know, I learned from my dad. He was a cowboy all his life. My mom's the one who made me go to college. She didn't want me to limit my opportunities, or so she said. But I'd been working for the Rocky Road since I was in high school. Jackson Dunn was a regular fixture at my house and followed me everywhere, so I kind of had an in."

"But you do like it, right? Being a cowboy?" Her brows remained furrowed, and she looked truly concerned for him.

He nodded to reassure her. "I do. It's in my blood, so to speak."

A knock on his truck window had him turning to find Stacy Mitchel, a waitress at the Lucky Lasso Hotel and Saloon.

He opened the window. "Howdy, Stacy."

"Hey, Layne. You know there are better places to make out in a truck, right?" She laughed, clearly pleased with herself.

He turned to Silver, who looked to be blushing. "Don't mind her. She's full of it." He turned back. "What can I help you with?"

Stacy looked around him at Silver before returning her attention to him. "I just bought a concrete fountain and got it to my truck, but the sucker is heavy. Any chance you could help a girl out?"

"Of course." He turned back to Silver. "This is the hardware store. I'll be getting a few things for the ranch. Any chance you need something from here?"

Silver nodded, her hand on the door latch as if she couldn't wait to get out of the truck. "Actually, I do. I'll meet you in there." And out she jumped.

"Great." As the passenger door closed, he opened his door and Stacy stepped away. She still wore her usual uniform, either coming from or going to work. Her three-sizes-too-large for her, red Lucky Lasso Saloon t-shirt, and short black skirt were known throughout town. "Where you parked?"

"Right over there." She pointed, but kept her gaze on Silver who strode into the store.

He walked by Stacy and found she'd rolled the fountain over to her truck on a brand-new wheelbarrow. "Come over here and hold the wheelbarrow."

Stacy, who was ten years younger, sashayed over, her blue eyes bright with curiosity. "New girlfriend?"

"No. She's a guest at the Rocky Road."

"Ah-huh. But the Rocky Road isn't opening until next month, according to Mr. Hardy."

"That's true, but this month there are three scientists staying there to check out those petroglyphs on the eastern mountain. Now, can you hold the wheelbarrow so I can get this into your truck bed?"

Stacy finally focused on the task and held the wheelbarrow in place.

He lifted the heavy fountain and placed it on the tailgate. Then he climbed up into the bed to lift it inside as he didn't want to scratch the bed of her truck.

"She's a scientist? I don't know. She looks familiar to me for some reason."

"Do you have a blanket or something I can put this on? If you take a curve, it's going to scratch your bed."

"Oh, yeah. It's in the locker near the cab."

He found the moving blanket and laid it down, then set the fountain on it.

"Did she say where she's from?"

He jumped down from the truck. "No, she didn't. Maybe you saw someone who looked like her in one of those hair magazines." Stacy liked coloring her short hair different colors. This month it was blue.

"That's it! I do know her. She's Dr. Silver Colins from that podcast on aliens. Oh, wow. I have to get her autograph!"

"Whoa, there." He jumped down in front of her. "You can't go rushing into Mr. Hardy's and ask for an autograph. You don't even know if she's the same person."

"But I do. I recognize her. Here." Stacy pulled out her phone and clicked a couple buttons, then held it up for him to see. The sound wasn't on, but sure enough, there was Silver, in a dark maroon silk blouse, some gemstone around her neck, and her face made up to make her look like a model. She appeared to be a completely different person. Even her hand movements were different, almost practiced, and her nails were painted the same color as her blouse. Now that he studied it, her lips were that color too. It was her and yet not her.

Stacy pulled the phone back and watched for a few more seconds, then stuck her phone in her tiny purse. "See, I'm right, aren't I?"

He gave her a nod, and she broke into a squeal.

"Wait." He stepped between her and the store. "Maybe you should ask her when she comes out."

Stacy's hands found her hips. "What's up with you, Layne? She's a celebrity. Everyone will want to meet her. Unless for some reason you were hoping to keep her to yourself." She gave him the side-eye.

"No, of course not. I'm just the guide for all of them. Just doing my job." He let his arms drop to his sides, trying to make himself appear relaxed even if he didn't feel that way. That in itself gave him pause.

Stacy grinned. "Well, good. If there's nothing personal between you two, I'm going in there right now to get me an autograph and to tell our town we have a freaking celebrity. Wait until Mr. Hardy hears!"

In less than a second, Stacy had stepped around him and was almost running back into the store, her new fountain and wheelbarrow forgotten.

Shaking his head, he picked up the wheelbarrow and placed it in the truck bed upside down between the fountain and tailgate so it wouldn't slide around. He hoped one of Stacy's brothers would be at the other end to help her unload. He slammed the tailgate and turned toward the store.

He didn't move. Silver was a celebrity? She didn't act like one or dress like one. When Amber couldn't believe he hadn't heard of Silver, he thought she was just pulling his leg. He didn't mind, it was just that...that she appeared so normal. Well, for a woman scientist. He stared at the hardware store, pretty sure he knew exactly what was going on inside.

He scanned the parking lot. There were seven vehicles, and he recognized every one of them. It would take forever to get checked out. Good thing he was on guide duty today because he wasn't getting back to the ranch before dinner time.

CHAPTER 5

SILVER ADDED three small brushes to the trowels, measuring tapes, and flags already in the buckets she carried. Their new sieves and shovels had arrived before they did, but the smaller items that were too bulky to bring on a plane were much easier to purchase on site, or nearby. She sincerely hoped Four Peaks had everything they needed, as she didn't want to delay getting started by having to take a day to go into Phoenix or whatever urban center was closest.

Now she just needed to find the batteries and she should have everything she needed. Everything but the popcorn up at the front. It smelled way too good. She walked around the end of an aisle and started toward the front of the store when she came upon an empty pen with a light set up on it. She stopped, smiling. They were getting ready for baby chicks or ducks. Springtime probably came early in Arizona. She continued toward the square check-out counter where she remembered seeing batteries on her way in.

"Dr. Collins?"

The woman named Stacy walked toward her from the side of the store. "Yes?"

"Oh, I knew it!" Stacy came right at her. "Dr. Collins, I'm a huge fan. I've watched every one of your podcasts and interviews. I just have to ask you, do you really believe there are aliens? Is it true there's going to be a movie? Could you sign my t-shirt? Please let me take a selfie with you. My brothers are not going to believe you're here."

Shocked that someone in the little town of Four Peaks would even know who she was, she took a moment to respond. "Um, yes, I'm here. If you have a marker, I'd be happy to sign your shirt." She gave Stacy a smile.

"Oh, wow. Thank you." Stacy lifted her head and yelled. "Mr. Hardy! I need a black marker right away!"

A little surprised, Silver winced. "Are the markers nearby? We can go get one."

Stacy waved off the question. "Mr. Hardy will bring it. Don't worry. He's the best."

Not in a hurry to answer any of Stacy's other questions, Silver pointed to the battery rack. "Mind if I grab a few batteries?"

"No, of course. Are they for your equipment?"

"Mostly for flashlights. We don't like to use our phones for lighting." She pulled a couple of packs off the stand and added them to the buckets. "Your shirt says the Lucky Lasso Hotel and Saloon. Is that here in town?"

Stacy looked down as if she'd forgotten she wore it. "Yes. I work there. Ava hired me right out of high school and I've been there ever since. I'm a waitress."

"Is the food good there?"

"Most of it. If you come in, I'd be happy to—"

"Here you go, Stacy. Is something marked wrong?"

Silver turned to find a gentleman in his late forties with a significant receding hairline, his brown hair in a crescent around his head. He had a lean face and a bushy mustache half the size of Layne's.

Stacy plucked the marker from Mr. Hardy's hand. "Mr. Hardy, I'm thrilled to introduce you to Dr. Silver Collins. She's an expert on ancient alien astronauts. They're even making a movie about her."

That wasn't exactly true. She reached out her hand. "It's nice to meet you, Mr. Hardy."

Mr. Hardy's mouth split into a wide smile, showing off a set of white caps that would make any actor proud. He grasped her hand and pumped it a few times. "You're a celebrity? What a pleasure it is to have you here in Four Peaks. Will you be here long? I would love to talk to you about a marketing opportunity."

Stacy stepped in front of the man, forcing him to let go. "Not yet, Mr. Hardy. Dr. Collins has promised to sign my shirt." Stacy held out the marker.

The man blinked. "Shirt? Is that what's done today? I have a number of Hardy's Hardware t-shirts in the back. I'll be right back."

As the man scampered off, Stacy turned her back. "You can use the whole back of this shirt if you like. I spell Stacy S-T-A-C-Y, no e. Maybe you could add that we are friends or something?"

Silver uncapped the marker and wrote. *Stacy, it was so good to see you in Four Peaks. It's always fun catching up on the latest theories with a fellow enthusiast. I look forward to stopping by and having your favorite meal. Keep the faith. Silver.* She made sure to make the S in her first name the largest letter, with her signature curly-ques. "There you go."

Stacy turned around. "Thank you so much. This is amazing." She looked over her shoulder trying to see what was written, finally giving up. "Don't forget our selfie. I need to prove you were really here. Wait until—"

"Do my eyes deceive me or do we have a model visiting our little town." A cowboy, probably not much older than Stacy, sauntered toward them in a black t-shirt and brown leather jacket. He had a deep voice, short dark-brown hair, and a chiseled jaw covered in scruff. As he came closer, she could see his light-blue eyes. That was a killer combination for most women, but she preferred more mature men. She'd left her twenties more than a few years ago and was glad. This man had *womanizer* written all over him.

Stacy beamed. "Perfect timing, Luke. I need to you to take a picture of us."

That caused him to slow his stride. "Why?"

Stacy took the two steps to reach him and handed him her phone. "Because I want one, dumb-ass. You do know how to take a picture with a phone, right?"

"Give me that." Luke took the phone.

Stacy hurried back as if afraid Silver would change her mind. As Stacy looped her arm around her, she whispered. "Thank you so much."

"Okay, look over here."

At Luke's command, they both looked at him, but he wasn't holding up the camera.

"I could stand here all day enjoying this view."

Silver barely kept from rolling her eyes. It was never a good idea to anger the local people, no matter where she was.

"Luke Hayden, take the damn picture." Stacy scowled at the cowboy.

At that moment, he held up the phone and snapped a picture. Even before Stacy went to him to look at it, Silver knew they would have to take it again.

"I found them," Mr. Hardy rushed up with a handful of tee-shirts. "Took a little digging, but I have five left. Could you come over to the counter and sign these for me?" Mr. Hardy set his free hand on her arm to turn her toward the cash register.

"Wait." Stacy grabbed her arm with the buckets. "I need another picture with her."

Luke pulled his own phone from his jacket. "I'm thinking I need a selfie with such a beautiful lady."

Silver felt a bit like a fish being torn apart by a family of bald eagles, something she'd seen on a site in Alaska.

"Mr. Hardy. You have a customer."

At the sound of Layne's voice behind her, she immediately relaxed.

"Oh." Mr. Hardy looked up. "Thank you, Layne." The man hurried off.

"Stacy, did you know the ice you bought and threw on your passenger seat is melting?"

"Well, damn. I totally forgot. I need to get that to Sandra's birthday party." Stacy let go and ran between the displays.

Silver looked up at Layne as he stepped next to her and stared at Luke. He didn't say a word. She turned back to Luke.

"I gotta pick up some screws. See you 'round." And with that, Luke disappeared down the closest aisle.

She turned to Layne. "How'd you do that?"

He shrugged. "Do what? Did you find everything you need?"

"I did. What about you?"

"I still have a few more things to get. How about you come with me?"

"Sounds like a good idea." She followed him to the back of the store.

He pulled out a list from his pocket and started pulling things from the racks of hardware. "Mind if I borrow one of those buckets?"

She handed him one, and he filled it to the brim within

minutes. When he was done, they headed to the counter where Mr. Hardy waited.

She took her items out of the buckets. "Ring me up for another one. Layne's using my third one as a basket."

Mr. Hardy grinned. "Of course." The man rang everything up and bagged it for her before turning to Layne. He never said a word about the t-shirts, yet she could see them on the stool behind him. Did he still want them signed? She didn't mind. She waited until Layne was all checked out. "Mr. Hardy, would you like me to sign those shirts?" She pointed at them.

He looked at Layne then nodded. "If you wouldn't mind."

"I'll meet you in the truck." Layne picked up his bag, then walked around her and picked up hers.

"Here you are." Mr. Hardy set the shirts on the counter and handed her the marker.

She signed all of them, then hurried outside, not wishing to run into Luke Hayden.

Layne was leaning against the tailgate of his truck, one leg crossed over the other. "That's all I needed. Where do you need to go next?"

She unclipped her phone and pulled up her list. "That was my main stop. I only need two more things. Is there a clothing store here that might have both baseball caps and large sun hats?"

He nodded. "There are two clothing stores, but neither has both types of hats, so we'll have to go to both. Anything else?"

"Four Peaks wouldn't happen to have a computer store, would it?"

"No, but there is a computer whiz in town. What do you need?"

She crossed her fingers before answering. "Amber forgot the cord to charge her laptop, so I need to get one. I know her brand, so I'm hoping we can find one."

Layne looked past her, his gaze following something behind her.

She glanced over her shoulder to see Luke Hayden get into his truck. She turned back to Layne. "You don't like him."

"It's not a matter of liking or not. He's just someone who needs to be watched."

"Why? Is he a bad boy?" That's what Luke made her think of, a young man with not enough responsibility and too much time, and from the looks of his truck, too much money. The term 'spoiled brat' came to mind.

Layne watched the truck leave the parking lot before answering. "Luke looks for ways to get into trouble."

"Has he ever gotten in trouble with you?"

"Once. That's all it took." He pushed off the back of the tailgate, walked to the passenger door and opened it. "Ready for the next stop?"

She walked up to him, but didn't get in. "What happened between you and him? He seems to give you a wide berth."

Again, Layne shrugged. "About ten years ago, he tried to get me riled up, hoping to instigate a fight. Stupid kid didn't pick his adversaries very well then. Or now. When I didn't react to his taunts, he took a swing at me. I stepped aside which just infuriated him more. When he came at me again, I taught him a lesson. I called legislator Hayden from the emergency room and told him his son had received stitches and was ready to go home."

"Are these Haydens any relation to Amanda?"

"Luke's her brother."

That was surprising. She'd bet that made holiday gatherings interesting. She was about to ask about that when the smell of popcorn wafted past her. "Did you get popcorn?"

His smile was back. "It's in the truck. You can't go to Mr. Hardy's hardware store and not eat the popcorn."

Incentivized now to get going, she climbed onto the front seat to find two bags of the popcorn sitting in the middle. "If you had told me we had popcorn, I would have rushed to get in here. Smelling it in the store made me hungry. I had planned to have some but got distracted. Thank you."

"You're welcome." Layne shut her door.

She immediately picked up a bag, which was still slightly warm. The popcorn was covered in butter and salt. She stuffed her mouth with it.

He got in, and in no time they were on their way down Main Street. She had finished her bag of popcorn before their first stop. After purchasing a baseball cap for Jade at a local clothing store, Layne took her to a western wear store, where she found a wide-brimmed sunhat for Amber. She couldn't resist a pair of red cowboy boots and another cowboy hat for herself. She'd never owned cowboy boots before, but she liked how they felt.

Layne waited patiently as she tried them on. "Your heel should slip a little in the back. If it doesn't, then they don't fit right. And if it slips a lot, they're too big."

She walked back and forth as the owner, Sheila, fetched a couple more sizes. "These feel like they'll fall off." She sat back down and waited. When Sheila came back, Silver took the smaller size from her. After pulling them on, she walked toward the back of the store and then toward the front where Layne stood, his shoulder leaning against the wall.

"How do those feel?"

"I think these are perfect. I can feel them slip a little, but they feel good." She sat back down and pulled them from her feet before putting on her tennis shoes again. When she stood, her feet felt like they had no support. "Wow, what a difference. Maybe I should wear the boots back to the ranch."

Layne pushed away from the wall. "I wouldn't. You want to

break them in slowly or you'll have blisters, and I doubt those will feel good when you're working on your site."

"Good point." She brought the boots to the counter with the black felt hat she'd found. It looked great on her white hair.

As she climbed into the truck again, she noticed Layne still hadn't eaten his popcorn. When he got settled in his seat, she held it up. "Don't you want your popcorn?"

"That's not for me. I got that for you."

"You did? But why didn't you take some for yourself? Are you watching your weight?" She personally couldn't see why. He wasn't lean like Tanner, but was broad and filled out well. She'd caught herself looking at his butt a few times.

He chuckled. "Not at all. I enjoy what I like. I'm just saving room for our next stop."

"The computer place? Does it have food as well?" That was concerning, especially if it wasn't actually a computer store. If it had food, that made her more wary.

"No. You'll see."

Finding his relaxed manner rather refreshing, she sat back to see where they'd stop. The Main Street of Four Peaks was like stepping back in time, for the most part. She had a feeling the proprietors of the various establishments had done that on purpose, most likely for tourism. She'd only seen two stoplights on the whole street, which appeared to be about two miles in length, but that was probably being generous. Beyond it on both ends appeared to be desert and mountains. The view of the four peaks she caught down side streets was quite impressive.

Layne put on his blinker and turned into what appeared to be a four-store strip mall. Though the building was the typical adobe look, the statue of a rearing horse in front of one shop, and outside another, a paper mâché saguaro cactus with a cowboy hat on top, and halfway down a holster with fake guns, continued the Old West theme.

She was so intent on studying the cactus and wondering what future generations would think if they dug one of those up in an archeological dig that Layne surprised her by opening her door.

"Ready?"

She unbuckled her seatbelt. "I'm not sure. Where are we going?" She jumped down from the seat and looked curiously at the four signs.

"There." Layne pointed to a plain white sign with black lettering and no western decoration.

She read it aloud. "Mrs. Silva's Ice Cream Shop."

"Yeah. I can't come into town without stopping."

She raised her brows at that. "Don't you come into town every day on your way to the ranch and back?"

He gave her a shit-eating grin. "Yeah."

Not sure if that meant he had ice cream every time or if he meant he stopped by to say *hi*, she followed him in. He was definitely happy to be there, because he walked faster than he usually did. That was telling.

Layne opened the glass door for her and a little bell rang. Then it rang again as Layne flicked it with his finger.

She stepped into a clean but sterile ice cream shop, just as a thin woman in her late fifties bustled through batwing doors at the back, the only nod inside to the western theme. Her black hair, liberally sprinkled with white, was pulled back in a tight bun, which did little to soften the appearance of her angular nose and large gray eyes.

"Layne Dawson, what are you doing here in the middle of the day?"

Layne leaned his elbow on the tall glass ice cream case closest to him. "You mean I need an excuse to visit my favorite woman in all of Four Peaks?"

"If your mother heard such shit come out of you, she'd hire

the National Guard to tie you down and wash your mouth out with soap."

Layne laughed, fully and loudly. "I love you, too, Aunt Rose."

Ah, so he was related. That made more sense.

"And who do you have with you? Is this a new hand the Rocky Road hired?"

Silver didn't wait for Layne to respond. "Hello, Mrs. Silva. I'm Silver Collins. I'm visiting the Rocky Road for the month."

"She's a scientist and anthropologist."

"An anthropologist?" The woman's eyes lit up. "That's fascinating. Are you here to study our townspeople? You know we don't have any Native Americans in the area. They left long before the Europeans settled here."

Surprised and pleased that she didn't have to explain what an anthropologist did for a change, Silver smiled warmly. "Actually, I am studying Native Americans, but those who lived here around 8,000 BCE or older.

Mrs. Silva looked at Layne as if to ask if it was true and he nodded, then she tapped the glass cooler. "Then you'll need a bowl of ice cream for such intense work. What flavor would you like?"

"What kinds do you have?"

Layne leaned down and spoke next to her ear. "Only unusual ones."

"Really?" She stepped toward the glass cases. There were three in total, and each had eight tubs. "I like trying new food flavors." She started at the front. "Blue Moon, Chocolate Truffle, Eggnog, White Cherry Chip, Banoffee, Coffee Nut, Peppermint Pattie, Hazelnut Cheesecake, Key Lime Pie, Chocolate Brownie, Chocolate Peanut Butter, Macaroon, Lemon Raspberry, S'mores, Snickerdoodle, Black Licorice, Ube—you have ube ice cream?"

Mrs. Silva nodded smugly. "I do. I have Philippine connections."

"Oh, I haven't had that since the last time I was in Asia and our guides wife made it for us." She looked at Layne. "She was from the Philippines where this flavor is a favorite. I must have some."

As her bowl of ice cream was being prepared, she leaned on the counter and watched. There were no waffle cones or sprinkles or syrup, just a metal bowl filled with the purple ice cream she'd chosen. "Have you ever tried making an ice cream like the Red Rubies dessert found in Thailand?"

Mrs. Silva set the metal bowl on top of the ice cream case and added a spoon. "No. Is it sweet?"

"It is. It uses water chestnuts drenched in a syrup that I think is grenadine, then they're coated in tapioca and mixed into coconut milk. It's delicious."

"I will definitely look that up. I could use my coconut base. Thank you, Silver." The woman turned to her nephew. "I'll get yours now." She went into the back.

Silver took her bowl to one of the little round tables set against the wall. She sat and took a bite, unable to wait for Layne. The nutty sweet flavor coated her tongue, and she closed her eyes. "This is amazing." She opened her eyes and looked at Layne who was staring at her. "Is your flavor a special one that she makes only for you?"

"Yes."

Mrs. Silva came out with a large ceramic bowl, obviously hand-made by a child, and handed it to Layne. "One day I'm going to get you to try something different."

He gave his aunt a grin. "Why, when this is perfect?"

His aunt shook her head, mumbling something under her breath as he came over to sit.

Silver looked at the ice cream piled like a mountain in the deep piece of pottery. "Is that coconut or mascarpone?"

He dug his spoon into it and lifted out a large amount. "It's vanilla."

She stared. "Really?"

Layne smiled around his spoon, which he'd just put in his mouth.

"That's too funny. Your aunt owns an ice cream shop with unusual flavored ice cream, and you like vanilla. Have you tried any other flavors?"

He held another spoonful of vanilla and looked at it as if it were his bliss before moving his gaze to her. "Chocolate chip, but I prefer vanilla. It's pure, perfect, creamy goodness." Again a large spoonful went into his mouth.

She took another bite of hers, but watched as he truly savored three more bites. "You like things simple."

"I do. I believe that if it ain't broke, don't fix it."

"That's an unusual philosophy, closer to Tibetan then to American. Our citizens are always striving for something—more money, a bigger house, a higher position, more children."

He studied her for a moment, the color in his hazel eyes reflecting the soft blue of the walls in the shop. "You strive for discovery, more knowledge about where humans came from."

Not a little flattered that he'd paid attention earlier, she felt her cheeks heat. "That may seem redundant when so much has already been discovered, and it was so long ago, but I feel as if the more we know of our ancestors, the more we can know about ourselves."

He nodded as if it made total sense. "Knowing that my great-grandfather was a cowboy does make me feel more comfortable about who I am. I never thought about it on a societal level."

Layne continued to surprise her with how quickly he

grasped her field of study when so many people struggled to understand it. "What about you? What do you strive for?"

"That things remain just as they are. It's not that hard though, so I wouldn't say I *work* at it. I just live it." He grinned.

There was something about his world view that was incredibly calming. "Did you ever push toward being in this particular place in life?"

"You mean in my aunt's ice cream shop with you?"

"No, I mean in your life." Too late she noticed the gleam in his eyes. He was teasing. "Seriously, Layne?"

He laughed, the deep sound exciting and lulling at the same time. "I suppose I pushed toward saving money for my house, but it wasn't really hard. When I had enough, I bought it. I find if you're patient, things will work out."

She sighed, unable to help herself. His life sounded peaceful, content. "You're a special person. I'm just not wired that way. My ancestors were obviously not content."

"So you're blaming your need to make a discovery on your genes?"

"I guess I am."

"Then maybe you should have bought those white jeans I saw you eyeing at the western store. With new jeans, you could have a new outlook on life."

She blinked, trying to follow his reasoning then smirked. "Nice try, cowboy."

CHAPTER 6

"TOO BAD THE Rocky Road doesn't own a mule."

Layne examined the pile of tools and supplies Nash had stacked on the ATV and had to agree. "It's just for this one trip, and then again when they leave. I don't think Tanner's going to want to invest in a mule when it's just for a couple days of work."

"He could always add it to the petting zoo afterward."

"That's not a bad idea, if you had it a couple of weeks ago." Layne tightened Honor's cinch.

Nash, who was an expert at cattle more than with mules, tightened the ropes over the bagged canopy. "What about that wild burro who's always hanging around?"

"George? That's not gonna happen. He's wild, remember?"

Nash finished his knot and stood straight. "I don't know. He doesn't seem to mind people at all, and he's never with the other burros. He's over at the front porch munching on the hay in the post hay feeder right now."

"What?" Layne headed for the open doors. They'd never had a wild burro come up to the porch of the house. Between the vehicles driving in and the people coming and going, the wild animals gave the residence a wide birth. Only George had come near the barn, and Layne had assumed it was because Jackson's raccoon had taken his apple.

Just outside the barn, Layne stopped in his tracks. Sure enough, the burro was standing at the hay feeder attached to a porch post, which the Dunn men used for their horses when they came in to make lunch for their father. George was distinctive because of the white diamond on his forehead. Not wanting to approach the burro from the rear since their kicks could be deadly, Layne gave the animal a wide berth before he leisurely ascended the steps to the porch to engage the animal head-on.

George ate like he was famished, but there was plenty of grass by the north mountain where Layne had seen him last. "George, what are you doing?"

The burro moved his snout out from the box and stared at him, but continued to chew.

"Are you feeling okay?"

George finished chewing then dipped his snout down to the feeder tray to scrape up the last of the hay.

Layne looked at his watch. If he hurried, he could refill the box. He turned on his heel and jogged down the steps, making the barn in no time, where he got another hay bale from the loft and strode out to where George was, standing about five feet from the hay box.

Layne slowed his stride as he approached George from the side. "If you stay there and not cause trouble, you can have more for breakfast. Do we have a deal?"

The burro's head lifted slightly, its nostrils twitching.

"I'll take that as a yes." Keeping the animal in his peripheral vision, Layne laid the bale across the open box, pulled his knife from his back pocket, and quickly cut the twine holding it together. He was in the process of pulling the twine out from under it, when his shoulder was nudged. He froze.

Slowly, he turned his head to find George sniffing his flannel shirt. Then the dark brown furry nose pushed under his elbow.

"Whoa, there." Layne let his arm lie on George's neck, not in a hurry to get bit. "If you want more to eat, you have to let me do my job."

George moved his head up against Layne's waist.

"Are you asking for attention?" Not sure he was reading the animal right, but well aware he couldn't just stand there all day, he stroked George's head with his arm, keeping his hand far from the animal's mouth.

George leaned into him harder, almost pushing him over.

"Well, I'll be damned." With one hand, he finished removing the twine while he stroked the burro with his other. After settling the hay in the feeder, he stepped back to see if George would start eating again.

George looked at him and then at the hay.

That was the thing with burros. They always took time to mull things over, but he didn't have a lot of time. Then again, the ladies weren't going anywhere without him, so he waited to see what George would do.

The burro walked to him and nudged his arm again.

"You cannot be a wild burro." He stroked George's head down the white diamond between his eyes and back again. He'd known George was different, as he was always alone and his coloring was gray and not brown, but he wasn't the only gray burro in the area. But this behavior was concerning. If George wasn't wild, he could get into trouble.

The wooden front door of the adobe residence opened and Amanda Hayden Dunn stepped out in her scrubs, blonde hair pulled back in a ponytail. Immediately, she walked across the porch. "I couldn't believe what I was seeing on the security camera. You really are petting a wild burro. You know that's not smart, right? Is the stress of guiding our scientists getting to you that much?"

He chuckled, which George seemed to like. "No, they're fine. I'm pretty convinced that George is domesticated."

"George?" Her brows rose with her question.

"It's what I named him when I first noticed he was hanging around. It's a lot easier than saying 'that burro that's been hanging around'."

"If he's domesticated and running loose, he could get into trouble."

"My thought as well. He was at the shelter at the north mountain a few days ago. Now he's here eating from the hay feeder. And *he's* the one who asked for the attention."

Amanda frowned. "Aren't you taking our scientists to set up their site today so they can start work?"

"I am. I was just adding hay to the feeder to try to keep him around where it's safer."

"That makes sense. At least Cami isn't here."

He'd completely forgotten about Brody and Hannah's dog. He couldn't put off the ladies, but he didn't like leaving George on his own, now that he knew how vulnerable he was. "Hannah's not reviewing the finances today, is she?"

"No, why?"

"I just want to be sure he's safe." He laid his hand on George's back. "I don't know where you came from, buddy, but you've got a new home now."

"Maybe we should find his original home first, and then talk to Tanner." Amanda crossed her arms over her chest, which wasn't a good sign.

"I'm not worried about Tanner. I'll take responsibility for his care."

Amanda raised her brows. "You? The man who's talked

about buying another horse for two years but doesn't want to take on the responsibility of caring for it?"

She was right. "This is different. I've always said things will work out the way they're supposed to, so I guess there was a reason I didn't get a new horse. It was so I'd have the time to take care of George."

She eyed him skeptically. "I don't know about this."

He needed to convince her to keep George at the Rocky Road. The animal wouldn't survive in the wild. That was why George was always showing up on the ranch...and it was a *dude* ranch now. "Just think how much fun your guests would have with a burro wandering around."

Amanda's eyes widened and she uncrossed her arms. "You're right. If he really is domesticated, we need to find a way to keep him here. What about the corral?"

"No. He's been free-range for too long. He might panic. Food is a good start. Don't we have some metal tubs in the barn for the cattle in the birthing enclosure? If we set one up with water nearby, that will definitely entice him to stay."

Amanda's eyes lit with excitement. "We could even give the guests carrots to feed him like they do in Oatman. I love this idea! I'll get the water trough set up."

He eyed Amanda's scrubs. "You?"

She looked down at her clothes before frowning at him. "Yes, me. I can always change, and I'll get Isaac to help me lug it out of the barn. You have a job to do."

Isaac was Jeremiah's CNA and a strong guy, so he'd have no problem moving one of the metal tubs. "Yes. I better head over to the square. I'll just make sure George is occupied with the feeder before I leave."

"Good. I'll go talk to Isaac right now." Amanda spun on her heel and disappeared into the house.

Now to get George back to the feeder. He removed his hand

from the burro's back and immediately the animal stepped against him, pushing him and forcing him to take a step. "Hey, I can't stay here all day." He heard steps behind him.

"Dangerous, my ass. No pun intended."

He whipped his head around to find Silver standing not twenty yards behind him, a scowl on her face.

Though he appreciated her humor, it was clear his credibility as a guide had been blown. "This isn't a wild burro. This one is domesticated."

"Are you telling me Rocky Road has its own burro?"

He nodded. "They do now." He stepped around George's head and tapped the feeder. "I have to go now. We have a big day ahead of us. You better stay around here."

Luckily, George decided more food was welcome and started to munch.

Confident the animal was distracted, Layne headed for Silver. "My horse is saddled and Nash has already headed out with your equipment. Is everyone ready to go?"

She looked past him. "Aren't you going to say goodbye to him?"

He didn't dare look. The last thing he wanted to do was encourage George to follow them. "It's better if I don't. He's safer near the house."

She gave George a final look then turned back toward the corral. "We've been waiting over twenty minutes."

"Then we can stay an extra twenty minutes. Making sure an animal is safe is a priority on a ranch."

She walked beside him, but didn't look at him. "Even if it's a wild animal?"

He laughed, finding her ill humor over such a small delay humorous. "Yes, even a wild animal. But when we get back in, if you want to pet George, you're welcome to."

She stopped then. "That's George? You told me he was wild."

"I thought he was. I just discovered he's not. Someone had him, though who, I haven't a clue. Honestly, I should have figured it out sooner. Burros are not loners. They always have friends."

She started walking again. "Well, I think you're his new friend."

"I've had worse."

As they approached the corral where all the women and horses waited, Jade greeted him. "It's about time. We should have left already."

Before he could respond, Silver spoke up. "Our cowboy was making friends with a burro."

Jade raised one eyebrow at that. "I can think of more helpful animals to make friends with."

He walked over to Amber and gave her a hand up onto her horse. "Actually, a burro is one of the most helpful of animals. They have excellent hearing. They can hear danger that's still far off, plus they are good at carrying things. In addition, they're thinkers, and will make smart decisions instead of reacting like horses will. I've seen a wild burro stare down a mountain lion. Even that cat doesn't want to tangle with a kick from a burro."

Jade waved him off as she mounted her horse. "You sound like a fan."

He walked to his horse since Silver was already mounted. "I am. I've always liked asses." He winked before mounting up.

Amber laughed but Jade groaned.

He turned his horse to face them all. "I'm also partial to rocks."

"Rocks?" Silver cocked her head.

He grinned. "Yes, rocks like Amber, Jade, and Silver."

Silver immediately got it and chuckled. "That makes me the third rock from the cowboy."

"Oh, I like that. That means I'm Mercury." Amber smiled.

Jade, however, shook her head. "Only Jade is a rock, so it doesn't actually work."

Amber turned toward her. "What's wrong, Jade. You don't like being Venus?"

At Amber's observation, Jade clamped her mouth shut.

Layne turned his horse to lead the way. "I know that silver is a mineral and amber is actually a hard resin from a tree, but when you think of it, they are all used in jewelry and are considered precious."

Jade's eyes widened, her cheeks flushing, while Amber chuckled, but Silver tipped her hat to him, obviously approving of his set-down.

"Now ladies, I believe there is work to be done." He started them out at a walk, Amber once again falling in next to him, but as he picked up the pace, she fell back and Silver came up to ride beside him. He glanced behind him to make sure they didn't get too far ahead of the other two women. When the distance was growing long, he slowed down again. It wouldn't do to lose a scientist.

"Was Nash able to bring all our equipment in one trip?"

He looked over at Silver. She sat a horse well. "Yes. But getting it up the mountain is going take a number of trips."

"That's not a problem. We're used to schlepping our stuff all over the place. At least we won't have to wade through water holding everything over our heads. You don't realize how much you use your hands for balance when walking in chest-high water."

He was about to ask where she'd done that, but refrained. It would be some other exotic remote place she'd been to that he'd have to look up on the internet. "Do you ever stay home?"

Her laughter floated around them. "I am the ultimate nomad. Jade has a house and Amber has a room in her parents' house in between trips, but I just visit friends or go on vacation. It's not worth the effort of having a home when we are only free for one or two weeks at a time."

The idea of not having a home was more foreign to him than any exotic local she may have visited. "What about your family?"

"Oh, I visit one of them sometimes. They're all spread out. I have a step-sister that I enjoy spending time with. She's the closest to a home base. If there's going to be a family gathering, it's at her place."

"What about your mom and dad?"

"My mom lives with my other sister. I never knew my biological father, but my dad passed away about six years ago of a heart attack. My step-siblings have their own families now, so I pop in when I can."

He remained silent, trying to wrap his head around a life with no home.

"You seem confused. I know you have a home because you said that was something you had as a goal. Do you have siblings who are less settled? Not like me, but just in transition so to speak?"

"No. All my sisters and one brother are married. My brother married a surgeon over in Scottsdale. He and his wife live in Cave Creek. My sisters married a lawyer, a builder, a store owner, and a teacher. My youngest brother is still living at home until he can buy a house. This is his first year out of college. He's working over at Cholla Valley, the Haydens' ranch."

"Oh wow. How many siblings is that?"

"Six. And all of them have children except my youngest brother and myself. Our gatherings for Memorial Day, Fourth of

July, and Pioneer Days are very active. I have eleven nieces and nephews."

"Eleven?"

He grinned as her tone revealed her surprise. "Yeah. We have enough people in our family to man a football team, special teams, and all."

She studied him a moment. "How come you don't have children?"

It had been so long since someone had asked him that, he couldn't remember his pat answer at first. But at the sound of horse's hooves, he looked back. Amber was riding up to them.

"Should we be worried about that?" Amber pointed behind her to the south.

He slowed Honor to a halt. A squadron of about seven or eight javelinas rutted around a large agave plant. "No. Those are javelinas. They're too busy looking for food to be a bother."

"What's a javelina?" Silver looked over her shoulder.

That question surprised him since the animals were more common in South America than North America. "Many people mistake them for wild pigs, but they are far removed from that ancestor."

Amber scrunched up her nose. "Oh, then we've definitely seen those before. They stink."

"Yes, they are a bit pungent. They can't see well, so they communicate by scents and sounds."

Jade joined them then. "Will they attack humans?"

He was about to say no, but remembered a classmate back in high school who'd been tormenting them. "Only if provoked. Most of the animals, reptiles, and snakes out here are just surviving. They're not looking for trouble, just their next meal."

Jade nodded authoritatively. "Then as long as we don't run into a wolf or mountain lion, I guess we're safe."

He straightened in his saddle. "You still would be safe since

I'm here. We don't have far to go and Vic told me you all can gallop. Are you ready—"

"Race ya!"

"Amber, no!" Silver kicked her horse and galloped after Amber.

Layne sighed as Jade followed her friends. "Come on, boy. Let's stretch your legs." The last thing he needed was for one of the ladies to get hurt.

Luckily, it didn't take long to catch up. The women were inexperienced riders, and Honor was fast when he needed to be. The horse probably looked at the women like they were cattle to be herded. Racing past them, he then put Honor in their path and slowed. The ladies' horses slowed immediately.

He walked Honor toward them, catching the tail end of Silver's admonishments. Pleased he wouldn't have to lecture them, he simply waved for them to follow and they did, only stopping when they reached the shelter where Nash had unloaded the ATV.

Layne jumped down from his horse to give Nash instructions, but the man walked to Amber and helped her dismount. That didn't surprise him. Nash was friends with all the women in town, but had no girlfriend. Looked like he was working on that right now.

Silver got off Chestnut and immediately moved toward the equipment. She grabbed the folded canopy and a bucket. The other women joined her, quickly taking what they wanted and leaving a variety of items. Silver turned toward him. "We're ready."

He shook his head. "You do remember there's a forty-foot patch of shale to walk around, right?"

Though she didn't say it, he could see she had forgotten. "Yes, well, we still need to get our tools up there."

"Nash, take those shovels from Amber and Jade. I'll carry

the canopy. You each need one arm free for that section. Now let's go." He turned his back on Silver as she had opened her mouth to speak. Hopefully, she'd remember he knew more about maneuvering in the Sonoran Desert than she did, no matter how many mountains she'd climbed or how many deserts she'd crossed.

As he started up the slope, he tried to put himself in her boots. What was it like for her to always be ignorant of her immediate environment? She may know a lot about ancient peoples, but living in the past meant missing out on the present...and the future. He found himself feeling bad for her. To be so driven about her career that she missed out on today was sad.

Maybe he could show her the present was just as interesting.

SILVER SIFTED dirt through their tripod sifting screen, keeping her eyes focused on finding anything that might be helpful as the dirt disappeared below. She stood outside the three-sided canopy in the sun, which felt good since the temperatures had dipped overnight, and even in her sweater and fleece, it was chilly in the shade.

"I found another one. This one is pretty small. I'm guessing a bird." Jade, who sat on the ground near the petroglyph rock in her wool jacket, held up a small bone, which Amber promptly inspected before bagging it and labeling it. She turned to Silver. "Have you found anything yet?"

"No. It's been pretty uneventful all day. I wonder if we should start to move away from the face of the rock and toward the mountain. Only the artists would have stood right against the rock."

"That's true." Amber tilted her head. "But I thought you said it could be the roof of a structure."

"I did. It still could be, but maybe it's time to ask Benedict to send the GPR machine." Though their boss went by 'Dick' because he hated his given name, it gave her pleasure to refer to him as his mother named him, because he was such an ass.

Amber groaned. "I hate asking him for those special gadgets. He always puts up such a fuss."

"I'll ask him. I'm the one who thinks this is a roof."

"I hope it is, or we'll be done here in a few weeks. There's barely fifteen feet between this rock and the mountain." Amber held her arms out, indicating the distance.

"And if you take into account that manzanita tree with all the brush under it behind our canopy, we're down to about six feet at the center. I wish we could trim it back a bit."

Jade set down her trowel. "Don't even think about it. This is conservation land. They barely let us come here as it was. I read the permissions. Unless we find something earth-shattering, they won't consider allowing us to even break a twig on that tree."

Silver rolled her eyes at Amber. "I know. I was just wishing." They were always limited by whoever owned the land they worked. Government land was the most restrictive. Personal property tended to be free rein. "Too bad the Rocky Road Ranch doesn't own this far up the mountain."

Amber lifted her face to the sun for a full minute before turning to go back to the dirt at the base of the rock. "Maybe the GPR will find that cave you're hoping for. Better call Dick the Prick."

"Right." She set down the sifter, unclipped her phone from her jeans, and hit Benedict's name on her contacts list.

It rang twice before he answered. "What?"

"Good morning, Dick. How's your day going?" He hated it when she was nice.

"It sucks. What do you want?"

"We need the ground penetrating radar. It looks like we may have a cave symbol."

"Looks like it or you have one. Which is it?"

"We have the symbol. We need the GPR to see if the cave is here." She shook her head. He could never just say yes. Every penny spent on their work was like pulling teeth.

"So dig deeper. You have shovels, right? Put your backs into it."

She held onto her patience. He said the same thing every time they asked for needed technology. "Dick, if it's deep, we won't reach it by the end of the month, and if we have no proof it's here, we'll be done in two more weeks."

"Only two weeks? You can't. You have to work for a month or I'd have to give back part of the funds. You have to make it last a month. If you have to, make shit up."

The man hated returning money more than he hated spending it. It pissed her off royally. "We are not freaking making shit up! We're scientists. I told you that when you decided to exploit the ancient astronaut side of my work. Now we've got one rock with petroglyphs and six feet of ground in front of it. That's it. If we don't know something else is below us, there's no reason to stay. Either send the damn GPR or we're done here!"

"Fucking A. How do I know you're telling me the truth? Maybe you're making up this possible cave so you can use the GPR to find some hidden gold mine out there."

She counted to ten before responding. "If I wanted to find a damn gold mine, I certainly wouldn't do it while on the clock for you. The last thing I'd want to do is share anything with you. So send the freaking GPR or we're leaving!" She didn't wait for a response, ending the call.

"You're so much better at that than I am." Amber brought another bucket of dirt to be sifted.

Silver took a deep breath to get rid of the frustration of dealing with Benedict. "You just have to use your intelligence and not back down. He may know finances but you can talk him into a corner in—"

Rocks falling behind her had her spinning. Layne appeared to surf down the mountainside from his look-out above them. "What's wrong?" He stopped his descent by jumping to the small path next to her, his booted feet sending up dust.

"Nothing's wrong. Why?"

He scanned her, then Amber, then the surrounding area. "I heard yelling."

Amber set the bucket down. "I'll let you explain." She disappeared around the canopy.

Layne stepped closer to her. "What happened?"

She could almost feel the sizzle in the air around him. He'd come to protect them and his whole body was tense. It sent a strange feeling of gratefulness through her that had her feeling uncomfortably vulnerable. To give herself a moment, she stepped back to clip her phone back to her belt, but her heel caught the wall of the canopy and she started to fall back into it. She threw her arms out to catch her balance.

For the second time since coming to the Rocky Road, she found herself in Layne's arms. The first time startled her. This time, all she felt was desire as she was held against his hard chest. She was neither short nor thin, but pressed against his large body mass, she felt like she was both. She made the mistake of looking up at him.

His hazel gaze seemed mostly green as he looked at her as if he wanted to slowly take off all her clothes and lick every inch of her. His heartbeat echoed her own, thudding against his chest, and the hand that had landed on her back moved to the back of her head. In that instant, she recognized a kiss was about to happen and now was the time to stop it if she wanted to.

She didn't want to.

As his head lowered, she closed her eyes.

His lips touched her own with a tantalizing kiss that both stirred her senses and made sinful promises. Having no reason to resist, she opened her mouth and invited him in.

He hesitated for a split second before his lips opened and his tongue moved inside, savoring her as if she were fine cognac. It was a heady feeling.

She held onto his back tighter, to keep herself up as his tongue stroked against her own, filling her with the scent of cedarwood and leather. There was nothing demanding or rushed about the kiss, so much like Layne himself.

Too soon he ended their connection and pulled his head back. "Are you okay?" The question was filled with meaning.

She smiled. "Very okay."

His lips widened in a sinful smile. "Good."

As his hold loosened, she let go of him and found herself standing on her own two feet though still incredibly close. She would be lying if she denied the strong attraction she felt to him. He was manly in a very mature, confident way that was far too tempting to resist.

Since she couldn't step back any farther as she'd already proved, she waited for him to make more space. But as they stood there, she couldn't help imagining him shrugging out of his lined jean jacket that he wore open despite the cold. Or what he would look like beneath his blue plaid flannel shirt.

"Why were you yelling?"

His question brought her attention back to his face as her gaze had wandered down to his chest.

"That was just my boss. Benedict Nagle is the most infuriating boss I've ever had. He finds us the best sites to work on and is excellent with numbers, but getting him to spend any money is harder than chiseling gold from bedrock."

Layne frowned as he stroked the side of his bushy black mustache. "But doesn't he pay you and provide the lodging and equipment? Or does he make you pay for lodging and equipment?"

"Oh, he pays us and for the basic lodging, food, and minimal equipment. But with the more expensive items, he hoards them unless we can convince him why we need them."

"And you need something for this site?"

She was still very much aware that he had not stepped back. "We do. I asked him for ground penetrating radar to discover if there really is a cave beneath our feet like I think. He didn't want to send it. So I had to argue with him. I'm usually the one who calls him because he'll walk all over Amber, and Jade can't keep up with his illogical thought process. I simply explained to him how he'd lose more money if he didn't send the GPR. Yelling keeps the conversation at his level. I figured that out by the second time I requested equipment and found I get much better results." She smiled smugly.

Layne's brows rose even as he shook his head. "You're a very smart woman." His hand came up to rest against her cheek. "Smart and beautiful."

Her heart skipped a beat. It wasn't so much what he said but how he said it, the last word coming out on a breath. She'd rarely heard both compliments in one year, never mind in one sentence. Her normal reaction was to brush a compliment off, but the intensity in his eyes was too sincere, too real. "Thank you." Her own words came out in a whisper.

"Hey, Silver. Take a look at this." Amber peeked her head around the canopy catching sight of Layne before disappearing again.

At Amber's appearance, Layne took two steps back.

Silver forced herself to refocus on her work. After moving around the canopy, she walked to where Amber brushed off an object. "What is it?"

"It's an arrowhead, but it doesn't appear to be of the same time period as the other artifacts." Amber handed it up to her.

She examined the small stone piece, obviously worked by man. "You could be right. Jade, what do you think? My guess is much later, maybe the Folsom period." She walked over to the corner where Jade had stopped digging and handed it to her.

After studying it, Jade nodded. "Yes, this is much finer work. This could be two thousand years later. I can double check now or wait until we get back to the lodge." She handed it back.

Silver felt her stomach muscles tense with excitement. "Check it at the lodge. I don't want to waste daylight on research. This could be more evidence that there's a cave here used by more than one generation, either of the same group of people or multiple groups."

Jade looked across the area to Amber. "Where'd you find it?"

Amber pointed to a spot right at the entrance to the canopy. "Here. We might want to move the canopy to one side."

"But which side?" Silver shook her head. "First dig more on each side of this find. If you find something else, then we'll move the canopy in that direction."

"Good idea." Immediately, Amber start digging to the right of the spot.

Jade rose. "I'll dig on the other side. You keep sifting."

"Will do." Quickly, Silver moved to the back of the canopy and bagged and tagged the arrowhead. More sure than ever that there had to be a cave. But she needed to sift until they knew which way they should go next. After adding the artifact to the backpack used for transporting the items down the mountain, she stepped around the canopy, anxious to share with Layne what the new item could mean for her theory about a cave.

He wasn't there. Disappointed, she looked up the mountain

to find him back at the spot he used to watch out for them, the very spot where he and she had seen the roof image on the rock. She felt an urge to climb up and join him, tell him the exciting news, which surprised her. The only person she shared her career successes with was her sister.

Tamping down the feeling, she picked up the bucket Amber had brought and poured some dirt on top of the sifter. Then she started sifting, keeping her eyes focused on finding the smallest of artifacts even as her fingers brushed through the dirt, spreading it across the screen.

Unfortunately, her thoughts were not as focused as they needed to be. Layne's kiss had most of her mind occupied. While it had been a sensuous kiss that told her he was interested, it wasn't demanding, as if he needed her right that moment. Then again, based on what she knew of Layne so far, he never seemed to need anything right away. He was exceedingly patient and seemed to savor every moment of life. That was how she'd felt about the kiss, as if he'd savored her.

So what would happen now? She did like him. He was a handsome, confident man. He never did get a chance to answer her question about not being married, but she wasn't exactly in the market for forever. Her work had her traveling to a new location for one to three months or more at a time. He was perfectly happy staying put, yet neither of them had someone in their lives, at least not that she knew of.

Even as she continued to sift, adding more dirt, she shook her head. Layne was definitely not the type of man who would kiss her if he was seeing someone. He was old-fashioned to a fault. She had a feeling he was as honorable as they came.

Maybe she just needed to get out of her head and see what happened naturally. Layne didn't seem like a man who played games. He'd probably come right out and ask her out on a date or to dinner or invite her to his house. Or he might simply continue being their guide, helpful, reliable, and amiable. Even at the thought, she was surprised that she didn't want him to be the latter.

Footsteps from the other side of the canopy let her know one of her colleagues approached.

Jade came into view and set down another bucket of dirt. "This is all from the canopy edge. I figure we want to know if there's anything in that dirt first. My other bucket from the corner of the rock is half full. You want me to dump what you have left into that one?"

"Good idea. This way I can start on this promising track right away." Silver poured the new dirt in and moved the sifter back and forth. The work was tedious, whether sifting or digging or researching, but the small discoveries made it all worth it. If she could just—

"I got it!"

At Jade's yell, she set down the sifter and ran around the canopy. "What is it?"

Amber scrambled over, too.

Jade held the tiny object out to Amber. "I believe it's a Clovis point."

Silver moved behind Amber who sat on the ground. Amber brushed more dirt from what appeared to be a well-worked jasper stone.

"You're right. It is. This has to be from a more recent group than the artifacts closest to the petroglyphs." Amber held the two-inch piece up.

Silver took the small object and moved into the sunlight with it. It definitely was a weapon point, and whatever tool was used had been more advanced. "This is what we needed." She grinned at her colleagues. "It looks like we can move the canopy to the east and dig on that side all the way up to the mountain wall. Who knows what other items we'll find. Having multi-generations using this site means the chances of a cave below have increased tenfold."

Jade nodded in agreement. "So does this discovery rate as well as Layne's kisses?"

She rolled her eyes at Amber, who'd obviously seen more than she'd let on.

"Well, I had to let Jade know he was off limits." Amber gave her a cheeky grin.

She returned her gaze to Jade. "To answer your question, yes it does. It definitely does."

Jade's one eyebrow rose.

A vibration at Silver's waist told her she had a message, saving her from further explanation...for now. She unclipped her phone and read it, then grinned at Jade and Amber. "I just got a shipping notification. The GPR is on the way."

"Awesome." Amber lifted her hand to take the small stone. "I'll bag this. Let's get as much done today where we are now, and then reposition the canopy before we leave so we can start moving east tomorrow."

"That sounds good to me." Silver placed the artifact in Amber's hand, then headed back to sifting. She poured in more dirt, but couldn't resist sharing any longer. Leaving the sifter, she started the climb up to Layne. It wasn't difficult, but it did require she watch her step.

As she reached the ledge where he stood, he took her hand to help her step onto it. "You look happy."

She smiled. "I am. After you left, Amber found an artifact from a more recent group of people. Just now, Jade found another but an even more recent group. That means more than one generation of peoples were here, which makes the chances of a cave even better. I also got notice that the GPR I asked Benedict for has been shipped. This is promising to be a great site."

His smile was wide. "That's excellent news. I'm happy for you. Congratulations. Is there anything I can do to help?"

"Yes. When we're done today, we're going to move the canopy to the east, so we can dig more on that side. I'd love help doing that."

"Of course. If I remember your set-up, there's a manzanita tree in the middle, so you want it to the east of that?"

"Yes. With the canopy moved, we can even dig under that tree as long as we don't disturb the roots. I really think we are on to something here."

"Then we should celebrate." He pulled her close.

"Well, not yet. I don't want to jinx it. Once we have confirmation with the GPR, then I can celebrate. Of course, then the really hard work starts, uncovering the cave that I hope is there."

"Silver, every little triumph should be celebrated. It's what makes the disappointments in life livable."

Her hands rested on his biceps, which were hard, despite the fleece lining of his jean jacket. She could imagine him enjoying the sunset to celebrate the end of a long day of work. "I have a feeling you haven't had many disappointments."

A soft smile flitted about his lips. "No, not many." Then his lips descended upon hers and he kissed her again.

He leisurely explored her lips and mouth, her body seeming to turn to molten lava, just as hot and just as liquid. She held his arms tightly and did some exploring of her own. He tasted minty and manly, if there was such a thing. It had her wanting a lot more than his mouth.

The kiss didn't intensify, which just seemed to make her want him even more. Then before she was aware of it, he was kissing the corner of her lips and lifting his head away.

She opened her mouth to protest but snapped it shut, not sure what she would say. Kiss me more? Take me here? All of which sounded like a bad porno flick.

His hand squeezed her waist where it rested. "Since you don't want to jinx the possibility of a cave, we should wait for more celebrating until you know for sure, right?" His eyes seemed to twinkle with laughter.

"Right." She cleared her throat as the word barely vocalized. "Yes. I'll be on pins and needles until I know for sure."

Layne raised his brows. "That doesn't sound comfortable."

She blinked, not sure what he meant at first, but at the twitch of his lips, she got it. He was teasing again. She kept her face completely serious. "Yes, well, I've slept on worse."

All signs of humor disappeared in an instant as his gaze became intense and the gray in his eyes seemed to dominate. "That is not acceptable."

His reaction sent a thrill of desire through her. His over-protectiveness and old-fashioned values made her insides mush. She'd been around men all over the world who treated her and her colleagues in many different ways, but Layne was unique. If she wasn't careful, she would find herself becoming attached, which would not be a good idea.

She waved off the subject altogether, feeling a bit off-balance by her thoughts. "There was no help for it. Sometimes the accommodations near a new site that was just discovered are non-existent. But the new knowledge is so worth it." She smiled, hoping to ease his mind.

"You—and the other ladies should always have comfortable lodging. Your employer should make that happen."

She almost snorted, but held it back. "I'll be sure to let him know. Now, I should get back to work. We still have a lot to do." She lifted her hands from his arms to signal he could let her go.

He did and he didn't. Releasing her body, he took her hand again and escorted her back down the mountainside. When they reached her sifting spot, he finally let go and pointed to the canopy. "Let me know when you need that moved and I'll come back."

"Thank you."

Layne turned and started back up to his ledge.

She couldn't take her eyes off him. At first it was his tight butt in his jeans, but even as he disappeared out of sight, she still watched, seeing him in her mind, seeing him lowering his head and kissing her.

She seriously liked the way Layne celebrated. Now she had even more incentive to find a cave. Smiling, she returned to the sifter and began to shake it. Yup, she was looking forward to a full-on celebration very soon.

"Did you enjoy your rendezvous?"

At Amber's voice, she spun around. "What?"

Amber pointed up. "I came here to drop this bucket off and saw the steam from here."

"Are you upset?" She'd noticed all the flirting Amber had been doing with Layne, but Amber flirted with almost every man.

"Nah, enjoy. There's plenty more cowboys around here to get to know. Besides, he's a little old for me."

Relieved, Silver relaxed. "He's even older in his thought process, which I find curious."

"For once, just go with it. You don't need to analyze everything." Amber shook her head before turning and walking back to her digging spot.

Silver chuckled silently. Amber knew her too well. They all knew each other better than their own families. Picking up the shaker, she started sifting again, forcing herself to concentrate on the dirt and anything that might be in it. She needed to stay focused if she wanted something to celebrate later. And she definitely wanted to celebrate.

LAYNE STOOD PARTIALLY up the mountain from the site where Silver worked an odd-looking machine. It looked like a metal detector with wings. She walked back and forth in tight switchbacks between the rock and the mountain face.

He'd taken down the canopy for her earlier so she could sweep the entire site. According to her explanation, if there were any voids beneath her feet, the ground penetrating radar would show her on the screen. She was halfway done now, and she hadn't stopped. He wasn't sure if she would wait until she was done or if she'd tell Amber and Jade immediately, as they stood well out of the way, watching as avidly as he.

She wanted that new discovery, and for her sake, he hoped she found it. He liked seeing her happy. Most of the time she was focused and thoughtful, or concerned. She wasn't prideful, and handled her celebrity status with humility.

When Stacy had been so obsessed with Silver at the hardware store, he thought she was only a celebrity among a small fringe group, but while having his weekly dinner at his mom's Sunday night, two of his nieces insisted that he introduce them, and his brother-in-law had been equally impressed. Then he got a call from another sister and a nephew because his nieces sent out a family text. Now he'd have to convince Silver to meet them all. Maybe dinner at Mom's?

"Silver, do you see anything? I'm dying over here." Amber's statement got a nod from Jade and him.

"Not yet." Silver continued to walk back and forth.

She only had about twenty-five percent of the area left to cover. He looked at Amber to see how she handled the news. She held her hands together as if afraid to move. But Jade, who'd been focused on Silver, stopped watching and scowled at the petroglyph rock instead, obviously having given up hope.

He returned his gaze to Silver who continued her methodic walking. Though her movements were smooth, he could sense her tension as if he could feel her frantic hope. It wasn't looking good. His gut tightened at the thought of how she'd feel. He crossed his fingers, hoping against the odds that something would pop up.

Silver finally stopped when she was just below him. She turned off the machine and looked across the area to the other ladies. "There's nothing below us. Sorry I got your hopes up."

Amber ran over and put her arm around Silver. "It's not your fault our ancestors were content with a simple rock painting."

Silver didn't respond, which was tough to see.

Jade strode up to her. "Hey, you had to give it a shot. What if you were right, and we left and someone else found it? It's always better to be sure."

"Right." Silver nodded. "Now we know what we have to work with. So let's not waste time. We still have half this area to excavate."

Amber released Silver. "I'll put the markers back in. Jade, you grab the tools."

Layne stepped down the rocky path and stood next to Silver, waiting for her to look at him.

When she did, his heart stopped. Tears shimmered in her eyes.

He pulled her to him, wishing he could take her disappointment from her. To want something so much and not have it was a feeling he'd never had, but seeing it in her gave him a hint of what it was like, and he hated it.

After a few seconds, she squirmed in his embrace and he released her, perplexed.

"Don't." She sniffed. "Don't sympathize with me or I'll lose it. I just need to work it out of my system. I'll live. I'll feel better."

"When?"

Her gaze snapped to his at his question. "When what?"

"When will you feel better?"

"I have no idea. I just know I will. I always do. I have no choice, right?"

He wasn't sure that he agreed, but he could see he wasn't necessarily helping. "Okay. What can I do to help?"

"If you could set up the canopy where we had it on the east side of the tree, that would be great."

He gave a quick nod and set up the canopy for her. When he finished, he returned to Silver, who was studying the petroglyphs, a frown on her face. "Anything else you need?"

She turned to look at him. "No. Thank you."

"I wish I could do more." He glanced at the canopy feeling a bit useless, a very unusual feeling for him.

Her hand on his arm brought his gaze back to hers. "No. You did more than you know. Thank you for not trying to fix this or give me false encouragement. I appreciate that."

He wanted to tell her he was available if she needed to talk or just a shoulder to lean on, but his gut told him now was not the time. So he didn't say anything. He lifted his hat in salute before settling it more firmly on his head against the breeze, then he hiked up the mountain to his lookout ledge, as he called it now.

He reached his spot, but didn't sit in the canvas folding chair he'd set there. Instead, he stood in front of it at the edge of the ledge to stare down at the top of the petroglyph rock. The squiggly lines clearly ran into two straight lines that came to a point. It was such a typical symbol for heat rising in the Sonoran Desert and hitting a roof that it had to mean the same thing to man's ancient ancestors. So if that was the case, where was the roof? Had they built a wooden roof between the mountain and the rock and now it had all rotted away?

That reasoning made far too much sense, solidifying that there was no longer a roof to be found. Disappointed that he couldn't offer Silver another possibility, he finally sat. Even as he scanned the area for possible wildlife threats, his gaze kept coming back to her. She worked alongside her fellow scientists, determined to finish their investigation, even if there wasn't much left to investigate.

By the middle of the afternoon, even he could tell that the women had lost their enthusiasm. There was no chatter, and they moved about as if they were trudging through waist-high mud. He always found that stepping away from a problem offered new insights, or at least renewed energy. Rising from his chair, the wind almost took his hat from his head, reminding him that it had been increasing all afternoon. Even the little canopy below seemed in danger of collapsing. Maybe it was time to call it quits for the day.

He folded up his chair and carefully descended to their spot. He stepped onto the shelf where Jade stood sifting now outside the canopy, her movements slow and methodical. He actually had to touch her arm to get her attention.

"What?"

He held his arm out toward the canopy where Silver and Amber sat scraping the ground. "Come over here. I'd like to offer a suggestion."

Jade simply nodded and walked toward the others.

Silver and Amber stopped and looked up. Still, no one spoke.

"Ladies, I know you still have much work to do, but the winds are picking up, and I think for everyone's safety, and state of mind, we should return to the ranch now. I know it's early, but a restful afternoon, a good meal, and a night's rest will give you a fresh perspective. Plus, this wind is getting worse. The conditions should improve by tomorrow. I believe that would be a wise plan of action at this point."

He waited as they stared at him as if having a hard time focusing. He expected an argument, but each one in turn nodded their head and began to gather their tools. Once they had all they needed to descend, he folded up the canopy and took it with him.

The silence was deafening on the way down. Usually, they discussed the artifacts they'd found or what they hoped to find the next day. But they made it to the shelter without a word spoken.

What they needed was a distraction. Maybe a fire and roasting marshmallows would help, if the winds were quieter at the east end of the valley. Quickly, he tied the folded canopy to the post of the structure then helped Amber mount. As he led the women toward the ranch, it reminded him of when his teenage niece's team lost their softball playoffs. He'd been tasked with driving four of the team members home, and the silence in the truck was as profound as it was now.

That time he'd stopped at his aunt's ice cream shop and bought them all ice cream, which got them talking. Then he brought them to his mother's house to see the baby chicks. That had finally brought the girls out of their slump. But now he had three grown, intelligent women, and there was no ice cream between the north mountain and the guest lodges.

Silver rode next to him, Amber and Jade close behind as they all plodded along. It was as if the horses too could feel the disappointed mood. Not one for moping about, he started singing an old classic—*Country Roads* by John Denver.

Silver looked over at him and cocked her head as if she'd never heard singing before, which just made him smile. As he got to the refrain, he turned to look at the two behind them. Amber was grinning and Jade looked shocked. That just made him chuckle, but he kept right on singing.

When he finished, there was clapping behind him and Amber piped up. "Sing another, Layne?"

Not sure what country songs they might know, he decided on Garth Brook's *Friends in Low Places*. Amber actually joined him on the first refrain, and by the end of the song, Silver and Jade were participating, too.

When they finished, Amber clapped again. "That was fun."

Silver looked over at him. "You didn't tell us you were such a great singer."

He shrugged, not in complete agreement about his prowess, but pleased she liked it.

"You have a lovely baritone. Did you take lessons?" Jade's compliment had him turning.

"Only from my dad while riding the range." He turned back, pleased that he could get them talking again. Life was too short to wallow in the disappointments.

The rest of the way back, the women talked about favorite songs, a subject far from their careers. It was exactly what he wanted for them. Once they arrived back, Amber dismounted on her own. "I'm going into the hot tub. Anyone want to join me?"

Jade shook her head. "I feel like treating myself to some mahjong solitaire on the computer. My mind needs a break." With that she headed out of the corral.

"Suit yourself. How about you Silver?"

Layne wasn't sure if it was something in Silver's expression or he just sensed that she'd already returned to the non-existent cave problem.

"No, you go ahead."

"So I will." With a quick smile, Amber strode toward the lodge.

Silver remained standing next to her horse, absently petting Chestnut's neck.

He didn't like that she was back in her head again. "What will you do with your free time?"

Her gaze jerked to his as if unaware he was still there. "I don't know."

"I need to find George, then start working on the new gate to keep him on the ranch. Would you like to join me?" It wasn't a very exciting distraction, but it was something.

She didn't answer right away, obviously still holding onto the problem of the cave, but finally she nodded. "Sure. Why not? Do I need Chestnut?"

"I don't know. I didn't see George on the way in, so he's either in the south fields, by the house, or beyond the fencing. Let's check the house first. I added hay to the feeder there this morning, and refilled a tub of water, so hopefully he found it."

Silver walked toward him. "You did all that before meeting us at seven this morning?"

"Yes. Why?"

"You must be an early riser."

They walked toward the barn. "It's habit. Even on days I

don't come to the ranch, I still wake up early, but I just roll over if I have nothing scheduled that day."

Silver stopped and pointed. "Is that George?"

He followed her hand to where George stood, his snout down in a pile of garbage. "George, what did you do?" The damn burro lifted his head to look at him, then went back to eating whatever he'd found.

Layne picked up the pace. "The last thing we need is a sick burro." He stopped a few feet away from the overturned green plastic trash receptacle and examined the trash.

"I take it burros aren't supposed to eat trash." Silver stepped up next to him.

"Wild burros will eat whatever they want, but processed foods can make them ill." He moved next to George. "What are you eating?"

George lifted his head again, a long peel from a carrot sticking out of his mouth.

Layne grinned. "So I see."

George lowered his head again.

"He's eating the vegetable leftovers from the kitchen. That's not necessarily bad for him, but if he makes it a habit of knocking over trash cans, he's going to get in trouble." Layne righted the trashcan before stepping into the barn for a new trash bag.

When he came out, Silver was a few feet away, studying the ground. "Did you find a bug?"

"Come here a second."

He dropped the trash bag on the trash can lid and walked to where she stood. There was no bug, but there were lots of tracks.

"What are those? They don't look like burro footprints."

He followed a number of them toward the exit to Rocky

Road's driveway and then north. Looking up, he covered his eyes with his hand. "Javelinas."

"Those wild pigs?"

He turned to find Silver right behind him. "Yeah. Probably the same group we saw the other day. There's not much we can do about them, but at least I know now that George didn't knock over the trash."

"No, he was helping. He was cleaning up." She smiled, obviously pleased with her deduction.

"Of course. He was cleaning up. But now I better clean up the mess before George decides to try something he shouldn't eat." He started back toward the trash.

"I can help."

He didn't expect her to, but wasn't going to refuse the offer. "Thanks. I'll pull the food he's eating aside. If you can keep him occupied without him eating the plastic bag it's resting on, I can get the rest picked up."

"You have a deal if I can pet George, too."

He stopped at the trash can. "Deal." Bending over, he managed to move the trash bag a few yards away, then went about picking up the rest of the mess the javelinas had left behind. When he had it all bagged except what George had, he found the burro had left off eating and was standing farther away while Silver stroked him. Pleased that George and she were getting along so well, he quickly gathered up the rest of the trash and added it to the can, then set it inside the barn. He stepped back outside just in time to catch Silver giving George a hug. He had a feeling it was more for her than the burro.

She was a most unusual woman, and he liked that. He liked her, too. That gave him pause. He liked most everyone, and he liked the other ladies, too. But there was something about Silver that was different. She had layers, and he found himself wanting to learn more about her, even if she was only in town for a short amount of time. In fact, that made it easier, since he was quite happy with his life as it was.

Catching sight of him, Silver gave George a finally pat and walked over, her stride confident. "He was full, so I suggested he take a walk."

He greeted her smile with one of his own. "Great idea. Now to installing that gate, so he doesn't walk too far."

"Right. Just tell me what to do. It will feel good to accomplish something worthwhile today." Her smile faltered just a bit.

"Then come with me. I'll put you to work." He barely kept himself from setting his hand on her lower back as they walked into the barn, but he wanted to. In fact, there was a lot he wanted to do with her, and installing a gate was the least of it.

CHAPTER 9

SILVER CONTEMPLATED the evening's events as Layne drove her to a place he called The Stampede. She felt stupid that it took her until after dinner to understand what was happening. If she hadn't been so caught up in her own disappointment, she would have figured it out sooner.

But no. She hadn't even questioned why Nash, Vic, and Layne stayed and had dinner, or why Amanda and Tanner brought Jeremiah, Tanner's father, with them. Then when they'd decided it was a good night for a fire and hot chocolate, she'd joined in, not even wondering why they'd offered. But when Layne had invited her to The Stampede, and all conversation stopped, she'd finally put two and two together. "Thank you for distracting our whole team today."

Layne's lips lifted in a smile, even as he kept his eyes on the dark road. "You're welcome."

"You told Amanda what happened today."

"I did." He slowed at the stop sign to turn onto main street.

"Was the fire her idea or yours?"

"She suggested we all stay for dinner. I suggested the fire. Amber and Jade seemed to enjoy both."

"I enjoyed them, too."

He made the turn, glancing at her. "But you kept thinking about your one discovery and how you'd thought Four Peaks would be it."

"Was I that obvious? I really was trying not to think about it. I was just so sure. I keep thinking I'm missing something." She barely kept herself from whining. She hated whiners. Benedict was a whiner.

He took a right down a side street. "Haven't you had sites that were simply a rock?"

"Yes, we have had those, some with very little rock art, and others had a lot, but there was nothing else. We've had those kinds of sites right here in Arizona. Luckily, they don't take much time, and we can move onto the next potential find."

He turned into a paved parking lot before a large steel building with an old western barn painted on the front, the door made to look like it was in one of the barn doors. There were no windows.

He pulled into a space and turned off the truck. "But you thought there was something more at the north mountain because of the squiggly lines and roof."

"That, and because we found artifacts from a different century. That's rare when there is only rock art. I've only encountered that once before. So I was convinced there was a cave below based upon that."

He turned toward her. "And now that you know there isn't, it's hard to move on. Is it possible you could still find a unique artifact? Do you have any idea why the rock art would be from one period and the artifacts be from multiple ones? My question would be, why didn't the later visitors to the rock add to it. From what I've seen in Phoenix, when one graffiti artist paints on a wall, at least three others add their artwork. It's like an art magnet."

She opened her mouth to respond then shut it. She'd been about to argue, but Layne had some valid points. Why hadn't the next generation added to the rock? She unbuckled her seatbelt and faced him. "You're right. Could there be another place on the mountain with more petroglyphs?"

"If you want, tomorrow we can hike farther up and see what we can find."

And there he did it again. Made her feel better, giving her hope. "I'd like that."

"Good, now you ready to play some pool?"

"Pool? Is that what this place is?" She looked out the windshield.

"Of course. I always play pool on Tuesday nights."

"Always?" She couldn't help challenging him.

He shrugged. "At least for the last fourteen years."

"I can't think of anything I've done besides breathing for that many years."

He laughed. "You've studied our ancient ancestors, right? So now you get to come into my world."

As an anthropologist, she should be excited at the prospect of going into her first pool hall, but her excitement stemmed from much more personal motivations. "Lead the way."

Before she could blink, he'd hopped out of the truck and was opening her door for her. The last person who opened her door for her before Layne was a valet at The Jewel hotel in Cairo. She slid off the seat and stepped to the side as he closed the door. "I've never played pool before."

He took her hand. "You can watch a few games. Then if you'd like to learn, I'll teach you."

Surprised by his warm grasp and the tingling sensation it sent up her arm, she quickly recovered. "That works for me."

He opened the door to The Stampede for her and she stepped inside. Her first impression held true. The floor was painted concrete and the whole place was one large room, like a warehouse, except for a corner where there was a long L-shaped bar. There had to be at least sixteen pool tables down the center. Along the outer walls were cocktail tables and chairs, though few were being used. The scent of barbeque permeated the air.

"This way." Layne held out his hand toward the bar while his other hand settled on her lower back, sending a frisson of excitement through her. As they walked between two pool tables, Layne was greeted by the players not playing, but the men's gazes kept flitting toward her. Layne didn't stop to talk, but kept her moving until they reached the bar. "Howdy, Archie."

The older man with white hair turned around, his mouth open as if to greet Layne, but instead he just stood there staring at her.

"Archie, I'd like you to meet Dr. Silver Collins. She's a scientist staying at the Rocky Road Ranch."

Archie recovered quickly, but it was clear he'd been surprised to see her. He held his hand out over the bar. "Nice to meet you, Dr. Collins."

She smiled warmly at the man and shook hands. "I'm not at work, so just call me Silver."

"What can I get for you, Silver?"

She scanned the beer taps and hard liquor behind the man. "How about a whiskey on the rocks? Do you have anything local?" She liked trying local food and drink, no matter where she was working.

The man grinned, nodding in approval. "Sure do. One Johnny Ringo on the rocks, coming your way."

The bartender poured the whiskey and set it before her. Next, he pulled out a cold glass and set it under a tap.

She looked at Layne. "Big Saddle beer?"

"It's a local brew. I like to support our community. It's what keeps it going."

She nodded even as Archie placed the beer in front of Layne.

"Thanks." Layne held his arm out and led her to a pool table where two men had just finished a game. "Ready for me yet?"

"Not happenin' with me." The younger of the two walked away.

"I'm always ready for you, Layne."

Layne turned toward her. "Silver, this is Rory Lester. He manages the feedstore in town. Rory, this is Dr. Silver Collins."

The man's blond brows rose high, almost disappearing beneath his cowboy hat. "Nice to meet you. Do you play?"

"Not yet. Layne said he'd teach me."

Again the brows disappeared and the man looked at Layne. "You're going to teach her?"

The question was asked with such astonishment that she got the feeling Layne didn't often teach people to play pool. Just another indication that he was truly going out of his way for her.

Layne nodded as he took off his jacket and hung it on a nearby stool. "Yeah, but first I'm going to teach you who's the better player."

As the two men started trash-talking each other, she moved to the cocktail table where Layne had left his jacket and pulled her own off to hang it on the back of a tall stool. After hopping up to take a seat, she took a sip of her whiskey. It was rough, as she expected, but definitely drinkable.

Layne came over and set his beer on the table. "This won't take long."

Rory laughed. "I heard that."

As Layne and Rory played, she found herself getting distracted by Layne's physical attributes, like his tight butt as he bent over the table, or his broad shoulders when his back was turned, or his large hands as he handled the cue. He was the full package: great personality, caring, easy going, kind, respectful, protective, and a good singer. So why wasn't he married, especially when he said almost everyone in his family was?

After splitting two games, each with a win, Layne came over and finished off his beer. "He just got lucky. I'll win this one and then I'll show you how to play."

"No rush. It's quite entertaining." She nodded toward Rory who was lining up to break with the cue behind his back.

Layne strode over. "Show off. She's with me. That won't help."

A rush of heat sliced through her at his comment. She was with him, meaning, no one could hit on her. There he was, being protective again. She'd never liked it when men made it seem like she couldn't stand on her own two feet, but that wasn't how Layne made her feel. The fact was, he had her feeling a lot lately. She needed to be careful because if there was nothing more to explore on the west mountain, she'd be leaving in a couple of weeks. She wouldn't let an easy-going cowboy keep her from her goal.

The warning was more for herself. She was pretty sure that Layne just lived in the present, which she would very much like to do for the next couple of weeks.

"Told you." Layne grinned at Rory as the number eight ball disappeared into a pocket.

Rory lost gracefully. "I needed a refill anyway. You want anything?"

"No, I'm good."

When Rory left, Layne came back over. "Are you ready to learn to play?"

"Absolutely." She hopped off the high stool and walked to a rack of pool sticks hung on the wall closest to the table. "So which of these do I use? They seem to be different sizes."

His gaze ran from the top of her head to her new cowboy boots and back up, which had her heart picking up its pace.

"You're of average height. Take one of the middle ones."

She turned from him and took her time choosing a pool stick, certain he was checking out her butt. It was only fair. She'd been unable to stop staring at his. She returned to him with stick in hand. "Okay. Now what."

"Let me rack up the balls."

She waited impatiently, anxious to learn how to play. She rarely had time to indulge in local customs while at other sites, so hanging out with Layne in a pool hall was a treat.

He pulled the triangle frame from around the balls and then stepped next to her. "The first thing you need to learn is how to break. So hold your stick like this, bring it back and then follow through until you hit the cue ball."

She copied his stance, pulled the cue back and hit the white ball on the side, causing it to roll to the right past all fifteen balls in the center. Usually, she'd be embarrassed by her complete miss, but with Layne, she didn't feel judged. She straightened. "Told you I'd never done this before."

"Yes, you did. So let's see if I can help improve your aim." He retrieved the errant white ball and set it in front of her. "Now get into position."

She leaned over the pool table and lined up her stick behind the ball.

"I see why you missed. Your arm is off. Here." Layne leaned over the pool table next to her, his torso to her back, and gently pulled her arm into the correct position. "Feel that?"

She swallowed, because what she felt was hard desire coursing through her as he touched her. Damn. "So I just pull back like this?"

"No." Layne pressed his body closer to hers and set his hand on her upper arm. "Let your forearm swing like a pendulum from your elbow."

She made her arm move and hit the cue ball. It hit the first ball, making it roll a couple of inches, but that was it.

Layne stood, taking his body from hers. "That's perfect aim."

She straightened and faced him, hoping her cheeks weren't flushed. "But pathetic power. I saw you break this whole cluster across the table, sinking two balls in the process."

"That's from fourteen years of practice, not fourteen seconds. Try again, this time with power." He reset the balls and put the white ball down.

She looked at the balls determined to get it right this time, but the odd feeling of being watched had her turning to look behind her. Three men and one woman at various pool tables, suddenly looked away.

"What is it?" Layne turned his head to find what she was looking at.

"Nothing. Have you ever given anyone a lesson in playing pool here?"

He shook his head. "I have a pool table at home, so when I taught my nieces and nephews, it was at my house, not here." He paused to look over his shoulder again before continuing. "I guess people are surprised because I never bring a date here."

"A date?" Again her pulse started to speed up. "Am I your date tonight?"

His hazel eyes appeared almost all gray as he searched her own. "If you would like to be. I brought you here because I always come here on Tuesday nights and thought you could use the distraction, but to be truthful, I didn't want the evening to end."

"I don't want it to end either. I like the idea of being on a date with you, though I'm woefully out of practice. You might have to remind me how it works." She chuckled, hoping he'd understand.

His lips split into a wide smile. "Trust me. I'll take care of everything."

She stepped closer to him. "I have no doubt that you will. But I think if we're to save your reputation, it might be better if you taught me how to play pool at your house."

"My reputation?" His brows rose before his gaze scanned the room.

"Unless you'd like to play a few more games before you give me my private lessons?" Since they'd barely been there an hour, she had to make the offer.

His face froze for a moment before one side of his mustache twitched. "No, I'm good."

She smiled, excited at what the rest of the evening could bring. "Great. I just need a lady's room before we leave. Which way?"

Layne pointed back toward the bar. "See that exit—"

When he didn't continue, she prompted him. "Yes, I see the exit sign."

He looked at her, his eyes wide. "Does that exit sign remind you of anything?"

She returned her gaze to the sign. It was an old lighted sign, but part of it wasn't working because it was five rows from top to bottom and the second and fourth row wasn't lit, making it look like three rows of dashes with an arrow pointing left. "Just a broken exit sign. Why?"

"Imagine those dashes as squiggle lines."

Even as he spoke, the symbol on top of the petroglyph rock appeared in her head. "The rock. It's not a roof. It's an arrow!"

He turned to face her. "It might be."

She envisioned the space, her photographic memory helpful

for once. "Then the arrow points toward the mountain right where that red tree is growing."

Layne nodded, his smile back in place.

"You're brilliant!" Excitement welled within her. She dropped her cue stick, took his face in her hands, and pulled him down to kiss him with all the happiness filling her.

His arms wrapped around her and he kissed her back, turning her excitement into a different kind altogether. And then he stepped away.

She grabbed onto the pool table, as it took her a moment to get her equilibrium back.

"I'll settle up with Archie and put the cues back while you're busy. The restrooms are down the hall the exit sign is pointing toward."

At his mention of the exit sign, she looked at it again. Now that he'd pointed it out, the similarity was obvious. She grinned. "Sounds like a plan."

She headed for the exit sign, passing by a table with two women, who watched two others play. She recognized one of them as Sheila, who owned the western store. Sheila noticed her. "If you can catch him, be sure to treat him right."

She slowed her step and looked back. Both women nodded at her. That was odd. She continued on her way, quickly using the bathroom and returning to find Layne at the bar.

Layne watched her as she walked up. "Ready to head out?"

"I am. I'm looking forward to my private lesson."

He immediately checked where Archie was before responding. "Then let's go." He took her hand and led her out of the building.

But she was curious. "Why did you look for Archie when I said I was looking forward to my private lesson?"

He waited until they reached his truck to answer, then he

pulled her into his arms. "I didn't want him to overhear you. It could ruin your reputation."

She blinked. "Reputation? Do people still have those?"

"They do in Four Peaks. Plus, you're famous. I don't want people getting the wrong impression of you."

His outlook was so foreign to her, she couldn't process it immediately. Not knowing how to feel about such an old-fashioned idea, she remained silent as he reached around her and opened her door, allowing her to get settled in. Then he walked around and got inside himself, quickly starting the truck before driving to Main Street, where he continued farther into town.

She'd only had a few short-term relationships while at sites, since she moved from place to place so often, and never had one at a place she was at for less than six months. But Layne was different. There was something about him that fascinated her, even beyond the physical. Plus, she felt safe with him. Even her reputation was safe with him. At that thought, she smiled into the darkness. "Do you live far?"

"Just at the other end of town down a dirt road. When I bought the place, I wanted to be as far from my family as I could, yet still be in town."

"I thought you enjoyed being part of a big family."

"I do. But as the oldest, I like having my own space and a little privacy. That's not to say they don't come and visit...a lot."

As Layne turned down the dirt road to his house, she appreciated his sentiment. "I'm the oldest, too, and I can relate. It's funny, though, because I'm never alone. I'm either with Amber and Jade or with a friend or family member. I guess since my family was smaller, the urge to have my own space is not as strong as yours."

She kept her eyes on the road, curious what Layne's home would look like. They drove by typical desert landscape with cacti, shrubs, and the ever-present mesquite trees. When they turned onto a dirt driveway, she expected the lights from the truck to show the house, but they didn't. It wasn't for another half mile of curvy driveway that she finally viewed the home. It was a one-story adobe house that seemed to have additions attached, but they stopped at the front door before she could truly get a feel for it.

"Let me get some lights on for you." Layne jumped from the truck and unlocked the front door, quickly turning a light on that lit the front yard, which was actually just dirt. Then he opened her door. "Welcome to Casa Cómodo."

"Ah, Comfortable House. I like it."

He grinned. "Me too." Then he led the way until they reached the door and he allowed her to go first.

Her immediate impression was that it was larger inside then it looked on the outside. The ceilings were vaulted, and the kitchen/living room were open-concept with two archways, one at either end, which appeared to lead to other rooms. "Wow, this is big."

He helped her off with her coat and hung it on a hook near the door. Then he shrugged out of his jacket, hung it next to hers, set his cowboy hat on a side table, and dropped his keys.

She stared at him. His hair was fuller than she expected, and without his hat, it looked longer. "I've never seen you without your hat on."

He ran his hand through his hair. "I promise, I don't sleep with it on. Would you like a beer or something?"

"I'll take a water. Not sure I want to mix beer with my Johnny Ringo whiskey."

"Smart." He moved behind a large wood-topped island counter with a sink in it and opened the fridge. After pulling out a beer and a water, he came over and handed it to her. "Let me show you around."

She followed him as he explained the various rooms, which

included two bedrooms when his nieces or nephews slept over, a bathroom, a movie theater room, in addition to a room with a pool table. She was surprised that it wasn't messy, though it was lived in with a pair of boots left by a recliner as if he'd toed them off and never put them away, and there were dirty breakfast dishes in the sink.

"On this end, there's only my office and the master suite." He walked ahead of her and pointed out his "office," which looked more like a den with a desk added.

When they entered his bedroom, she stopped. "This is huge."

"Yeah. The people who designed the house had wanted a separate area they could rent out for added income, but their initial financing dried up and I got a great deal."

The main part of the room had three sets of glass doors to the outside that looked like they folded in for indoor/outdoor living. There was almost another wing with a kitchenette and another door, which she expected included the master bath. "The size fits you."

"Are you saying I'm large?" He frowned at her, but she could tell now when he was teasing.

She cocked her head, pretending to think about it. Then she walked around him, very pleased with what she saw. "Yes. From what I can see you are large. I like large."

"Good answer. So are you ready for your private pool lesson?"

Though pool wasn't exactly at the forefront of her mind, she did want to spend more time with him. "I'm ready, especially now that I know how to break."

"There's so much more I can show you." He led her back through the main room and down to the pool room. He selected a cue stick from the five on the wall rack and handed it to her.

Then he set up the balls. "Okay, now aim and give it some power, elbow back."

She did as he instructed and balls scattered across the green felt of the table. Triumph flew through her. "Yes!" She turned to where he stood behind her and caught him watching her butt. Hmm, so maybe pool could be more fun than she expected.

His gaze snapped to hers. "Now, you want to use the cue ball to sink one of the balls into a pocket. Whichever type you sink, striped or solid, will be your balls."

She kept her mind from going in a completely different direction regarding balls, and spun back around to study the layout. A striped ball was lined up perfectly in front of a pocket, so she leaned over and took her shot. The ball rolled into the pocket followed by the white ball. She stood and held her cue stick up. "I did it." Again, pleasure filled her as it always did when meeting a challenge.

Layne strolled over to the pocket she'd just sent the balls into. "Not exactly. By sinking the cue ball, you lose your turn and I can place the ball anywhere on the table." He lifted the white ball out.

She set the end of her cue stick on the floor and placed her other hand on her hip. "You didn't tell me that. I deserve a do-over."

He raised his brows. "A do-over?"

She gave him a cheeky grin. "Yes. You didn't tell me my limitations, so I get a do-over. You have heard of a do-over, haven't you?"

"Sure, when I was seven."

She laughed, enjoying herself way more than she expected. "Fine. I wouldn't want you to take your ball and go home."

He came back around the table, still holding the ball, but this time he didn't just walk, he moved like a mountain lion about to attack.

Though a thrill moved through her abdomen, she held her ground. "How nice of you to bring it to me." She held her hand out for the ball.

He continued to walk by her, moving with purpose before stopping to place the white ball on the table.

"Seriously?" She pretended to be perturbed, pouting as if the game was important.

He leaned over the table and aimed his stick, then he stopped and looked at her. "Seriously." Without taking his eyes from her, he sent the white ball into two solid balls which split, sending one into a corner pocket and the other into another solid ball, which promptly fell into a side pocket.

She stared in awe. "How'd you do that?"

He stood. "Practice." He moved his position and promptly sank another ball.

Obviously, Layne planned to finish the game on her, but she had another idea.

As he leaned over to take aim again, she walked behind him and ran her hand over his hard round butt, something she'd been wanting to do all night.

He missed his shot then turned toward her. "You play dirty."

She widened her eyes innocently. "There's nothing dirty about admiring what a nice ass you have." Moving to the other side of the table, she looked for the easiest shot. Despite the fact she'd been admiring Layne all night, she had watched him play three games at the pool hall, and thanks to her memory, she used his same technique to put on some back spin, aiming low but level. As her ball rolled into the pocket and the white ball returned toward her, she threw her hands up. "And that's how you do it."

"Impressive."

She wasn't sure if he referred to her shot or her breasts,

because his gaze was centered on her cleavage revealed by her V-neck sweater. Since her sweater had risen up her waist when she lifted her arms, she purposefully pulled it back down, showing more.

His gaze remained on her chest a moment longer before he looked away. "Where did I put my beer?"

She didn't answer as a new idea formed for winning the game. It wasn't that the game was critical and more about the fun they were having. Knowing that Layne found her attractive was reassuring, because for over a week, she been ogling the man when he wasn't looking.

She walked to the other side of the table near where he now stood, beer in hand. With her back to him she scanned the balls. There was no easy shot, but she was happy to try a harder one. She bent over, lined up, and shot. Her striped ball missed the side pocket, bounced off the side of the table and rolled diagonally into a corner pocket. She'd been aiming for the side pocket, but she'd take it. Straightening, she nodded. "Yup, meant to do that."

"No, you didn't." Layne's voice held humor in it.

She smirked at him. "But you can't prove it."

"When you get better at this game, you'll need to call your pocket."

She let her gaze wander down to the front pockets of his jeans and his zipper. "Hmmm, I didn't realize I had to call a pocket." She brought her gaze back to face. "Would you like me to call my next ball?"

He swallowed, then shook his head. "This is your first game. That wouldn't be fair."

She should have guessed he'd say that. He was obviously a good man. It was probably better not to tease him, but he did a bit of teasing himself, so maybe he'd take it in stride. Turning back to the table, she lined up another shot, but her ball hit three other balls, sending one of his into a pocket. "I get to take yours out, right?"

He set his beer bottle down and strolled toward her. "No. I get to keep that one. Thank you."

"Oh, I think I need more than a thank for that."

He wrapped one arm around her and kissed her. Again, as before, the kiss was leisurely, like they had all the time in the world, which just sent her sex drive into high gear. Then he let her go and moved past her.

She wanted to fan herself. How could the man kiss her like that then move onto shoot...and sink a ball? He didn't just sink one, but the next three as well. There was only one solid ball left on the table, the eight ball. He was going to win.

She couldn't let him distract her with a kiss and win. She needed to do something else, something to get his full attention on her.

Layne moved to the other side of the table and leaned over.

Since she was ready to do more than play pool, she pulled her sweater over her head, leaving her in her aqua bra. She leaned down too, letting her cups rest on the side just above the pocket.

Layne's gaze flitted to hers, and she grinned.

Then his gaze lowered to her breasts and he shot.

THE EIGHT BALL went straight into the pocket beneath her. Silver straightened, shocked. "How'd you do that?"

Layne gave her a sly grin. "You gave me something worth shooting for."

"Shit. That wasn't the plan."

He set his cue stick in the rack next to him and strode around the table toward her. "You mean you wanted to play more pool?"

Realizing how illogical she'd been, she laughed. "No, I didn't want to play more pool, but I did want to win."

He stopped no more than two feet away. "And what would you want for a prize if you won? A teddy bear? Cotton candy? A bottle of whiskey?" His voice had deepened, coming out rough and sexy.

The sound skittered down into her core, starting a slow burn. She leaned her stick against the pool table and set both her hands on the flannel covering his broad chest. "No. I would want *you*. But since I didn't win, it's a moot point. What do you want for a prize?"

His hazel eyes seemed almost green as he focused on her mouth. "You. All of you."

Goosebumps ran across her bare arms at the intensity of feeling he conveyed. She believed him. Moving her hands up to encircle his neck, she took the step that brought them together. "Then I win after all."

He lowered his head and whispered in her ear. "We both do."

The touch sensitized her skin, and she pressed herself closer. Though his flannel was soft, she'd prefer his bare skin. She moved her hands lower toward the first button of his shirt, but he pulled her tighter against him and started kissing beneath her ear and down her neck.

His hands on her back moved in opposite directions, one to slip beneath the waistband of her jeans to cup her ass cheek, while the other moved beneath her bra. With barely a pause, she felt it unhook and loosen about her. Oh, he was good.

Since she couldn't unbutton his shirt, she moved her mouth to where it was open and licked his skin.

That got his attention, his mouth stopping its progress over her shoulder. He lifted his head and settled his lips on hers.

She opened for him immediately, but he took his time before slowly delving inside her mouth.

He tasted of beer and man, and that had her belly moving like the moon jellyfish of Spain. His hand cupped her head, tilting her face, his body pressing her closer as his tongue discovered her own.

She grasped his shirt beneath her hands, her body reacting to the feel and scent of him. He smelled of cedar and leather, and every womanly part of her wanted him.

When he brought the kiss to an end, he loosened his hold a bit and looked at her. He didn't say anything, just studied her face like he'd never seen it before, sending another thrill of excitement racing through her.

She took advantage of his distraction and managed to unbutton two buttons of his shirt before he reacted. He covered both her hands with one of his, his gaze never leaving her face. "Are you sure?"

"One-hundred percent sure."

His chest expanded beneath her hand as he took a deep breath. Then he let go of her hands and her body and stood perfectly still.

Since he had given her the green light, she unbuttoned his shirt to his waist, then let her bra fall down her arms, catching it in one hand and dropping it on the pool table. Without hesitation, she pulled his shirt from his jeans and spread it, her bare hands running over his solid chest. It was no surprise that a light line of dark hairs ran between the mounds of his pectoral muscles.

As she stood on tiptoe to push the soft shirt over the top of his shoulders, he pulled her against him. She let go of the shirt and looped her arms about his neck, loving the feel of his hard chest pressed against her bare breasts. She sighed with contentment.

The vibration of a silent chuckle beneath her cheek caused her to look up at him.

He grinned at her. "You sound satisfied."

"I am...so far." She finished pushing the shirt down his arms until one hand was free, then he took over, throwing the shirt onto the pool table.

Now they stood close, but not touching,

Layne laid his hands on her jeans-covered hips and turned her so her back was to the table. "Hop up."

Not a little excited about what he planned, she did as he requested.

He stepped up to her, spreading her legs before taking her face in his hands and thoroughly kissing her. Then he sucked on her tongue, sending pleasurable shivers along every nerve ending.

She held onto his shoulders as he bent her over onto the pool table, the green felt soft on her back even if it was rock hard beneath. She swallowed a moan as his mouth left hers and he began to trail kisses, licks, and nips along her neck to her collar bone.

Her nipples hardened in anticipation, now straining upward, impatiently waiting their turn.

But Layne appeared to make love like he lived life, enjoying every moment for what it was, and by the time his mouth reached her nipple, it was so hard, it ached. His lips covered it, gently sucking the tip before laving her areola with his practiced tongue.

She arched up into his mouth, wanting, needing more.

He slipped his arm beneath her back and gave her what she wanted. He sucked her nipple deep into his mouth and hummed.

This time she did moan, loving the sensation until he pulled back and took a nip at her tip, which sent an arrow of need straight to her core.

His mouth released her before he blew on her wet breast, making it even harder.

She wet her dry lips. "I want you."

His gaze met hers. "You will have me."

As he lowered his mouth to her other breast, she didn't have time to wonder when as pleasure swept through her. When he finished giving that nipple equal attention, he pulled her back up to a sitting position and kissed her until she was lightheaded.

She'd never been kissed so much during sex, not when she'd been so ready. Instinctually, she understood that Layne would not be rushed. Shit. If she was right, she would be hotter than the sun by time she had him.

He used his hands on her ass to pull her forward and off the table. Then he knelt at her feet.

Without him holding her, she leaned against the pool table for support.

"Lift." He patted her cowboy boot.

She lifted her foot, and he took off first one boot, then the other.

When his hands reached up and unbuttoned her jeans, she sucked in her breath, not because they were tight, but because she couldn't wait. Finally, they were getting somewhere.

Layne unzipped her pants and pulled them down over her hips.

She stepped out of each leg and stood there in her blue panties and blue socks, anxious to see what he'd do next. He didn't disappoint as his hands reached up and he pulled her panties down to reveal her trimmed mons.

He stopped at her thighs, staring at her. "You're a brunette?"

She chuckled. No man had ever asked her about her hair color in the middle of having sex. Then again, no one took it so slowly before. "I was. My hair went white early, just like my mother's."

His gaze moved from her mons to her head. "So it's natural."

"That's me." She held her arms out wide, not ashamed that his gaze moved to her breasts again. There had to be something she could do to speed things up. The longer she stood naked before him, the hotter she got.

He finished pulling down her panties, then rose.

Immediately, she pulled on his belt buckle. This time, he let her open it and unbutton his jeans, but when she reached for his zipper, he caught her hands.

"Not yet."

Not a little frustrated she huffed. "When?"

He placed her hands on the sides of the pool table then ran his large calloused ones over her breasts and down her sides to her waist. "Hop up again."

After catching her breath at his touch, she quickly sat her butt on the side, the height just a little too high for her feet to touch the ground, but now that she was paying attention, it could be the perfect height for intercourse.

Layne spread her legs to get close. Despite his jeans, she could feel the hard bulge that let her know he was as hot as she was.

"Lie back."

She wouldn't make him ask twice, even though with her hips on the rail, she was lying downhill.

He leaned over her and kissed her.

She wrapped her arms around him, his back warm and muscular, wanting to feel him between her legs, but at her angle, she couldn't push her hips higher. His hand rested on the inside of her thigh, teasing her with its stillness.

Layne's tongue became demanding, causing spikes of need to ricochet through her body. So caught up in his kiss, she missed the movement of his hand until his fingers found the folds between her legs.

She tried to move her pelvis up, but she had no leverage, leaving her at his mercy. That realization seemed to turn her muscles to goo. As his fingers leisurely explored the opening to her sheath, she sucked hard on his tongue, wanting more, wanting him.

He must have understood her message, because he broke the kiss to pay homage to her breast, just as one of his fingers slowly entered her.

"More." Her word came out on breath, her body strung so tight with need, that she could barely talk.

Luckily, Layne got the message and before his finger had fully entered her, he pulled it out and added another to slowly traverse her wet sheath. She moaned as the friction from his roughened fingers met the sharp excitement of his teeth nibbling at her nipple.

Her breathing turned shallow, as all her focus was on the building pleasure from his fingers slowly moving in and out of her, while her nipple remained in a constant state of arousal.

Then without increasing the speed of his hand between her legs, his other hand came up to pinch her other nipple. It was the final straw. Every atom in her body reacted, causing an explosion of nuclear proportions to go off inside her, obliterating all thought as she dug her fingers into his back and screamed her ecstasy.

The feelings went on and on as his ministrations didn't stop, holding her to a pinnacle she'd never reached before, bearing her away into another level of existence—swirling colors blinded her behind her closed eyelids, even as all feeling converged to the center of her being and lifted her weightless into the stars.

CHAPTER 11

LAYNE FELT the second Silver began to climax, her sheath squeezing his fingers, trying to keep him still. But it was her scream of complete surrender to her rapture that sent a spike of need through him so hard that he almost lost control. His whole body seemed to fight him, and his concentration centered on holding back his own release, until he could experience the same bliss inside her.

Finally, he got control of his movements and lifted his head from her breast, though he continued to move his fingers inside her until he knew her orgasm had subsided.

Her breathing remained shallow and her eyes closed. Gently he pushed her silver hair away from her face, spreading it out across the green felt on which she lay.

Every moment of her climb to orgasm had been erotic, her reactions candid, letting him know exactly how much pleasure he gave her. That he'd brought her such joy filled him with elation. So much so that he wanted, no *had to*, bring her there again.

This time, though, he would join her. Even at the thought of what it would be like to slide into her, his cock reminded him that sooner would be better. He didn't want it to be fast. He wanted to enjoy every minute, every second of joining with her.

He didn't question the strange, almost otherworldly need to go beyond a simple orgasm with her. As always, he trusted the universe, fate, nature, whatever it was. He pulled his fingers from her warmth before wrapping his arm around her and pulling her limp form upright.

Her eyelids fluttered until she looked at him and opened her mouth. No sound came out, but she clearly mouthed the word "wow."

He gave her a soft smile. "Wrap your arms around my neck and your legs around my waist."

Her efforts were weak, but she managed.

Then he lifted her from the edge of the pool table and strode out of the room, not stopping until he'd reached his bed.

Gently he laid her on the thick navy-blue quilt.

She stretched, her limbs seeking to fill the king-size bed, but not coming close. "This is silky. I like it." Leaving one hand above her head, she lifted her other toward him. "Join me."

He studied her, letting his eyes view her from top to bottom. Against the dark material, her body looked warm, light, inviting him to touch her. That's exactly what he planned to do. He toed off his boots and unzipped his jeans before stripping them down, his erection now free of its confines. Leaving his pants on the tiled floor, he pulled off his socks, then knelt on the bed next to her.

Her gaze fastened on his cock, which made it start to ache. "I was right. You are large."

"And you're observant."

At that, she laughed softly. "So I've been told. Luckily for me, I have a photographic memory, so I'll never forget seeing you like this."

Something about her words dulled the pure contented

feeling he'd been floating in. He wasn't sure if it was that she'd remember him, or that she would need to remember him because she'd be gone, but whatever it was, a niggling concern wormed its way into his psyche, and with it a need beyond simply intercourse. He needed to make her his. The feeling was so strange to him, that he froze.

Silver must have sensed something, because she knelt up and placed her hands on his chest. "You okay?"

The warmth of her touch seemed to release him, and he cupped her face in his hands. "Almost."

Her eyebrows rose. "Almost? Is there anything I can do?"

Words tornadoed through his head, making it impossible to focus... *mine—now—take—bind—catch—love*. It was too fast to decipher. Instead, he kissed her, tangling his tongue with hers, feeling driven in a way he'd never felt before. There was something about her.

He pulled her down onto the quilt, rolling her beneath him without releasing her mouth. The need to stay connected ran hard up his spine. Though it shocked him, he couldn't deny it any more than he could deny breathing.

She spread her legs wider as he lay nestled between them, inviting him in, where he *had* to be.

But this wasn't him. He liked enjoying each moment for what it brought. Rushing forward was not his way. Savoring a woman, her scent, her taste, the very feel of her was what made sex worth the time.

Despite his thoughts, he found himself lifting his hips, seeking her entrance with his tip.

Her hands traveled down his back to grasp his ass, squeezing it, causing his balls to tighten.

Desperate, he broke the kiss and leveraged himself so he could lick at her nipple, but despite his best intentions, he found himself sucking it into his mouth as she arched into him.

"Layne. Take me now."

If she had used any other words, he may have stood a chance, but "take" reverberated through his head like a stampede, pushing him forward whether he wished to or not.

He didn't just wish to. He *had* to. His body strained as he forced it to move slowly, spreading her sheath as he entered her. Gritting his teeth against plunging hard, he moved deeper until finally his pelvis met hers.

The relief he expected at being inside her didn't come.

"Hmmm, you feel so good." She titled her hips slightly, and he slipped a bit deeper.

Still, it wasn't enough. What was wrong with him? Even as the thought surfaced, he was pulling out. But before he could think of anything, he slid back in, much faster than before.

"Yes. More."

As much as he tried to slow his movements, something primal within him had him thrusting faster and then faster.

Silver's vocalizations grew louder as he pumped into her, sending sparks on his out-of-control burn, until she squeezed him hard and let out a scream of pure joy.

Her pleasure drove him over the top and he filled her, claiming her as his. His own shout of triumph filled the room. Still, he thrust until he was completely spent. But absolute satisfaction remained out of reach.

He snaked his arm beneath her, holding her against him as if she'd run away now that she was fulfilled.

Silver's breaths still came fast, even as his slowed, and reluctantly, he leveraged himself on his elbows to give her more room to breathe.

He didn't understand what happened or why. He never took a woman so hard. Was that why, despite feeling the thrill of his orgasm, he still felt that there should be more? He lowered his head and gave her a light kiss on the lips.

She smiled, though her eyes remained closed. "Are you sure you're from this planet? Because that was definitely out of this world."

Usually, he'd chuckle over such a ridiculous comment, but he still felt odd. "Born and bred here in Four Peaks."

She opened one eyelid. "Maybe your mother had a visit by aliens? I would swear in any court that you are more than human."

He forced a half smile. "I'm not sure my father would agree with you."

Her laugh vibrated through him as she opened her eyes. "I have a feeling your father puts your mom on a pedestal if he's anything like you."

Staring into her soft green gaze, part of his unease disappeared. "I do admit, Mom is the boss most of the time. But Dad steps in when needed. It's what makes their marriage work. They celebrate their fortieth anniversary next year."

Silver reached up and ran her hand through his hair. "That explains why you're so confident and content. I envy you that."

"Why would you say that? You are the same." He liked thinking of them as the same.

She shook her head. "I'm confident in what I know, but hardly confident about my life, and contentment always seems out of reach. I'm always on a rollercoaster, excited one day and disappointed the next."

He turned his head and kissed her wrist. "You speak of your work, not your life."

She pulled her hand back, her green gaze locked with his own. "You're right. I never thought about the two being separate. I'll need to cogitate on that."

He raised his brows. "Cogitate? Is that the type of word you use for 'think about' when you do your podcasts?"

She gave him a rueful smile. "I suppose it is. I have to pull out every educated word I know when talking about aliens possibly having visited our ancient ancestors. I don't know where Dr. Collins comes from when Silver is completely contented to be right here." Both her hands ran over his shoulders and down his biceps.

"See. You are content."

Her hands stopped. "You're right. I wish I didn't have to go back to the ranch tonight."

The thought of her leaving had him feeling possessive all over again. Shit. "You don't. You can stay here. I'll be going to the ranch in the morning anyway."

Her eyes widened before a slow smile curved her lips. "You mean I could stay here all night?"

He nodded, holding his breath for her answer.

She lost her smile as she thought about it.

If she preferred to go back, he'd take her. But he wanted her to stay. He never wanted anyone to stay.

"I probably should go back since none of us were excited about the dig when I left. The right thing to do is return and tell them of your new interpretation of the symbol on the petroglyph rock." She paused as she considered. "Then again, they're most likely already asleep."

Letting out his breath, he pulled out of her and rolled them to the side, afraid she would leave. "Then you'll stay?"

She snuggled up against him, one hand on his chest as she lifted her head to look at him. "Yes. If you don't mind."

Relief poured through him at a highly disproportionate rate. He didn't care. She was staying, and that was all that mattered. He grinned. "In that case, we're going to need a snack."

"A snack?" Her gaze left his face and moved to his groin as she licked her lips. "Or dessert?"

Shit. He could feel himself growing hard again already. "A snack...then dessert."

She laughed. "That sounds good to me. Let's do it." Before he could respond, she'd rolled out of his embrace and rose from the bed. "What are you waiting for? An invitation?"

He grinned as he linked his hands behind his head. "Maybe."

"Then I humbly request your presence in the kitchen to help me with the whipped cream."

"How do you know I have whipped cream?"

She rolled her eyes, even as one hand found her bare hip. "Your aunt owns an ice cream shop. Ice cream is dairy and sugar, so is whipped cream, and you have the same genes."

She was way too smart. "Why would you need help with whipped cream?"

"Because, I'll need you to lick it off my breasts after I use it."

His entire body tensed, his erection getting harder. Slowly, he rolled to the edge of the bed and sat up, pulling her to stand between his legs. "You mean here?" He moved his mouth to her breast and sucked.

Her hands grabbed onto his shoulders.

"Yes, that's the spot."

She tasted so good. Still sucking, he pulled his mouth from her breast. "And here." He moved to the other one and licked at it before taking the nipple between his teeth and rolling it, then tugging it toward him, forcing her closer.

"Yesss." Her word was more like a hiss as her head fell back.

He let go and rose. "Then I'd be happy to help you in the kitchen."

"Right."

She seemed to have lost her train of thought, so he took her hand and they walked naked down the short hall to the center of his house. That she didn't ask for a robe or her clothes had him admiring her all the more, and not just physically. There was a quiet confidence about her that he hadn't encountered in a woman before. She didn't try to impress people or make excuses. He liked that about her.

He led her to a stool at the island then walked to the fridge. Opening it, he scanned the contents. "Do you like chocolate chips in your pancakes?"

"Who doesn't? Is that going to be our snack?"

He pulled out the chocolate chips, butter, maple syrup, milk, and whipped cream then elbowed the refrigerator door closed. "Yes, but I only have semi-sweet."

She cocked her head. "That's fine. I don't think I've had chocolate chip pancakes since I was eleven. They remind me of home."

"How long ago was that?"

She looked away then back. "That's twenty-two years ago. Wow."

"Then it's about time. I don't go a week without eating a stack."

"I can believe that. Can I help?"

It wasn't rocket science to make pancakes, but he wouldn't mind watching her move about his kitchen naked. "Sure. The pancake mix is in the bread box on the counter."

She hopped off the stool and strode to the counter behind him.

He turned to watch, but as his body reacted, he focused on getting a mixing bowl from below the island.

"I haven't seen a bread box since I visited my grandmother when I was young."

"Yeah, Mrs. Allen made it for a fundraiser years ago. She had a dozen of them and no one was buying them, so I got one. It was the plainest one she had."

Silver set the mix on the counter next to him before turning to look back at the wooden box. "Bright yellow sunflowers were on the plainest one?"

He moved to a cabinet and pulled out two plates. "Yeah. You should have seen the other flowers. I didn't know there were lime green and aqua blue tiger lilies."

She laughed, the sound loud enough to enjoy at a pitch that was smooth like the low of a steer. "Maybe she wanted to be unique."

"She succeeded." He added the ingredients together. "Can you stir?"

He pulled an apron from the pantry and put it on before starting his griddle. Then watched as she stirred.

She made sure everything was completely mixed, carefully pulling any mix off the sides of the bowl.

He sprayed the griddle, then turned back for the bowl.

Her gaze swept over the apron top about his neck to the bottom that fell to his knees. "Cute. Let me guess. A Christmas present?"

He grimaced. "Birthday present from my eight-year-old niece."

"That must be why all the painted smiley faces."

He started dropping batter on the grill. "Yes, it was a phase she went through. She even dotted her 'I's' with little hearts for a while there. I love wearing this to grill when we have a family gathering. She's a teenager now and swears she's going to buy me a decent apron, but hasn't yet."

"I hope she never does. That fits you."

He wasn't sure if she meant the happy faces or the size. Either way, he took it as a compliment and flipped over the pancakes. It didn't take long to have a good-sized stack, and he set it on the counter. He untied the apron and took it off over his head, dropping it on the counter behind him. When he turned back, Silver had sprayed whipped cream in a perfect spiral around her top pancake then brought her plate around to the other side of the counter to sit.

He stayed on his side of the counter, partly to enjoy the view of her and partly to hide exactly how much he enjoyed it. He gave her a fork and butter knife and watched as she cut the pancake in eighths. "Are you always so neat?"

She had the first bite half way to her mouth and stilled. "Am I?" She examined her pancake. "I guess I am. I don't think I'm neat so much as I like everything in its place, nothing falling over the sides. When you travel as much as I do, knowing where I put everything helps with not losing stuff." She popped the bite of pancake into her mouth.

He quickly looked down at his own plate—syrup ran down the pancakes and over the side onto the counter. He cut a chunk from the stack and took a bite.

"So do you ever cook regular food for yourself, or do you use this big kitchen for breakfast only?"

At her question, he finished chewing, realizing he needed some milk to wash down his meal. "I cook twice a week." He moved to the fridge. "Would you like a beer, water, soda, milk, or juice?"

"What kind of juice?"

"Orange."

"I'll take a water. So only twice a week. Why that many times?"

He handed her a bottle of water and she took the cap off, taking a sip before he could ask if she wanted a glass. "Because every Sunday I go to Mom's for dinner. She says she doesn't trust that I'm eating right."

Silver's gaze ran down his chest to his stomach. "I don't know what you're eating, but it's being worked off very nicely."

He patted his abs. "Just cattle ranching."

"What about the other days of the week?"

"I cook at home on Mondays and Thursdays. Tuesdays, as you saw, I go to the Stampede and usually get a sandwich there before playing. Fridays, I hit the Lucky Lasso Hotel and Saloon for dinner, and usually go to Boots n' Brew for the live music. On Wednesdays and Saturdays, I have the leftovers from what I made earlier in the week. I found if I'm going to cook, I might as well make enough for two, and then there's less work later."

She nodded. "And you do this every week? I mean, the same schedule."

He'd taken a large bite of his pancakes, so he held up his hand for her to hold on as he chewed.

"No, you don't have to answer. I already know. Your week is always the same."

He swallowed. "Usually, not always. There are unexpected events, a niece or nephew needs a ride, and expected ones like birthdays and Pioneer Days. I think there will be more change to my schedule once Rocky Road opens the dude ranch operation full-time. Amanda likes the ranch hands to participate in some of the evening activities. I don't mind. I like meeting new people, like you." He smiled even as his gaze roamed over her naked torso.

"You said everyone in your family is married except you and your youngest brother. Do you get pressure from your mom to tie the knot?"

He was about to put the last piece of his pancake stack in his mouth, but set it down. This was a conversation he had with every woman he brought home, though usually not so soon. "I used to. But a year ago, when I turned thirty-five, she stopped nagging me. She finally decided I was too set in my ways to change them for someone else."

She took a sip of soda. "I get it. My family is always asking if there's a special someone in my life. I've explained over and over that I don't stay in one spot long enough to have a special someone. Not that I haven't had a few relationships, but it's just not going to happen. What man wants a wife who's gone for a month or three at a time?"

Though he understood why she didn't marry, it was still hard to believe. Every woman he knew wanted a husband and kids, eventually. "What about children?"

She waved her hand. "Been there, done that."

"You have children?" Despite her silver hair, she wasn't that old, unless they lived with their father. Even at the thought that she had a child with another man, he felt his comfortable contentment vanishing.

She laughed. "No, not exactly. But since both my parents worked, and I was seven years older than my siblings, I've already done my part. You see, my biological father wanted nothing to do with me, so Mom was raising me alone before she met my dad, and then she had three more kids. I became the built-in-babysitter at the age of nine. I did everything from heating bottles and changing diapers to walking my siblings to the bus stop, to curling my sister's hair for the prom or dropping my brother off at his high school job. I've already contributed to humanity, as far as I'm concerned. My siblings can add more little people to carry on our species. I'm out." She snapped her fingers as if that made it so.

Despite the fact that he understood, he'd never met a woman who thought as he did. They weren't supposed to think that way. Say it, yes, but really mean it? He hadn't met one... until now. "You're very unique." He reached across the counter and took her empty plate.

"Thank you. You are too, in my experience."

He set the dishes in the sink and ran the water over them before looking at her. "I never thought of myself as unique. I'm just a cowboy."

Her gaze softened. "No, Layne. You're not just a cowboy. You're a unique cowboy with strong values, a relaxed confidence, a sharp intellect, and a killer body." Her gaze ran over him. "Which reminds me. Didn't you promise me dessert?"

At her reminder he stiffened, but in a good way. "Yes. You said something about whipped cream."

She hopped off her stool and moved to the fridge. After opening the door, she pulled out a can of whipped cream, then halted, a slow smile filling her face. "It looks like you have four cans of this. Good thing, because I think we'll be needing at least two cans." She pulled out a second can and closed the door with her hip.

His heart started to pound as she made her way round the counter and handed him a can of whipped cream.

After uncapping her own can, she shook it. "I hope you don't mind, but I'm going to go first. I've been wanting to do this almost all night."

He expected her to turn the can on herself, but when she knelt on the tile floor, his cock jumped.

She grasped it in her hand and proceeded to pile whip cream on his erection. As her mouth moved to lick it off, he grabbed the counter on one side of him and the island on the other. It was going to be a long night...and he planned to enjoy every second of it.

SILVER RODE BESIDE LAYNE, the cord on her cowboy hat the only thing keeping it on her head. The wind whipped through the valley like a wind tunnel, and with the further drop in temperatures, it was bone chilling.

She was well aware that Layne wasn't happy. Both he and Amanda had insisted on them all staying at the ranch until it warmed up to something reasonable, saying that it was too dangerous and they risked exposure. She understood that. She'd had hypothermia once before. It wasn't fun. Jade had also experienced it. They just got too involved in their sites to notice when the weather turned cold.

Jade and Amber had wanted to come, too, after hearing about Layne's interpretation of the symbol, but since she'd barely got him to agree to let her just do a quick swipe with the GPR, she'd known he'd call it off before letting them come along. Convincing her colleagues that was the case had been difficult, but they finally agreed. They also agreed that she had the most pull, since she'd been sleeping at Layne's the last few nights.

Even as she thought about his invitation, she smiled, despite the wind trying to tear her scarf from her face. He'd suggested that since she might only be in Four Peaks a short time that they appreciate their time together, because he enjoyed her company. For a confirmed bachelor like Layne, that meant a lot. She wouldn't even think about the spike of excitement his words sent to her heart.

After tying the horses beneath the shelter and covering them with blankets, they started up the mountain. Layne still didn't say much, but as her foot slipped, he was right there, grabbing her elbow to steady her. Once they made it past the shale, the wind lessened to just a breeze. As they made the ledge with the petroglyph rock, she plastered herself behind it. "That wind is nasty. I'm so glad it's not as bad up here."

"It's the wind tunnel effect of the valley. The higher you go, the less strength it will have. But it's still cold, so let's get this done quickly."

She whole-heartedly agreed. She had high hopes, but if there was nothing to be found, she was anxious to finish up and move onto the next possible site.

He opened the backpack and pulled out the GPR.

Thanks to her photographic memory, she didn't need to look at the symbol again to see where it pointed to. Instead, she faced the rock and moved to stand where she knew the symbol to be. Then she turned around. "I knew it."

"Knew what?"

She pointed to the manzanita tree. "The symbol points to the tree."

"Are you sure?" He moved to stand next to her.

"Yes. I'm going to crawl under there first and see if I can find an opening." She took five steps straight across, then knelt on the ground. Manzanita trees had bare main branches, but they weren't that tall, even in an older tree like the one against the mountain side. And since the tree bloomed in the winter, the pink flowers, which were somewhat protected from the wind, hid a lot.

"Try not to break any branches. If there's nothing to find, Game and Fish will not be happy with you, especially with such a mature tree."

She got onto her hands and knees and looked beneath it. "I know. It must be well over a hundred years old. I'll be careful." Crawling forward, she could see that the tree went quite a ways back, which made it a safe place for prickly pear cacti, aloe, and grasses to grow beneath it. The tree's trunk appeared to grow out of a crevasse about eight feet back, which was common for plants living on mountains. She dropped to her stomach and shimmied in farther, making herself as small as possible. One red branch, though, ran along the ground as she got closer to the origin of the tree. She crawled over it, careful not to touch it.

She'd just reached the rocky side of the mountain when Layne spoke.

"Can you see anything?"

"Not yet." She couldn't see much between the angle of the rock wall that blocked out the sun and the blooms overhead, so she reached her hand past the main trunk of the bush. Air hit her hand.

Her heart jumped at the possibility that there was a cave entrance, but with the day being so windy, there was no way to know where the air came from. Even where she was under the large tree, there was a slight breeze. She pulled her hand back and licked it then stretched it forward again. This time she was sure the wind came from the mountain wall itself, but it could be funneling down the crevasse to escape under the tree and into the underbrush.

Squeezing her arm down along her side, she unclipped her phone from her jeans and brought it up in front of her. She switched on the flashlight and held it in front of her. It cast shadows on the rock face behind the tree to prove there was more than one tree trunk. There didn't look to be a gap in the wall, but she couldn't tell without getting closer. Studying the large branches in front of her, she made her decision. She pulled herself up and over a red branch to squeeze between two significant branches and slowly lifted her legs through, but she curled into a ball to not damage any smaller branches as she stopped. Getting out was not going to be fun.

"Silver, are you okay in there?" Layne's voice came from above her and to her side.

"Yes. It's pretty tight, but I felt air flow."

"That could be the wind."

She rolled her eyes, smiling. "I know. I'm trying to get close enough to check it out."

When he didn't reply, she held up her light again. The pink flowers and red branches cast a pretty glow, which reflected off the wall of the mountain, but not two feet from her looked to be a black patch. It wasn't going to be easy, but she wasn't giving up now. Twisting, she brought her feet and legs over the next branch, which was higher, before backing her body through the narrow opening between the branches. Once through, she turned the light ahead of her.

"Holy shit!" She stared at the tall narrow opening in the rock face of the mountain wall.

"What? Are you okay?" Layne's worry colored his tone.

"It's here! We found it! There's a cave here." She stepped forward through the opening to find the cave opened up to at least twelve feet wide and ten feet high. She moved her light from side to side and up and down. Rock art covered the walls and her heart began to race. Could this be it? Could it be what she'd always dreamed of?

"Is it large?"

"I'm checking." She walked toward the back of the cave only to find it curved, going farther into the mountain. She scanned the dirt floor and walls. The art had changed, and excitement bubbled deep inside her stomach as she continued forward. The walls were covered!

"Silver?"

Layne's voice sounded far away, so she retraced her steps. "I'm here. It keeps going. I think there are multi generations of art here. This could be what I've hoped for all my life. I'm going to explore farther."

"Wait! Don't go too far. You don't know what's living in there."

She studied the ground, focusing her light at the base of the walls and in the middle. "I don't see any animal prints."

"What about snake prints?"

Her excitement dimmed. Only big snakes left prints and smaller ones didn't. He was right. She shouldn't explore more on her own. What if the cave split? Still...she shined the light of her phone around the corner again. There was no end in sight. Then her light dimmed.

She looked at her battery. "Well, crap." She was low. Quickly, she took a few pictures to show Jade and Amber then strode back toward the entrance, watching for any movement on the ground. "I'm coming out. It's going to take a while."

"I'm right here."

She smiled at that. Yes, he was. It was like he'd appointed himself her bodyguard, and what a body he had, too.

Shaking her head to get her mind back on track, she studied the many branches in front of the narrow entrance to the cave.

"Layne, are you still standing where you were when I crawled in?"

"I am."

"Okay, don't move. I need your voice to help me navigate back out."

"Do you want me to sing?"

The man was a certified genius. "Please."

As he began singing a country ballad called *Your Man* by Josh Turner that she'd loved back when it first released, she turned her left shoulder toward his voice and studied the branches, using her light for the last time, she found her foot marks on the dirt and crawled over the first branch. Keeping Layne to her left for one more branch, she then headed toward his voice.

She shimmied through the low branches before getting on her hands and knees and finally crawling out.

He stopped singing in the middle of the refrain and helped her to her feet.

"Thank you." She didn't hesitate, but pulled his head down for a kiss.

He wrapped his arms around her and held her close and leisurely kissed her as if they had all the time in the world and the cold wind was no more than a passing stranger.

She broke the kiss. "We did it. We found it. It could even be *the* discovery I've been hoping for. I saw what I believe are two periods of rock art in there and the cave goes on and on. I couldn't see the end of it with my phone light. Of course, that doesn't mean it kept going. It could end three feet past my light, but it's so much more than what we expected."

His smile was wide as he gazed at her, his arms still holding her close. "Tell me something. Does that mean you might stay longer than the end of the month?"

"Yes. I don't know how long, but definitely past the month's end."

"Then I'm pleased for me."

She hadn't let herself think much about their new relationship, but at his words, she saw a myriad of possibilities from heartbreak to love, all of which made her nervous and excited at the same time.

"Do you want to see the inside? I took a few pictures."

He nodded and loosened his hold as she pulled up the pictures for him to view.

"They're not that clear as my battery was dying on my phone. That's why we don't rely on our phones for light."

"That looks like a lot of art." He handed her the phone.

"It is. We have to contact Game and Fish and get permission to trim back this tree. It wasn't easy squeezing in there and getting any equipment in will be impossible. There's so much more to study now."

He pulled her close again. "Then we'll need to celebrate tonight."

"I'd like that. Can you imagine? All of this would have been left undiscovered, if you hadn't asked me to The Stampede, and I hadn't asked where the bathrooms were?" She paused, then laughed. "If people ask, maybe we leave that small detail out."

He grinned. "Or not. It is what happened. Then again, the fire marshal won't be pleased to learn that an exit sign with lights blown was never reported."

That had never occurred to her. "No, that wouldn't be good. I don't want to get anyone in trouble. I'll think of a way to explain it while leaving all that out."

"Why would we have to explain it at all?"

At his question, it reminded her of all that would happen if the site really was as important as she thought it was. "If this is as big as I hope it is, we will be interviewed on podcasts and probably local television. There will also be people who come to Four Peaks in hopes of connecting with their roots—be they Paleoamericans or ancient aliens."

He frowned and his mustache twitched, a telltale sign that he grimaced. "Ancient aliens? Are you saying we may have people who believe they were abducted by aliens staying here?"

"Probably not. It's more people who want to prove they are descended from aliens. You do remember I'm an ancient astronaut theorist in addition to being an anthropologist, right?"

His arms loosened about her. "Yes, I remember. Do you really believe in aliens?"

She didn't even hesitate. "Yes. It would be the epitome of arrogance to think the only sentient life in the entire universe, with its quintillion planets, is only on Earth. It's less that I believe and more that it makes logical sense that there are other species, many of whom could be humanoid."

"So in addition to scientists, we could be overrun with tourists and roots seekers. Is there any way to keep this discovery a secret?"

In all her years of searching, she'd never thought about what it would do to the local area if she did indeed discover something groundbreaking. She'd seen the evidence in other places, but they had already been discovered. Those villages and towns had mostly benefitted from the scientists, improving the economy, but in some places, it was not as beneficial. "We can keep it secret for a while until my boss insists on a media announcement, anyway. First, we need permission from Game and Fish, funding from the Sully Family Foundation, long-term accommodation arrangements, and more equipment."

He still looked uncertain.

"But first we need to celebrate. Are you ready to tell the others the great news?" She smiled widely, hoping to convince him that the cave was ultimately a good thing.

He turned his head to look at the manzanita tree and didn't say anything. Finally, he turned back to her, nodded, and let her go.

She didn't like that he wasn't as excited as he had been, or that she felt she was being selfish. She'd just have to make sure they kept the discovery close to the vest. She'd be vague with the state department about the cave. Just having evidence it existed should be enough to get permission to at least trim the manzanita, so they could get their equipment in.

The walk down the mountain was much quieter than the walk up, and the ride back to the ranch was dead silent. She wasn't sure what was wrong, but something definitely was. After she dismounted, he came over to her. "I'll bring Chestnut into the barn. I'm sure you want to tell Amber and Jade about your discovery."

"Thank you. But don't you want to tell Amanda and Tanner?"

He shook his head. "No. You can let them know. I'm going to head back to my house once I take care of the horses. Jackson's coming over this evening. He wants me to look at his house plans, so I'll see you in the morning."

Now, she knew something was wrong. He'd invited her back to his house every day for the last four days, even taking her to The Lucky Lasso. "Right. Is everything okay?"

He pulled her in for a kiss, but it wasn't sensual in the least. In fact it was quite chaste. "Everything is fine. I just have a few things on my mind and I need to do a couple of things before Jackson shows up."

Her instinct told her he wasn't telling the whole truth, but she had no right to pry. Hopefully, he'd talk to her tomorrow. "Okay. I'm going to miss you."

"Have a good evening." He lifted his hat briefly, then walked the horses past her and into the barn.

Now that was definitely not good. He hadn't lifted his hat to her since the third day they'd had him as a guide. Something was definitely wrong, and it had to do with the cave and the media. That much was clear. The suspicion that it had to do with her, the alien connection, and his town, caused a rock of tension to settle deep in her stomach. But what she really needed to figure out was why she felt like she'd lost her best friend, when she'd never even had one.

CHAPTER 13

HORSE HOOVES POUNDING the earth behind her had Silver turning to find Vic galloping down the ATV road.

Upon seeing Silver, the woman slowed and changed direction to intercept her. Vic jumped down from her horse and walked over with Faithful. "Hey, haven't seen you in a dog's age. How's the digging going?"

She held out her hands which were filthy. "Dirty."

Vic extended her arms out to the side. "Tell me about it. I got in an argument with a stubborn cow."

Silver scanned Vic's black fleece vest, black shirt sleeves, and blue jeans which were covered in light tan dirt. "It looks like the cow won."

Vic shook her head. "Haven't met an animal I can't control. Sometimes, you just have to sweet-talk 'em if showing them who's boss doesn't work."

"It sounds like dealing with my boss."

"Whoa. Then you need a new boss."

She nodded. "I've been thinking that for six years."

"I wouldn't last six days. I wasn't sure I'd make it that long with Layne in charge, but he came around."

At the mention of Layne, her unease returned. "Do you mean you had to sweet-talk him?"

"Hardly. He just needed to be educated on what a woman ranch hand could do. At least he can learn."

She'd noticed that as well. Maybe Layne just needed more information from her. She hoped that's all it was. "I wish my boss could learn, but he's a dead end in more ways than one."

"Good thing you're here and he's not then, right?"

"Yes, it makes my job easier."

Vic patted her horse on his neck. "I best be getting Faithful stabled and check in with Tanner before heading home."

As Vic started past her toward the barn, she tried to refocus on the cave, but her mind kept returning to Layne's change in behavior. She trudged up the stairs to the lodge and opened the door.

"Did you find anything?"

"Will we be staying longer?"

Jade's and Amber's questions reminded her that she should be jumping with excitement. How could Layne's mood completely obliterate the fact that her lifelong goal might be within arm's reach? She took a deep breath, trying to get her head back where it should be.

Jade waved her hand and returned to the book in her lap. "Never mind. I know that look."

Amber, who lay on the couch, lost her smile. Silver put her hand on her hip. "As a matter of fact, I did find something."

"Really?" Amber sat up, hope in her pretty blue eyes. "What?"

She took her time taking off her warm fleece coat and hanging it on the peg near the door. Then she sat on the bench there and untied her warm boots.

Jade set her book on the end table. "Well, what did you find or are you going to make us guess?"

"Is it a cave? A burial site? Another set of petroglyphs?" Amber's questions brought a scowl from Jade.

Silver walked over to Amber and sat next to her. "I found a cave."

"No." Jade rose out of her chair and sat on the arm to face them.

"Yes. There's a cave behind that manzanita tree." She finally smiled as she pictured the opening in her head.

Amber pulled her legs up and crossed them under her. "Did you go inside?"

"I did. And it's deep."

"How deep?"

She turned to Jade. "So deep that even after walking to a bend and shining my phone light, I couldn't see the end."

"And wall art?"

She nodded in response to Amber's question. "A lot, and more than one generation."

"Woo-hoo! Or should I say *yeehaw*? Is that what Layne said?"

Silver didn't meet Amber's gaze. "He was excited, but concerned about what this discovery might do to his town."

Jade nodded. "He should be concerned. The three of us can keep quiet, but you know Dickhead."

Yes, she did, and that concerned her. "I'd like to give Benedict just enough information to get permission to trim back that tree, so we can get inside with equipment. It's a very old tree with other plant life living between the branches. I barely made it in there. Jade, I'd like to work with you on what you send to him, to word it so it sounds like it might not be much, but enough to get us permission."

"And don't forget we'll need funding."

Amber's reminder was a good point. Silver looked at them both. "Let's hold off on future funding and really see what we have here. We're here two more weeks. It should only take a few days at the most to get the go-ahead from Game and Fish."

"If they give it," Jade added.

"They will, if we word it right. So are we agreed to keep this quiet until we see what we're into?"

They both nodded, giving her a little relief.

"We can start planning tonight." Amber looked at her. "Unless you're going to Layne's tonight."

"No, he has Jackson Dunn coming over."

Jade studied her. "Everything okay with you two?"

She shrugged, not sure how to answer. "As far as I know."

Jade continued to look at her until Amber jumped up. "This is cause for celebration. Let me see if Nash can find us some champagne."

Silver quirked a smile at Amber. "So much for keeping this quiet then?"

"I'll just tell him Jade discovered a new angle on the art. He's not that interested in archeology. But get him started on livestock and he can talk from now until the end of time." She laughed as she moved to the door where her coat hung.

Silver had to ask. "Have you hooked up with Nash?"

"No, he's just a friend. I was kind of hoping, since he's super handsome with that light brown hair and clean-cut look. Plus, his green eyes are to die for."

"He seems very polite, too."

"Oh, he is, and kind and funny and attentive. But there's just no spark. I guess we'll just have to stay in Four Peaks longer, so I can see who else is available." With that pronouncement, she broke into a grin, buttoned the top button of her coat, and slipped out the door.

Jade didn't waste a second. "So what's really going on with you and Layne?"

"I wish I knew. Everything was fine until I mentioned the

media. I get the feeling he hadn't really taken the whole ancient astronaut theory into account. I'm afraid he's making some assumptions about me now that aren't true."

"And does that bother you?"

"It does."

"Why? It hasn't bothered you before when you hooked up with someone."

At Jade's question, she stilled. "You're right. I don't know why it bothers me. Maybe because he's such a down-to-earth kind of man and I don't like losing his respect?"

"Hmm, you may want to think about that a lot more."

"Right." She was just afraid of what she might discover.

Since when was she afraid of a new discovery?

———

Jackson pointed to the architect's plans on Layne's kitchen island. "So if I were to move this half bath next to the hall closet, that would do it?"

Layne took another sip of beer to stall. "Listen, I know you like my childhood home's layout, but you may be putting a little too much focus on something from the past. Don't you want to make this your and Dani's house?"

Jackson stared at him a moment then started to roll up the plans. "Never mind. I'll figure it out."

Layne splayed his hand across the paper, keeping his friend from continuing. "I'm sorry. My mind is on something else. You should make your new house however you want it. If you want it like the house I grew up in, then yes, a half bath next to the hall closet is right."

Jackson let go of the plans and lifted his own beer. "You mean the house *we* grew up in. I practically lived at your family's house." He took a swig and swallowed. "Glad to hear you're not pissed at me. What's got your panties in a twist?"

"I thought I made it clear, I don't wear panties. I don't wear anything."

Jackson laughed. "I know. I know. Boy, you must be pissed if you're picking on an expression. Last time I saw you this angry, you laid out Luke Hayden. That was what, seven years ago? Not that he didn't deserve it. That one always deserves it."

"I'm not angry." Even as the words came out, he smirked. He sounded like a damn five-year-old pouting.

"But something's definitely up. Is it one of your family members? Someone at the pool hall? Tell me, it isn't Honor, is it?"

"No, my horse and George are doing fine."

Jackson set his beer bottle down on the island counter a little harder than usual. "That wild burro that Shotgun tangled with?"

Obviously, Amanda had not filled in all the Dunn men about George. "Yeah, him. It turns out he's not wild after all."

"Well, fudge. And here I wasn't happy with him for eating apple cores. He's lucky he's survived this long."

"Fudge? Been changing up your swear words for little TJ?" The humor behind it had Layne relaxing a bit. He liked hanging out with Jackson. Now that he was getting help with his PTSD from his years overseas, he was more himself. Maybe Jackson should be added to his weekly routine.

"Yeah. It's a real habit. I need it to be, because switching back and forth between real swear words and substitutes just doesn't work for me, and I really don't want another stare-down from Dani. She's such a great mother to my daughter."

"I'm glad to hear it. Maybe you two can give TJ a sibling. Watching your mouth for two makes it even more worth the effort."

"Not yet. I still have too much to work on with the therapist. The flashbacks aren't as regular, but I'm still getting them."

At the reminder of what his friend had gone through, Layne felt guilty for being such an ass with his tiny little problems. Jackson might be almost eight years younger, but he'd seen a lot more of both life, and specifically death, than he had. "There's no rush. You're still young. Give it time."

"Unlike you, who is way beyond having children?" Jackson raised his brows.

"Far beyond that. Why fix what ain't broke?" It was his familiar refrain, but even as he said the words, his worry returned, and he couldn't quite manage his usual smile.

"Okay, what's up. Going from mildly pissed to just fine is normal for you. Switching from perfectly fine to serious only happens around runaway bulls."

"Bulls are serious business."

"Don't try to change the subject. What's up?"

"It's Silver."

Jackson frowned. "Silver. I know it's not as valuable as gold, but I didn't know you'd invested in it."

He shook his head. "Dr. Silver Collins, the anthropologist staying at the Rocky Road."

"A woman?"

He held back a frustrated sigh. "Yes, a woman. You know what they are, right?"

"Wiseass. She must be one of the scientists. I don't know their names. Tanner has had me busy on the new grazing area, so I haven't met them yet. Have you started something with her? A scientist isn't your typical type."

"I don't have a type."

Jackson chuckled. "Oh, yes, you do. Single, independent, pretty, a little tough, easy going, and definitely not looking for a relationship."

Shit. Silver fit all that criteria. "What does that have to do with her being a scientist?"

"I'm thinking scientists are very focused and goal-driven. They have to be, in their line of work. Pretty smart, too. Probably career-oriented as well."

"Are you sure you haven't met Silver?"

This time Jackson laughed.

It wasn't a common sound, so Layne was happy to listen.

"No, I haven't met her. But I was in the Army. We have our own scientists, especially in the weapons and medical areas."

"Silver studies ancient civilizations and tries to determine what they valued, what their social structure was like, and how they lived on a daily basis. She and her colleagues have been excavating around the petroglyph rock. At first, it looked like that was all they'd have to do." He paused, remembering how crestfallen they all were, particularly Silver.

"But..." Jackson looked at him, waiting.

"But it looks like there might be more. If they get permission from Game and Fish, they could be here longer than the original month."

"Ah, I see."

Layne frowned. "What do you see?"

"I see that you have started a relationship with Silver, knowing it would end soon. But now, there's a chance she'll be around a lot longer and you feel obligated to either break it off, so she doesn't expect more, or suffer through it until she does finally leave."

He wasn't happy that Jackson knew him so well. "As a matter of fact, Silver isn't looking for anything long term either, so she could as easily break things off." And the thought of that did not sit as well with him as it should.

"Then I don't understand. If she's as willing to break things off as you are, what's the problem?"

And there was the question that had been nagging at him since she'd mentioned keeping the new discovery a secret as long as possible. She would soon be in the spotlight again. Though she didn't say it, there would be groupies of sorts descending on Four Peaks. She would be far too busy with her work to come over. That scenario should have pleased him.

"Holy fuck."

Jackson's swear caused Layne to jerk his attention to him. "What's wrong?"

"You don't want to keep it casual." The words were barely over a whisper.

He shook his head, but the seed had been planted and all his feelings over the last week converged. "Shit." He banged his two hands down on the counter and spun away. It couldn't be true.

"It's okay, Layne. It happens to the best of us."

He turned back toward Jackson. "What happens?"

"Love. It's a human failing. It's also a human joy."

"I am not in love."

Jackson just stared at him, a slight smile on his lips.

"I just don't want her to leave yet. I enjoy her company. She's traveled everywhere and practically sets the world at my feet. She's super smart but just as humble. You should have seen her at Mr. Hardy's when Stacy treated her like a celebrity. Then Mr. Hardy wanted her to sign shirts and Luke Hayden started talking her up. I had to get her out of there because she was the only rational one in the bunch."

Jackson remained silent.

"It's not like she's looking for anything long term anyway, which is perfect. She'll probably get an apartment in town or her grant will put her up at the Lucky Lasso. For all I know, they won't need a guide from the ranch anymore, so I won't even see her." But as he imagined the scenario he'd just painted, his heart squeezed inside his chest.

"We still have a couple of weeks to enjoy each other's company. I'm sure that will be plenty."

Jackson took a sip of his beer, then finally replied. "It's okay to love her, you know."

"No. It's not. My life is perfect just as it is. I'm comfortable with a good job, a nice home, and I enjoy my time with others in town. I have an occasional hook-up that works for me, and no responsibilities beyond Honor and now George."

This time Jackson spewed his beer across the counter as he was drinking.

"Hey, watch it!" He backed up and grabbed some paper towels from the counter next to the refrigerator. He wiped his arm and shirt first then started cleaning the beer-splattered island.

"No responsibilities?" Jackson wiped his mouth with the bottom of his T-shirt, showing off his overdeveloped abs. "How about this house? Not to mention you coach your nephew's baseball team, play chauffeur to your niece, unload the truck of supplies for your aunt, help your dad with chores he can't do anymore, and serve as the foreman at the Rocky Road Ranch. You have plenty of responsibilities."

"If you consider all those responsibilities, then I obviously don't have time to add another one."

Jackson shook his head. "A significant other isn't a responsibility. It's someone to share the responsibilities of living with. Trust me, I know."

"You have a baby girl. Of course, you'd look at it that way. No, my life is complete just as it is."

"And if Silver left town tomorrow, you wouldn't miss her?"

"I...I would miss her. Like I said, I'd like some more time with her."

"How much time?"

And wasn't that the million-dollar question? "I don't know." He shrugged, forcing his tight shoulders to move.

"A week? A month? Until the end of the year? Five years from now?" Jackson stared at him, actually expecting an answer.

"I told you. I don't know. Maybe until she's completed her work on the west mountain." But if what Silver found in that cave really was her big discovery, it could be years. Did he want to be with her that long? Longer?

"My friend, you are in a rut. It may be a comfortable rut, but it's still a rut. You do the same thing every week. Go to the same places every week. You see the same people every week."

"And what's wrong with that? I change it up once in a while, and my 'responsibilities' change it for me too. In fact, on Tuesday I took Silver to The Stampede and I've never taken anyone there, so you see, I'm not stuck. I can be flexible."

"You took her to The Stampede?" Jackson's eyes rounded.

Layne crossed his arms over his chest. "I did. So what do you say to that?"

"I say that you're in love and afraid. You're afraid that your life will change. Take it from someone who hated change. I almost missed out on Dani because I didn't want another change in my life, and that would have been the biggest mistake I'd ever made. My therapist says that when we control the change, we handle it better because we don't feel like we're a victim of it, but the boss of it. I'm telling you, Layne. If you love this woman, you need to be proactive and go after her. You need to jump out of your rut and pursue an even better future for yourself."

Layne stared down at the counter, hearing more than he wanted to. "I've never been in love. I'm not like you or my brother-in-law, who think their women walk on water. I'm a realist. I call it like I see it."

Jackson rose from his stool. "Fine. Then tell me what her faults are."

"She's...She..." He searched his mind for Silver's faults. There had to be some.

"I rest my case." Jackson started to roll up his house plans.

Desperate, he latched onto to the only thing he could think of. "She doesn't know enough to grab the reins of a runaway horse."

"You know that's pathetic, right?"

He did. "Sometimes she gets so caught up in her work, she puts herself in danger." He grinned, completely pleased with himself.

Jackson tucked the plans under his arm. "Then I guess she needs you to keep her out of harm's way, now doesn't she? See you on the ranch, Layne." With that, Jackson strode out the front door, leaving the house eerily silent.

"I'm not in love." He sounded pathetic. "I simply like her. We're still in the getting-to-know-you stage. I'd know all her faults if I knew her longer."

He picked up Jackson's empty beer bottle and threw it in the recyclable trash. Then he swallowed the last of his own beer and added his bottle to the garbage as well. He liked his life just as it was. He could as easily leave the empty beer bottle on the counter all night. He could go into his den and watch whatever movie he wanted. He could even go out and drive over to Nash's or stop in at Boot's n' Brew. He hadn't gone last night. He wasn't stuck in a rut.

He stood in the kitchen trying to decide what he should do next. The absolute quiet of the house seemed to press in on him. For the last four nights, Silver had been over, but she was back at the ranch.

The heat clicked on, reminding him it was cold outside, as a quiet hum filled the house. He should talk to Tanner about putting George in the barn on cold nights, if he'd go. Maybe he should do that now. He could always stop in and see how Silver's planning was going.

"No. I don't need to see her to have a good night." Making his decision, he headed for the front door. He'd go to his mom's house. There were always family members hanging out there. He could give them crap about being married or help one of his nieces or nephews with something. They all loved him.

He shrugged into his lined jean jacket and set his white cowboy hat on his head before grabbing his keys. It was Saturday night. The last place he needed to be was home alone in a quiet house.

He stilled halfway through closing the door. Since when didn't he enjoy being home by himself?

Shaking his head, he closed the door and locked it. It didn't matter. He could do whatever he liked. Striding to his truck, he jingled the keys in his hand. When he reached it, he climbed in and turned on the heat. His life was perfect just the way it was.

He drove down his driveway and onto Main Street, headed for his parents' house. It was Saturday, so his youngest sister should be there with her two kids. She usually went there on Saturday night to help Mom with making dessert for dinner the next day. Of course, his mom would want to know what was up at the ranch. She loved knowing how her kids' jobs were going and if they were happy. She'd also ask about all the Dunns. It was her routine.

He stopped at the red light at the end of town and waited. It took him a full minute of sitting there before he swore, "Well, shit." He'd gone right by the road to his parents' house, the road he traveled every week, the one he'd grown up on, all because without thinking, he was driving to Rocky Road Ranch.

Shaking his head, he waited for the green light and made a U-turn. He was not going to the ranch tonight. His gut was telling him if he did that, there'd be no turning back, and right now, he wasn't even sure how to move forward.

"YOU'RE A GOOD, BOY, GEORGE."

George pushed his nose against Silver's hand since she'd stopped petting him.

"I know. You like a scratch right here, don't you?" She scratched his neck as he leaned into her touch. "You're so funny. I don't know how Layne could have thought you were wild."

It was way too early to be out and about, but she was excited and couldn't wait to share the news with Layne. Not seeing him for four days had really played with her psyche. She hadn't realized how much she'd become accustomed to talking things over with him. She didn't just miss their talks, but there was an easiness about him that she missed, as well as his handsome self.

She grinned. "I think you're handsome, too, George."

"Your standards are quite low. If I'd known, I wouldn't have taken your words to heart." Layne strode toward her, his usual smile in place, his white felt cowboy hat on. He wore his jean jacket open, showing his green plaid flannel shirt beneath, and a pair of blue jeans that ended at the uppers of his brown boots.

"George is handsome for a burro. You, on the other hand, are handsome for a man." She stopped petting George and sauntered toward Layne, who leaned against the first stall, legs crossed, his hands in his jacket pockets. Despite his stance, she rose on tiptoe and planted a kiss on his lips. "I missed you."

He didn't embrace her, but he did smile. "Tanner took advantage of you ladies not needing me for a few days."

She lowered her heels and cocked her head. "You could have stopped by or joined us for dinner."

"I knew you were busy and I didn't want to disturb you."

It sounded like an excuse to her. They obviously needed to talk. It was her sole purpose for being in the barn. She knew he'd have to saddle his horse for their ride to the mountain. "It wouldn't have disturbed us. Nash and Vic came over the other night. You could have joined them."

He looked over her head. "I was busy."

She stepped back, then turned toward George. "I'm busy too, but I would have made time for you. I guess you really don't want to be around an ancient astronaut theorist, as I suspected."

He walked past her and stopped in front of her, making her halt. "You think I care about you being a celebrity?"

"No, I'm quite confident you don't care a whit about me being a pseudo-celebrity. You're far too confident in yourself to worry about that. Wait, haven't you been avoiding me because I'm an ancient astronaut theorist?"

"No. According to my two nieces, that's dope, cool, and over the top awesome."

She laughed. "Dope, huh?"

He nodded.

"Then why have you been avoiding me?"

Layne laid his hand on George's back and the burro stepped closer, forcing Layne to move to keep his balance. "Relax George, I'm right here. To answer your question, I've been doing some thinking."

She appreciated that he didn't tell her he wasn't avoiding

her, but knowing it was true hurt. "And you couldn't think if you saw me?"

"No, I couldn't. You look too good and I enjoy your company too much. You would distract me."

Now, she was thoroughly confused. "So you needed to think about something else and I would have been a distraction? Is it that you're worried about Four Peaks being inundated with alien believers?"

"What? Heck, no. Four Peaks would love it. This town has been trying to get on the tourist map for a century now."

She lifted her chin, determined to get to the point. "Then maybe you should tell me what you were thinking about so hard that you couldn't see me."

He looked directly at her. "I've been thinking about us."

Her heartbeat started to race. "What about us?"

"We have to be realistic. You don't know how long you'll be here before jetting off to your next destination. I've always been happy to have a casual encounter. But..."

She hadn't really expected him to be so blunt, but she should have. Layne didn't play games or equivocate. Part of her wanted to know what he was about to say and part didn't. The part that wanted to know won out. "But what?"

"That's just it, I don't know. I find I like having you around."

Now *that* was something she could work with. "I like being around you, too. I think we work well together and we play well together."

He gave her a serious nod, even as he continued to stroke George's back as if he didn't realize he was doing so.

She held her hands out. "So why not continue as we've been. I know for a fact that I will be in Four Peaks past the end of the month now."

"You will?" His brows rose, and maybe there was a bit of hope in his gaze?

"Yes. We just got word yesterday evening that we've been given permission to trim the manzanita tree. We just have to do as little trimming as possible. They're sending out a Game Ranger. They don't want too much cut, I guess."

Layne let out a deep breath as if he'd been holding it. "So you'll be here in Four Peaks for how long?"

"At least another month, based on what I saw in that cave with my phone light. If there's more to this cave, and I think there is, it could be much longer."

His gaze moved from her for a moment then as if he'd made a decision, he stopped petting George and stepped toward her. "The dude ranch opens to customers in mid-March. Where will you stay?"

"Benedict will put us up in a hotel or short-term rental."

He took a step closer. "If you like, *you* could stay with me."

Her stomach tensed, but her heart raced. "You mean live with you temporarily?"

"Yes." He took another step, so close his breath touched her forehead.

Though she wasn't sure it was such a great idea, everything in her was telling her to say yes. "I'd like that."

He gave her a devastating smile before he pulled her to him. "Good."

She couldn't help smiling too, her body relaxing into his, telling her she made the right decision. Then he kissed her and all was right with the world again, or at least her little corner of it.

"Umm, I don't mean to be rude, but Vic asked me to saddle the horses."

At the sound of Nash's voice, Layne broke the kiss and looked over her head. "So, saddle the horses."

"Okay." Nash walked by them and headed toward Chestnut's stall.

Despite the interruption, Layne just grinned. "I have to saddle Honor and then I'll be out. I'm guessing you ladies are anxious to get to the site. Who did Amanda hire to cut the tree?"

She pointed at him.

"Me? Did she happen to provide pruners and a chainsaw? Those lower branches are large."

"As a matter of fact, she did. They're sitting on the porch of the lodge. I'll see you over by the corral."

"Don't we have to wait for the Game Ranger?"

She was about to answer when Nash nudged Layne away from a stall. "No. I'm supposed to bring the man out on the ATV. Too bad Brody couldn't do it—then he could saddle his own horse and ride out by himself."

Curiosity had her butting in. "Who's Brody?"

Nash grinned. "He's Tanner's youngest brother, and my best friend. He married Hannah. Not sure if you met her yet. Brody's a Game Ranger now, but he's taking a leadership class because he aced the initial training, so he won't be coming. I haven't seen him in weeks. He's been taking that class and looking for a house up in Kingman where he might get assigned. He's like that, very focused."

"I see." She looked to Layne who nodded rather vigorously. "I'll be by the corral." She turned and exited the barn, feeling far more excited about the day than she had when she woke up. As she rounded the corner, she found Jade and Amber waiting for her.

"What did he say? Did you tell him to explain himself?" Amber frowned, clearly thinking the worst.

Silver nodded, but didn't say anything.

Jade raised one eyebrow. "Well, come on. You have to tell us. We've been on pins and needles waiting for him to show up again and find out why he disappeared on you."

She stopped in front of them. She always thought of them as

colleagues, but they'd become something more, or rather she thought of them differently. They were her friends. They'd been her friends for a long time...she just hadn't recognized that fact. "He was thinking about us."

Amber's eyes rounded. "Oh, that doesn't sound good."

"Actually it is. He wants me to move in with him temporarily, since we'll be staying in Four Peaks for at least another month."

"Temporarily?" Jade frowned.

"I know what you're going to say, but for me it's perfect. We don't know how long our team will be here, and I'm not sure how strong my feelings are for him, so it works. No pressure. Just time to get to know each other even better."

Amber stepped up and gave her a quick hug. "Well, if you're happy, then I'm happy."

"And if this cave turns out to be something significant?"

She knew exactly what Jade was thinking. There would be no easy way to move out, but she'd cross that bridge if and when she got to it. "I'm going to take this one step at a time. Just think, won't that be a great problem to have?"

Amber grinned and even Jade cracked a smile before replying. "Yes, it is. Now let's get back to work."

Her friends were as excited to see the new cave in person as she had been to show them pictures. Having told them about the additional generation, they were ready to start investigating. She couldn't wait for them to see it. She couldn't wait to show Layne as well. "It's weird. If it wasn't for Layne, we may have never found it."

"I think we need to name it after him." Amber nodded as if that made it so.

Jade looked at Amber. "Layne Cave or Dawson Cave?"

Silver spoke before Amber could answer. "Definitely Dawson Cave. Then his whole family can be proud of it, and he has a big family, including two nieces who think ancient aliens are 'dope'."

Jade pushed away from the corral fence. "Then Dawson Cave it is, and here come our rides to get there."

She turned around to find Nash leading Jade's and Amber's horses, followed by Layne leading Chestnut and Honor. His stride was relaxed and confident as a friendly smile lifted his bushy mustache.

My man.

The thought surprised her. He was only her man temporarily. No use getting ahead of herself.

Layne handed her Chestnut's reins. "You good?"

It was obvious he referred to her mounting her horse, but she decided to take it another way. "I'm great."

"Me too."

Her heart skipped a beat as he gazed into her eyes.

"You two ready?"

At Jade's call, Silver forced herself to break eye contact and look to her horse.

Within moments the four of them were on their way, and in what felt like no time at all, they were at the base of the mountain and climbing their way up to the site. Once they arrived at the rock, she explained where she thought they would need to cut the tree.

Layne shook his head. "That's not where you came out."

"True, but when you were talking to me when I was inside, you were to my left."

Amber looked around. "Too bad we don't have a pole or rope. Then you could go inside and feed it out."

Silver shook her head. "With all the undergrowth and the old branches, it would be impossible to push it out straight."

"What about one of your lights?" Layne gently pulled her backpack with some of their equipment off her back and unzipped it. "The sun hasn't hit this side of the mountain yet. If you were able to crawl in there, you could shine the light outward from the entrance, and we could mark where the trimming needs to be done."

The man was brilliant in a no-nonsense way. "That could work, if I hurry." She studied the rock face behind him. She had maybe twenty minutes before the sun bathed them in light.

Jade pulled one of their strongest lights out of the backpack and handed it to her. "Here."

She took it then immediately went to the side of the bush where she'd crawled through before. Dropping to her hands and knees, she then put the light inside her coat and started forward. Just like before, she had to contort her body to get through.

Finally, she stood in the crevasse opening, "I made it! How's the sun?"

"You have maybe five minutes." Layne's voice was far to her right.

She fished the light out of her jacket, and switched it on, shining it straight ahead. "It's on."

Seconds ticked by.

"I don't see it." Amber's voice held a bit of whine to it.

"Come more to the north." She moved the light up and down, trying to get it through the thick bush, the light pink flowers not helping.

"Is that it?" Jade's voice sounded a lot closer.

"I'm moving it up and down."

"I see it." Layne's voice sounded directly in front of her.

"Yes!" Thrilled that she wouldn't be crawling through the underbrush anymore, she moved the light faster.

Layne spoke again. "Shine it on the farthest left of the opening, your left."

She did as he requested.

"Here's the sun!" Amber yelled, just as light filtered through the flowers giving the rock at the entrance a pink glow, even though any direct sunlight was just a few tiny dots.

"Not to worry. I've got it figured out. I'll start trimming because the tree seems at its thickest here, probably because here is where it gets the most water."

She leaned against the side of the crevasse. "Shouldn't we wait for the Game Ranger?"

"Did they say he would tell us where to trim, approve our plan, or watch to be sure we didn't do anything wrong?"

At Layne's question, she thought back to the conversation she'd had with the woman on the phone. "Now that you ask, they didn't say anything specific, just that a Game Ranger would be out."

"Then I'll go ahead and get started. It will be awhile before I get to you, but I suggest moving into the cave a bit to stay safe."

She shook her head and smirked even though he couldn't see her. Like she didn't know to stay clear of a chainsaw. "You mean back in with the snakes?"

"No! Don't play with any snakes. If you get bit, I'll break every branch on this tree to get you out of there in time, Game Ranger or no Game Ranger."

Warmth filled her chest at his determination to keep her safe. It reminded her of when they first met, him redirecting her runaway horse before grabbing the reins and saving her from certain catastrophe. "Okay. I'll steer clear of all snakes."

"Thank you."

She swallowed a chuckle at the grumpiness in his voice. Layne wasn't usually grumpy, but he didn't joke around about safety.

Since she had a strong light, she turned around and walked into the cave. This time she could see the petroglyphs more clearly, and there were far more than she'd realized. Slowly, she circled the first "room," committing to memory the various geometric designs and squiggles. Then she stood in the middle and turned in one place. Just once around and she felt dizzy. Could that have been part of the purpose? She'd have Jade research that.

The chainsaw started, so she moved into the next section, which was less of a room and more of a corridor. It had to be at least forty feet long. Here the rock art started to take on rough images of animals and people that she would equate with a three-year-old drawing. Now that she could see them clearly, the drawings could be from the same era but used for a different purpose, less of a spiritual event and more of a history, possibly. Or, as she first thought, they could be another time period. They wouldn't be able to determine that until they did some excavation and dated any artifacts.

As she reached the sharp curve at the end of the straight corridor, she resisted going farther. This was a team effort, and she wanted to know what Amber's and Jade's first impressions were without influencing them. Keeping the light away from the opening so she wouldn't be tempted, she walked back toward the spiritual room as she'd begun to think of it.

The chainsaw had stopped, but she could hear Layne cutting smaller branches very close. "I think you're almost here."

"I hear you. Hold on."

She rolled her eyes. It wasn't as if she were going anywhere.

A thin branch moved in front of her, sending some of the pink petals to the ground. "You're right here." She moved the branch.

Layne chuckled. "Not quite, but I'm close."

She listened and watched as the branch moved again, until after more minutes than she would have guessed, the little branch disappeared and she could see his face. "You did it! We now have an entrance."

He smiled widely as he peered at her through the flowers.

"Well, that *was* my assignment. Let me get the rest cleared so you can actually step out."

She waited impatiently now as he painstakingly picked specific branches that would clear the way to the ground. Finally, there was a four-foot-long tunnel that was shorter than she was through the pink flowers of the tall and very full tree. Ducking her head, she walked through and out into the warm sunshine. "We have access."

"Yes!" Amber beamed. "And it's such pretty access."

Sliver looked around. "Wow, I would not have guessed this is where it would come out, it faces directly east."

Jade came to stand next to her and then looked over her shoulder at the entrance. "That makes sense. Many spiritual sites face east for the rising of the sun. Even Catholic churches face east, with the entrance located at the west. I imagine when the ancient people of this area found this cave, they saw it as a divine sign."

Amber came up behind them. "Or the aliens showed it to them."

Silver turned back to look at the entrance. "You never know."

Layne held the pruning shears and surveyed his work. "I'm not going to do anymore. I know the pathway is not very tall, but the less damage we do, the sooner the plant will recover. Never mind Arizona Game and Fish—if Brody Dunn heard I killed an old manzanita tree after he forced all the ranch hands to do as little damage to the desert as possible, I would never hear the end of it. And with Brody that actually means *never*."

Amber touched the pink petals. "I think it's pretty. Who would have thought a tree would have flowers in the dead of winter?"

Jade picked up Silver's backpack and handed it to her. "I

hope the tree makes a full recovery, but since we have access to the cave now, let's see what we're working with."

Layne's arm shot out just as Jade moved toward the access point. "Whoa, not without me. You don't know what you'll find in there."

"Sure we do. Silver said we'd find petroglyphs proving Paleoamericans used the space." Jade tried to push past Layne's arm, but that wasn't happening.

"I'm your guide. You have me here to keep you all safe. That means I go in first, with my gun. For all you know, there could be a hibernating black bear at the back of this cave."

Both Jade and Amber looked surprised, even as Silver questioned him. "Is there really black bear in the area?"

"There is. Now let me pack up these tools and I'll go in first."

She nodded, thankful she hadn't gone any farther into the cave. "It's only fitting that a Dawson enter Dawson Cave first."

Layne had just set the chainsaw on the ground next to his pack when he stilled. He rose slowly and looked at her. "Dawson Cave?"

She grinned, thrilled to reveal the name to him. "Yes. We decided it should be named after you because we might not have found it if you hadn't interpreted the symbol correctly."

Amber piped up. "We thought about Layne's Cave, but we wanted your whole family to be proud of it. It will be added to maps and files and studies."

"And don't forget histories." Jade nodded sagely.

Despite the other women's input, Layne's gaze never left her, and Silver felt his appreciation down to her toes. "I hope that's okay. We have to name it something, so why not after the person who helped us discover it."

Silently, he walked toward her and everything seemed to disappear as his gaze held her own. When he reached her, he took her head in both his hands and kissed her. It was no chaste kiss, but a deep, loving, thorough kiss that left her breathless when he pulled away. He let go of her face and looked at her colleagues behind her. "Thank you. I'm honored."

As he turned back to finish putting away his tools, she looked over at Jade and Amber who were both wide-eyed. Amber mouthed the word '*Wow*,' but didn't vocalize it.

Once Layne had everything put away, he held his hand out palm up. "I'll take that."

She'd forgotten she still held the light and gave it to him. "I have another. We always have extra lights because we never know when a battery will die on us."

"Smart." He turned it on, and they all headed through the pink petals and into the darkness beyond.

Silver grinned. Walking through the tunnel of flowers was like being in some cheap amusement park on an old-fashioned ride called the Tunnel of Love. She lost her smile. Could that be because that's what it felt like to fall in love with someone? Like walking past the lure of outside appearances and going in blind?

LAYNE HAD to admit the cave was interesting, though cold. He exhaled and saw his breath as he stepped aside to allow Jade to go ahead of him. It was a good thing he made sure the women stepped out into the sun once an hour, and now it was Silver's turn.

More interesting was having Silver move in with him. To keep her work out of the main living areas, she'd commandeered one of his guest rooms and made it an office. It had only been a week, but he was enjoying learning new things about her that he liked, and discovering the small traits that they had to negotiate. Of course, he found himself picking up after himself on a more regular basis, which was enlightening, as he usually cleaned up only on Saturdays. Now, without having to clean up that day, he ended up with the whole day free to spend with her. He liked having her around. He just wasn't sure for how long.

He hadn't mentioned anything to his family yet, but he was toying with the idea of bringing Silver to his parents' house on Sunday. Last Sunday, he'd gone alone, as Silver had to remain at the lodge late, meeting with Jade and Amber who were still staying there. That had been convenient as he wanted a bit more time with her before the whole town knew they were a couple.

Leaving the opening of the cave, he clicked his flashlight on and followed Jade farther inside. No one was in what the women called the Spiritual Circle Cave. There were so many spirals and squiggly lines in it that when Silver had had him stand in the center and turn in a circle quickly, he'd lost his balance. She believed that was part of its purpose.

When they reached the Clovis Corridor as the ladies had dubbed it, Jade opened her laptop and lifted a clear plastic sample bag she'd tucked inside it. "Take a look at this."

He stopped and studied the small black chip in the bag. "Is that charcoal?"

"I think it is. I haven't tested it yet. But if it is, it means they must have brought it in from somewhere because to burn fire in such a closed cave system, they would smoke themselves out."

"That makes sense. So that must mean this cave was not a place where they lived."

"Correct, but that also makes our job harder. There's no exact way to date rock art, though the science is getting closer. We rely on artifacts found nearby to date it."

They'd told him that when they started digging near the petroglyph rock. "So you're saying there probably won't be many artifacts since they didn't live in here."

"Exactly, but charcoal can be radiocarbon dated. This little chip could be a big break. Let Silver know when you find her."

"I think news this big, you should tell her when we pass back through."

Jade gave an authoritative nod. "Good point. I will."

He continued down the tunnel and upon reaching the end, he moved into the Transition Room, a smaller arched cave with more art on the walls, where Amber was busy setting up a grid to the left. She looked up and smiled before returning to her work. There was so much art on the walls of both the tunnels and the round cave rooms that he could imagine the whole cave filled with artists chiseling away, like monks, all in one room, busily copying ancient texts. He didn't understand the art, since he'd never been into art anyway, but he did find it interesting that all of it was carved from about two feet off the floor to just over six feet, about as high as the top of his hat.

He left Amber and walked through another corridor, not yet named, before striding into the third wide circular room, much larger than either of the other two rooms. It had not one but four tunnels leading even deeper into the mountain. The women hadn't named this one either, but he thought of it as Apache Junction after the town on the southeast side of Phoenix. Silver told him the Apache tribe was from a much later period of occupation than the cave room. She believed it to be more likely after the Clovis tribes, possibly a group called the Folsom, which predated the Pueblo.

Though she was the stranger in Four Peaks, she knew more about the history, or rather prehistory, of the local Native American tribes than he did. Then again, when it came to ancient history, he'd been most interested in the dinosaur period. The junction room, like everywhere else in the cave, also had rock art. He likened the Dawson Cave to an art history museum, without all the lighting. Silver said more lights and equipment would arrive as soon as her boss locked down additional funding.

Confidently, he headed for the wide tunnel farthest to the right, where the soft scrape of dirt could be heard. He found Silver sitting on the ground, scraping away at the earth. "Did you find anything?"

She looked up and smiled even as she shook her head. "Not yet. But the GPR says there's a void of some kind under here."

He opened his arms wide. "All this isn't enough?"

Smiling, she rose and dusted dirt off her jeans. "I know. You'd think I'd be happy with all this. If Benedict can get additional funds, we could be in here a year or two and still not be done investigating."

"A year?" That was longer than he'd expected.

"Yes. If this cave has centuries or more of spiritual practices and rock art, it could easily take that long, but it all depends on funding." She turned her head to look at the spot where she'd been digging.

His gaze fell to the small square hole she was making at the farthest point in the cave. Now that he thought about it, she was quite far from the other women, and he was under the impression they liked to work in order, which meant Silver searched for something else. "But you think there might be more."

She turned toward him, moved forward, and wrapped her arms around his waist, looking up at him. "You know me well already. Then again, I'm not that complicated."

He looped his arms around her. "All women are complicated."

"Not me. I simply want to discover something that hasn't been discovered before."

He raised his brows. "And a cave system with rock art throughout it that may cover hundreds of years of civilization has already been done?"

She chuckled. "Actually, we're talking thousands of years here. I know. I should be thrilled with this, and I am. There have been similar discoveries, but as far as I know, nothing that covers what years we are estimating, at least not in North America. Though there are larger canyons with possibly more petroglyphs right here in America. We haven't counted yet, but I don't think this has the most. Maybe if it had some of the oldest images, but the older ones are at the front and the younger ones back here."

"So you're saying that despite what a large discovery this is, it doesn't add any new knowledge to the human database."

"I like the way you put that. Yes, but that's only at first glance. We've just begun our investigation, and we may discover something that's unique. We'll just have to do the hard work to find out." She pressed herself closer to him. "I'm guessing you came to find me because I need to go outside and warm up, but you're doing that quite well."

He shook his head, disentangling himself from her arms. "As much as I enjoy warming you, it's better for you to get fresh air as well. You told me that yourself."

"You're right." She looked around the dead end as if searching for something she hadn't seen before, then turned back toward him. "Let's go, so I can resume my work."

He took her cold hand in his warm one and headed back the way he'd come. As they came to the opening of the junction room, he paused, unable to resist commenting on the level of the rock art. "I've read that humans were shorter in the past, but if the art on these walls goes above my head, then maybe these people were taller. Or do you think the ancient people of the land stood on something in order to complete their art? I've heard of graffiti artists hanging from bridges just to get their artwork completed in the right place."

"That's an excellent question. Of course we can't be sure, but on high canyon walls, we believe there were boulders they stood on that are no longer there, or like us, they hiked up."

"So what about inside these caves?"

She walked them over to the closet wall and took his light to shine it on the wall. "I'm sure they stood on something or could have used each other for leverage."

"That makes sense. I wonder if they carried people on their shoulders like I do with my younger nieces and nephews."

Silver didn't respond. Instead, she lifted the light higher revealing perpendicular lines from the artwork into the darkness of the ceiling.

He frowned as it looked like maybe someone had worked hard to make it taller. "Did they dig out this cave?"

"Not likely. There's evidence of them digging the tunnels in here, probably to make them more passable, but the three relatively round cave rooms are natural. We'll get a geologist in to confirm that though. See those marks higher on the wall?"

"Yes. That's why I asked about them digging these out."

She shook her head. "That's not digging." She let go of his arm and handed back his light. "Let me grab my lantern."

As she disappeared down the tunnel, he kicked himself for mentioning the height of the artwork. He needed to get her outside to warm up.

She came back into the space and moved opposite him, lifting her lantern higher. "Shit, there's something up there. We need more light." She strode toward the no-name corridor and yelled. "Amber, come here, and bring your lantern!"

He lowered his flashlight. "Maybe we should investigate this after you warm up."

"No. There's some kind of figure on the ceiling. I have to know what it looks like."

Hurried footsteps sounded in the corridor, and Amber appeared in the arched opening. "You called?"

"Shine your lantern at the ceiling. There's something up there."

"I hope it's not bats." Amber laughed at her joke before lifting her lantern.

As Amber's light converged with his, more lines could be

seen. "Is it more rock art?" From what he could see, it looked like giant wings.

"I don't know yet." Silver moved to another area of the room and shined her lantern toward the ceiling. "Holy crap." Her words came out on a breath as she stared upward.

He moved his gaze to the apex of the room and found what looked like a giant bird carved into the rock, but instead of having a beak, the head looked more like a lion. It reminded him a little of the Native American Thunderbird, but it was different. "What is it?"

When she just stared at the ceiling, he looked to Amber, whose gaze was riveted to the winged creature. She shook her head. "I don't believe it." Her words were also barely above a whisper.

"Jade." Silver's voice came out on a breath.

Obviously, it was something big, and Jade needed to see it too, so he yelled. "Jade, you need to see this!" She was the least excitable of the three, so maybe she could explain it.

It took a few minutes before Jade finally walked in. "What? Freakin-A!"

As she stood rooted to the spot, staring at the ceiling, he guessed the discovery was monumental, so he waited.

Finally, Amber spoke. "It can't be."

Silver's face split into a grin. "It is. It's unbelievable, but it's here, in North America."

Jade shook her head. "I can't believe we found a link."

He had no idea what it was a link to. "Is it a Native American Thunderbird?"

Silver finally took her gaze off the ceiling and looked at him. "No. It's a Sumerian Thunderbird."

"And that's different?"

Her smile was wide, lighting up her eyes in the low light. "It's very different. The Sumerians lived in the Middle East, what is now Iraq, over six thousand years ago. They worshipped beings called the Anunnaki who supposedly descended to Earth from the sky. Anthropologists, historians, and archeologists have noticed the similarities between the Thunderbird of both peoples, but there has never been any hard evidence that they were connected. This is it!" She pointed toward the ceiling.

Though he didn't understand the details, he did get the gist of what she was saying. "So this is the discovery you've been looking for?"

Tears filled her eyes. "Yes."

Jade, who had her camera in hand, snapped pictures. "Dickhead has to see this."

Layne was too busy watching Silver to look at the ceiling again. She practically glowed with happiness in the light of the lanterns. What caught him off guard was how exhilarated he was for her. It was the same feeling he had when his niece won the state softball championship or when his father was honored for his years of volunteer service...only this was even stronger. He felt her triumph was shared with him.

And in that moment, he knew. He knew what Jackson had tried to tell him was true.

He loved Silver.

He wanted to make her happy always, not just for a while. He wanted to support her success forever. He wanted to...to get her warmed up. At that thought, he abruptly turned off his flashlight.

"Hey." Jade frowned at him.

"The image will have to wait if you need my flashlight or that lantern Silver is holding. She needs to go outside. Now."

Silver looked surprised, but she didn't say anything as he took the lantern from her, set it down, and guided her out of the cave, through the pink flowers of the manzanita tree, and into the sun on the ledge. She stood silently for a moment and tilted her face toward the sun, her eyes closed. Two tears tracked down the side of her face.

He knew they were tears of happiness, but even so, he didn't like seeing her cry. "Feels good, doesn't it?"

She opened her eyes, sighed, then looked at him. "Everything feels good right now, the still warm air, the sun, you." She took his hand in hers.

"You do realize it's only fifty degrees out."

"Really? It must be close to freezing back there where I was working, then." She stepped closer to him, so their arms touched as she enjoyed the relative warmth.

He would insist that they buy thermometers and set one wherever each woman worked. They'd already admitted they lost track of time when engaged in their study. But right now, he remained silent. Silver needed to process her monumental discovery, and he was quite sure that was exactly what she was doing as she stared at the mountainside and beyond.

It was a good fifteen minutes before she spoke again. "Now that my dream has come true, I'm not even sure where to start. Is that strange?" She stepped forward and faced him, turning her back toward the sun.

"No. This is something you've strived for your entire career. I imagine it's how Thomas Edison might have felt after inventing the light bulb or how Snively felt when he discovered gold."

She cocked her head. "Snively? I've never heard of him."

"He started the gold rush here in Arizona."

"Yes, I can imagine he was pretty psyched to find gold, and Edison thrilled his invention worked. As much as I've studied the discoveries of others and even a few small ones that were new, like the rock over there, I've never discovered such a large site that could change the history of mankind. It's not only exciting, but overwhelming, and based on that Thunderbird, a bit scary."

He didn't like the idea of her being scared, so he pulled her against him. "Why is it scary?"

"That rock art on the ceiling links two civilizations that until now could not be linked because they are thousands of miles away from each other, not to mention having an ocean between them. Back over six thousand years ago or longer, they didn't exactly have ships or airplanes. So if that art can be directly linked to Sumerian art, it changes mankind's history. But it's more than that. It will bring change to the Rocky Road Ranch, the town of Four Peaks, the people in it. Even the county and state will be affected. This could well change what's taught in schools." She shivered.

As he began to understand what her discovery meant, his need to protect her grew stronger. "You may have discovered this, but you didn't put it there. You are no more than the messenger. You don't need to take this on your shoulders."

She rested her cheek against his chest. "You're right, though it's not quite that simple. Still, you really help me put things into perspective. I'm so glad you're here."

His heart swelled, wanting to say the words he felt, but not knowing her feelings, he kept it to himself.

She yanked her head back and looked at him. "You said Four Peaks wanted to be on the tourist map. Wait until the alien believers hear about this! The town won't have nearly enough rooms or food."

"And that's because this art somehow connects to aliens? I admit to not being well-versed in that particular area."

She chuckled. "No, I don't suppose you would be. Remember how I said the two civilizations had no way to travel to each other?" At his nod she continued. "The ancient astronaut theory states that the Thunderbird was an alien being. So if that image is here as well as in the Middle East, the logical summation would be that its proof these aliens visited both cultures, or it could go a step further and suggest that these aliens transported humans across the globe."

As farfetched as it sounded, there was a certain logic to it. "That does make sense in an out-of-the-box kind of way. So if this discovery is going to affect so many, are there steps that need to be taken to reveal the news? I know you had said you were keeping this cave just between you, your boss, and the foundation that funds you. Is there a certain way you go about making things public now?"

She raised on her toes and pulled his head down, giving him a rather satisfying kiss before pulling out of his arms.

"What was that for?"

She grinned. "Do I need to have a reason?"

"No, but I get the feeling there is one."

She laughed, the sound easing the tension he'd been feeling on her behalf. "You're right. I just wanted to thank you for pointing out the obvious when I can't see it. I can always count on your common sense. There are protocols for all of this. We've started following them, and since this new discovery is simply part of the whole cave, we continue to follow those steps. Of course, we'll need to have a private meeting with the state parks liaison, Amanda, the funders, my boss, and probably the mayor of Four Peaks, if that's what you have here."

"No, we have a Town Council and a Town Manager. You may want to also include Amanda's father in that. He's a state legislator and has done a lot to conserve land in this area. He could be a good ally."

"That would definitely be beneficial. There's so much to do, but we'll take it one step at a time." She turned around to go back into the cave then stopped. "Aren't you coming? We can't do this without you. At least, I know I can't." She held her hand out to him.

He took a deep breath, a feeling of contentment filling him once again as if he'd lost it somehow. "You can count on me." Striding between the pink flowers holding Silver's hand, he imagined his life changing from what he'd always had into something else. And for the first time since he was five, when he told his father he was going to be a cowboy just like him, he was open to that something else because it included Silver.

CHAPTER 16

"SILVER? HELLO, SILVER?"

At the sound of Amber calling her name, she pulled her gaze from Layne, who sat at a long table at the other end of the clubhouse, in a meeting with the rest of the ranch hands and the Dunn family. He'd offered to explain, in simple terms, what the new discovery meant so she wouldn't need to, which she appreciated. Just because she could stand in front of a camera for a podcast or video, didn't mean she was comfortable speaking in front of a lot of people. And there were a lot of people at that table.

"Dr. Collins, please pay attention."

She blinked and looked at Jade. "I *was* paying attention. Just to another conversation."

Amber bumped her shoulder against her. "You can't hear what they're saying. You're just ogling your man, and I can't say I blame you."

She snapped her head around to look at Amber, who winked. Silver sighed. "Sorry. I'm just not used to a man going to bat for me."

Jade looked over her shoulder as she sat on a love seat opposite Silver and Amber, a roaring fire in the stone fireplace nearby, keeping them warm and cozy. Then Jade turned back. "I believe he's a bit old-fashioned in that way. If you think about a generation-and-a-half earlier than his age, that's him."

"I do believe you're right. I'm not as up-to-date on recent generational anthropological insights, but maybe I should do a bit of research for my own knowledge."

Jade waved her hand. "No need to. I have files on each generation back to World War I. They may be a bit outdated as I did the research as part of my Master's thesis, but they will cut down your time. I don't think we'll have a lot of spare time on our hands for the next decade."

"If Dick the Prick can get the funding." Amber lifted a chocolate chip cookie from the dish between them and held it up. "I don't know about you, but I'm feeling a bit nervous about him being able to obtain the whole cookie." She promptly took a bite.

Jade pursed her lips for a moment before speaking, "I agree. Dickhead is like a bull in a china shop. Getting funding to cover this entire exploration is going to take finesse that he doesn't have. I wish he'd allow me to speak to the funders."

Silver silently agreed. Jade was far more sophisticated than any of them. "He won't let you because of his ego. I wish we worked for someone else. There's got to be another business owner who's interested in our ancient ancestors."

They both laughed then Jade shook her head. "Not likely."

"Besides, the Prick couldn't care less about any ancestors. He just loves the 'administrative' fee he charges on the grants."

She had to admit, they both made good points. "True. I often feel like our successes are *despite* him instead of *because* of him."

Her gaze wandered back to Layne. He wasn't speaking now, just listening as everyone at the table weighed in on his information. The man was the most patient person she'd ever met. He was also the most content. She'd never encountered anyone so satisfied with their life. Maybe if she ever got to visit Nepal, she might find a Buddhist monk with those traits, but everyone she knew, including herself, strove toward something. Not Layne Dawson. He was happy with his life just as it was. So what did that mean if she were to stay in town for years?

Amber elbowed her. "You're doing it again. I swear I've never seen you so captivated by a man before. Even that Italian, Antonio, who was drop-dead gorgeous, couldn't hold your attention that long."

"Well, Antonio was nice to look at. But his moods were always up and down. He didn't seem to have a neutral speed. It was like living with a roller coaster."

Amber laughed. "Now that's one roller coaster I wouldn't mind riding."

She chuckled herself. "Yes, well. That's great for sex, but not so much for an adult relationship."

"And Layne is relationship material?" Jade reached for a cookie as if her question wasn't the epic one it was.

Silver let the question hang in silence for a few minutes, knowing the answer, but not knowing the end game. "He is. But there are a couple of issues standing in the way."

"Such as?"

She could always count on Jade not to let her squeeze by with a shortcut on a dig or a guess when an answer could be researched. So it was no surprise that Jade wouldn't stop until she was thoroughly satisfied. "First, he's a confirmed bachelor. He's had girlfriends before, but draws the line at marriage."

Jade opened her mouth, but Silver continued. "Not that I'm looking for marriage. In fact, I think the last time I thought of marriage was when I was ten." She grinned at the memory of telling her mother that she hoped never to marry so she wouldn't have to take care of brats.

Amber faced her. "But surely you're open to a long-term relationship with Layne. You two look great together, and I've never seen you argue. He's the exact opposite of Antonio."

Jade nodded. "Maybe too much opposite? A woman needs an attentive lover."

"Oh, Layne's attentive. He savors every minute."

"Do you mean sex lasts more than a half hour?"

At Amber's question, she felt her cheeks flush. "Much longer."

Amber squealed quietly. "You're so lucky."

Even as she thought about the nights she and Layne had sex, her body began to heat, so she quickly switched topics. "The second issue is I'm not sure how he feels. We've admitted we like each other, and besides a couple of awkward adjustments, we appear to live together fairly well. But he could just as easily ask me to leave next week. As I said, he's a confirmed bachelor who is very happy with his life just as it is. I'm a temporary adventure, I think."

Jade shook her head. "It doesn't matter how he feels if *you* don't feel anything. In that case, you would just move out and continue your work. But if you *do* feel something..."

"I do feel something. I'm just not sure what it is. I admire and respect him. He sees things I don't. He's always on an even keel unless he's being protective, but even that's not over-bearing."

"You mean like Martin was?" Amber shivered.

She nodded. "I believe your ex needed to be in control of your every move. That's not protective, that's manipulative and scary. I'm so glad you were able to get rid of him."

"I couldn't have done it without you two."

Jade reached across the table and patted Amber's knee. "We

look out for each other. And from the looks of this new discovery, we're going to be together for a very long time."

Silver cocked her head. "If Benedict can get the funding."

"And if we accept Layne into our circle." Amber grinned.

She felt her breath rush out of her lungs as if she'd been holding it for minutes. He did fit in well with them, even looking out for Jade and Amber. "I don't know if he'll continue as our guide come March. He's the foreman here at the ranch. He's needed for the cattle operation. I doubt they'll let him continue with us."

Amber shrugged. "I don't think we need a guide. We know where the site is and can get to it on our own. What do you think, Jade?"

"How often would you have gone outside to warm up yesterday, or today for that matter, if Layne wasn't there to remind us to do that?"

Amber slumped back into the cushions of the love seat. "I'm sure we could set an alarm or something."

Amber's grumpiness struck Silver as funny, and she grinned. "I'm pretty proud of him for looking out for us and for understanding so much. Do you know, the other night while I was typing up some notes, he was on the internet reading about the Clovis people? The man may be stuck in his ways, but he doesn't shy away from learning new things."

"Like learning to love you?" Jade's voice was quiet, but no less startling.

At the thought of Layne loving her, she felt both elated and scared at the same time. "I don't know."

"Which brings us back to how you feel about him." Jade crossed her arms.

Before she could conjure a response, Layne rose from his chair and walked toward them. Her stomach tied in knots at how the family may have taken the news of the discovery. Since he wasn't smiling, her knots just got tighter.

"Ladies, I can't believe there are still cookies on that plate. Don't be shy." He reached down and took one. "The Dunns agree that this is not only an important discovery, one they are very much excited about, but also that moving forward should be planned carefully. If you wouldn't mind joining us, I believe some of the answers they're looking for would be best coming from you."

Jade rose immediately. "We'd be happy to answer questions."

Amber stood as well. "I'll try not to get too excited and wander off track. I haven't been able to share this with anyone since we discovered the cave."

Silver finally rose. "What do you mean? You talked poor Nash's ear off until midnight."

"He such a good listener."

As Amber and Jade made their way to the table, Layne stepped in front of her. "I have a question."

From his tone, she could tell it was important, yet he didn't appear tense at all. "I'm happy to answer it, if I can."

"What happens if the owner of your company can't obtain funding for you to stay here and detail the cave?"

She should have known he'd ask the tough question. "It's easier for Benedict to get private funding. It's tougher to get foundation funding. He always has to do backflips to get it because he's a for-profit company. If he can't get the funding from either source, I'd be forced to abandon the project and move on to whatever site he can find funding for."

"And would another team of researchers come here to continue what you started?"

Even as he said the words, anger filled her. After making the discovery of her career, the last thing she wanted was someone else to learn all there was to know about it. "If the news of this gets out before we receive funding, that is a possibility, which would piss me off royally."

Layne's lips lifted in a soft smile. "I imagine it would. I would suggest stressing the need for keeping this new discovery quiet until the funding is secure. Four Peaks is a small town with access to social media, so things could spread like ants discovering a picnic."

She relaxed as she understood his reason for asking. "I understand. I will do as you suggest. I'll also call our boss tonight and find out if he made any progress after receiving the photos Jade sent him. Thank you being our champion. We need one, now more than ever."

"What about you? Do you need a champion?"

She smiled, shaking her head. "I already have one."

"Yes, you do. Shall we?" He held his arm out to her, and she took it like they were walking the red carpet instead walking across the tiled room of the dude ranch clubhouse.

What she thought would take a few minutes turned into an hour. Everyone at Rocky Road was excited about the new discovery. But they also had a lot of questions relating to the potential impact on their dude ranch, the cattle, the town, and the desert itself. Though the brother, Brody Dunn, was not present, his wife Hannah was, and she asked a lot about the impact on the wildlife as well as the financial side. According to Layne, she was a whiz with numbers.

By the time the meeting was over, there was a plan in place with everyone assigned certain duties and another meeting scheduled in three days, when Silver hoped to hear about funding. A fire was built in the quad and a number of people stayed to enjoy it, but the married ranch hands headed home, as did she and Layne, not that they were married.

By the time Layne pulled into the driveway of his house,

she was anxious to get moving on her first task, even if it was almost nine at night. Once inside the house, she set her cowboy hat next to his on the side table in the entry way. She'd never noticed before, but his was much bigger than hers.

As he closed the door and locked it, a new habit that he'd started after she moved in, she waited for him to face her. "I'm going to my office to call Dick. I want to find out what happened when he called the Sully Family Foundation and if he's started talking to other possible funding sources."

Layne frowned. "Isn't it a little late to be working?"

"I know, but something this big needs special attention. I'll be in to shower in a few minutes. This isn't just important for Rocky Road. This is important to you and me as well."

"You and me? How?"

"First, let me make this call. Then I can explain." She gave him an encouraging smile before turning in the opposite direction of the master bedroom. When she reached the guest room she'd made into an office, she sat on the bed and clicked her boss's name on her contacts list.

After five rings, he finally answered. "What?"

"Good evening to you, too, Benedict."

"Don't call me that. Why the hell are you calling so late?"

"We need to know your progress with the Sully Family Foundation."

"My progress? What progress? You tell me you made this big discovery, send me a picture of some bird, and expect me to go back to a funder I spoke to not a week ago asking for more money?"

At the realization he hadn't done anything, her heart sank, and she took a deep breath to keep from yelling. "Yes, I do. Calling them so soon would alert them as to how important this new rock art is."

"Why the hell is another carving on the wall important. You must have over a hundred of those."

"Because—" *asshole*, "it links the ancestors of the Native American tribes to the Middle Eastern peoples of six thousand years ago."

"That's nothing new. Man has lived across the globe since the beginning of time."

Benedict was wrong on so many levels of that statement that she ignored it. "How could Middle Eastern people interact with Paleoamericans when they didn't have planes?"

"They could have used a boat or walked if the continents were connected. Trust me. This isn't going to get us more money. I barely got the funding I did. Call me when you have something seriously good."

She could sense his anxiousness to get her off the phone. Frustrated with the man who only knew the history of the world from movies and YouTube videos, she could see her discovery slipping through her fingers like prehistoric goo.

As a last-ditch effort, she threw him a bone. "Not even if it means proving the ancient astronaut theory?"

"What? You mean that aliens visited Earth? It could prove that?"

His astonishment was telling. Obviously, he'd only used her interest in the theory as a media stunt. As pissed off as that made her, she still needed him to find the funding, so she gave him what he wanted. "Yes, it *could* prove the theory if additional evidence is found, but we won't find anything without funding."

"Hold on."

She could hear him scrambling around, no doubt firing up his laptop.

"Okay, just give me the shit I need to sell the ancient alien theory. I've got a family here that is a sucker for that stuff."

Despite his complete lack of ethics, she explained again what was there and why it connected, along with what else they would need to find.

"Well, fuck. This is good shit. You should have called me when Jade sent me those pictures. All she said was there was a link to the Sumerian culture that had never been found before. Who the hell would care about Sumer?"

Silver grit her teeth. Jade had sent him far more, but unless the word 'alien' was in the text, Benedict only read half of it. "Then you'll go back to the Sully Family Foundation and see if they're interested?"

"Oh, I have far larger foundations than Sully I can call tomorrow. Fuck, I could even get us in the door with the National Sensient Beings Foundation. This is juicy shit. About time you bitches came up with something I can work with. If I need any more information, I'll come to the site. Might take a few of my own pictures, just to be sure they're authentic. I'll be in touch soon."

She was done dealing with him. She couldn't even manage a polite goodbye and instead just hung up. What an ass. If only she didn't have to work for him, but then again, she wouldn't have made the discovery of a lifetime if he hadn't found the funding that brought them to the Rocky Road Ranch.

Nor would she have ever met Layne. She let her gaze sweep her new office, recognizing that though she'd made it her own, it was still very much him. How long would their "temporary" living arrangement continue?

She rose from the bed before heading for the other wing of the house. As she walked into the bedroom, Layne came out of the bathroom, completely naked with his hair still wet. She stopped to enjoy the view. Damn, the man was built, not body-builder built, but honest-day's-work built, and it had her own body reacting.

"What'd he say?"

She lifted her gaze from where it had wandered and met his. His eyes were their usual mix of blue, gray, and green. As she thought back to her conversation with Benedict, she shivered. Somehow talking with that man always made her feel like she'd crawled through mud...under a barbed wire fence, ripping her clothes in the process.

"He said fuck, shit, hell, and bitch. But at least he has new ideas on funding sources. Do you know that man hadn't made a single funding call since Jade sent him those pictures? Even the Dunn family grasped the importance of the Thunderbird faster than that dufus." She paused. "He even acted like Jade hadn't communicated how important it was. That's because he has such a small brain, he can't read beyond the first sentence of a text or e-mail. I swear a dinosaur could understand better than he can."

The scowl on Layne's face made her feel a little better. That he disapproved of her boss as much as she did made her feel a bit more sane.

"I feel like I've been slimed after talking to him. I'm going to shower and wash my hair. I want to clean him off, so I can enjoy you thoroughly." She couldn't help looking Layne over from head to toe again.

"I'll help."

"You'll help what?" Knowing how protective Layne could be, she envisioned him pounding Dick into the desert dirt, which was actually a rewarding image.

"I'll help you shower." Layne closed the distance between them and immediately lifted her dark blue sweatshirt off.

She cocked her head at him as soon as the sweatshirt was gone, leaving her in the white tank she'd worn instead of a bra. "Have you ever washed a woman's hair before?" Even as she said them, she wished the words back. But before she could shrug it off, he answered.

"No, I haven't. But I'm willing to learn. I've found you to be a good teacher."

Her heart sighed at his words. However, when her tank was pulled from her torso, excitement hardened her nipples.

In record time, for Layne, he had her completely undressed. Taking her hand, he led her into the master bathroom. He started the water in his walk-in shower, and though she always used just the rain showerhead, he turned the knob so the hand-held also sprayed downward. He tested the temperature then stepped to the side. "Let's get you cleaned up. Dirt from the desert is one thing. Grime from a man's mouth is something else."

She smiled, too pleased that he understood how she felt to question his presence in the shower with her. Instead, she stepped in front of him and into the warm spray, closing her eyes and tilting her face toward the waterfall of the rain showerhead.

Warm water hitting her back from the handheld caused a ripple of excitement to fly through her. Layne meant exactly what he'd said, that he'd help her shower. It was an amazing feeling to be sprayed from above on her front and on her back by Layne. It was comforting and exciting at the same time. When he set the handheld back on its hook and reached the shelf from behind her to squirt her body wash into his rough hands, her senses opened up completely.

He started with her shoulders, spreading suds as he went, then focused on one arm, her hand, and each individual finger. Done with her right arm, he switched sides and gave the same attention to the other. She rinsed each one in turn, even as he soaped up her back and butt, carefully running his fingers between her butt cheeks before crouching down and washing each leg and every toe.

She was about to turn around to rinse her back when his hands came around her front and began washing her collarbone and chest. As each hand soaped up her breasts, her nipples hardened until he gave them the attention they craved. She found herself leaning back against him as he tweaked and pinched her hard nubs far beyond washing. Now she was truly wet everywhere.

Still, he didn't allow her room to turn around, but soaped up her abdomen, her mons, and between her folds. More than ready for him, she tried to step forward into the spray, but he wrapped his arm about her waist as he reached for the handheld showerhead again. He turned her to face him and began to spray the soap from her body. He started at the top and worked his way down. As he crouched before her, he pushed her legs apart and focused the spray to rinse her folds, using his fingers to be sure no soap remained.

About ready to jump him right there in the shower, she tried to nudge him to stand, but instead, he switched the showerhead to massage and then angled it at her clit. She pressed her hands against both sides of the shower to keep herself standing. The pulsing action of the water sent vibrations through her sheath that had her panting for release, but not giving it to her. "Please, now."

He must have heard the need in her voice because he dropped the handheld and backed her up through the rain shower and against the tiled wall. Layne never made love quickly, but his mouth took hers instantly and within seconds, she felt his erection slipping between her folds and plunging deep inside her.

The surprise entrance into her wet sheath sent her to the edge of her orgasm, causing her to catch her breath. She held on tight, her arms around his neck as she lifted one leg to allow him to slip deeper.

A low growl came from deep within his chest, vibrating her own, just before he lifted her by her thighs to bury himself completely inside her, pinning her to the shower wall. The action sent sparks shooting through her core, and she crossed her ankles to hold him inside her.

His mouth dominated hers in a way he'd never done before, even as he pulled out almost to his tip and thrust back inside. Every thrust made her feel claimed, wanted, protected, and oddly safe. His movements, always controlled, weren't, exciting her all the more. Then he tilted his pelvis and rubbed against her clit and her orgasm burst through her, sending her into the stars.

CHAPTER 17

AS SILVER'S sheath contracted around him, Layne let himself go, filling her with his release, the primal need to make her his still clawing down his back and through his balls. He continued to pump inside her, his ecstasy tinged with triumph. Even as he thrust for the last time, the satisfaction he usually felt was missing, and in its place, pure fear.

He could never let her go.

Her panting slowed as her fingers played with the wet hair on his neck.

He opened his eyes to the tiled wall of the shower, the water still running behind him.

Silver's head moved, and she kissed his earlobe. "At least we don't have to go far to clean up."

He could imagine her smiling as she said the words. They reminded him he needed to let her down, but he didn't want to. "I planned it that way."

Her chuckle reverberated through her, and he felt it everywhere. "I like that about you. Everything you do is done with intention."

Finally, he pulled his head back to look at her. "Good, because I intend to make love to you after dinner."

Her breath caught before she spoke. "So I'm dessert?"

Immediately, he envisioned her soft folds with his tongue licking between them before tasting the sweetness of her release. "Yes." Even as he said the word, he began to harden already.

Her eyes widened. "Wow, you really know how to make a woman feel wanted."

He didn't just want her. He wanted to love her. He wanted her to love him. But he couldn't get the words past his throat. Instead, he stepped back into the spray of the shower, coating them with the warm water as it sluiced between their connected bodies.

Her laughter echoed against the tile, easing his unfamiliar angst.

"I promised to wash your hair."

"So you did." She tilted her head forward, letting the water soak it all over again.

He stepped back some more, so the water ran against her back only. "I'll need to let you down to do that."

"I know. Maybe I don't need my hair washed after all and we can just eat dinner like this, feeding each other?"

That she felt the same about separating eased his mind and he grinned, a new idea forming. "Turn off the water."

"Um, you know we'll need water for my hair, right?"

He just nodded.

"Okay. Move me closer."

He stepped back into the spray coating them both as she turned the water off. "Now what?"

Without a word, he stepped out of the shower and continued with her into the bedroom.

"Layne, you're dripping water all over the tiles of the bedroom."

"So." He kept walking until he reached the bed. "Are you ready?"

She looked behind her than faced him. "We'll get the quilt wet."

He shrugged.

A mischievous smile tilted her lips. "I'm so ready."

"Then release your feet."

As she did so, he grasped her tightly and turned to sit on the bed. Her sheath tightened around him as she straddled him and he lay back on the bed. With his feet planted on the floor, he raised his hips, lifting her before settling back down. "Would you like to ride?"

"Absolutely."

He relaxed against the quilt, ready to bring her to another orgasm when she leaned over him and nibbled at his nipple, sending a shock directly to his balls.

She let go and grinned. "Prepare to be ridden."

His cock twitched inside her even as she moved her hips and rubbed her pelvis against his. As much as he wished her to enjoy herself first, he had a feeling she planned to make that impossible. And he was perfectly content with that.

Layne looked over at Silver in the passenger seat and grinned. Not only had they been late in waking up, but even now she'd dozed off. He should regret keeping her up all night making love, but he didn't. Since he couldn't seem to say the words, he'd shown her, in many ways, how he felt.

He turned onto the driveway of the ranch and stopped beneath the sign welcoming visitors to the Rocky Road. He moved Silver's white hair from her cheek and lightly brushed her cheek with his knuckles.

Her eyelids fluttered open and she looked at him, smiling sleepily.

"We're at the Rocky Road. I didn't want you to wake up because of a bump. I know you like to hold on."

She blinked then looked about her. "Oh wow. I can't believe I slept the whole way. Last thing I remember was you turning onto Main Street."

"You didn't miss much. Main Street hasn't changed since the last time you saw it. Actually, I can't think of any changes to it in over fifty years."

She rolled her eyes. "How would you know? You're only thirty-six."

"Okay, then it hasn't changed in thirty-six years."

She lost her smile. "It will probably change in the next thirty, or even three, if what we found makes the splash I think it will."

He took her hand. "That's okay. Remember, you just need to follow the steps. And keep me informed of what they are." He let go and put the truck in drive, and they started down the mile-long rocky road.

"Speaking of steps, remember long ago, as in last night, when we got back to your place, and I said I needed to talk to Dick?"

He nodded as he avoided a particularly bone-jarring hole.

"I told you that what I learned wouldn't just affect next steps, but us as well."

At that, he let the truck roll to a stop, his contented mood of moments ago evaporating like virga. "Yes, you did. So has it?"

She cocked her head. "I will know for sure in a few days, but yes. My boss is very confident he can get the additional funds now, so that means I'll be staying in Four Peaks for at least a year, if not indefinitely."

He wanted to ask her to live with him more permanently, but his throat closed, and despite swallowing, he couldn't seem to speak. So he gave a short nod to show he understood.

"Right. Well, I'm not sure what you think, but I was wondering if maybe, if you wouldn't mind, and you understand I have no idea how long or short it maybe be, that maybe you would be okay with me staying with you?"

His heart tripped, but it relaxed his throat enough to speak. "If that's what you'd like to do?"

Her gaze softened and she smiled. "Very much so. I love living with you. I really do."

At her words, despite the fact they weren't *the* words, his heart settled back into rhythm. "I'd love for you to live with me."

"Really? I mean, wow. That means so much to me."

At her statement, he unbuckled her seatbelt and pulled her across the seat. "It means a lot to me, too." Then he gently kissed her, showing her his feelings, hoping she felt the same way.

When he released her, she looked into his eyes as if trying to read his mind. "Just when I think I know you, you surprise me."

"Then I guess you'll just have to keep learning more about me."

"I agree. I'm looking forward to that." She held his gaze a moment longer, then scooted back over to her side of the truck and buckled her seatbelt. "But right now, we better get to the ranch. Jade and Amber aren't going to be patient much longer. As it is, they're going to grill me about why I'm late."

Layne put the truck back into drive. "And what will you tell them?"

"The truth."

He raised his brows as he maneuvered between two large

craters and drove the truck up over a bump. "I hope you won't go into detail."

She waved off his comment. "Of course not. I'll just tell them I had the most amazing night of my life making love with you. That should do it."

He grinned, his ego thrilled by her words, probably more so because she hadn't used the word "sex." Because last night, to him, it was far more than that.

Finally, he pulled into the yard of Rocky Road Ranch and they got out of the truck. There was an obvious rental sedan parked in front of the house, and at the other end of the porch was George, who stood staring at the empty hay feeder. "It looks like George is hungry and the Dunns have a visitor. No one drives a sedan down that driveway unless they're clueless about the ranch, so it can't be someone from town."

"I wonder if Tanner contacted the state already?"

"I doubt it. Tanner hadn't seemed quite as excited as the rest of the family last night. But I guess we'll find out. Are you sure you don't need me today?"

Silver stepped in front of him and gave him her sly smile. "Oh, I always need you. But as far as the discovery site is concerned, no. Today is a planning and research day. However, if you get bored hanging out with the cowboys, feel free to come visit us cowgirls." She flicked the brim of her straw cowboy hat.

"I will." He pulled her to him and kissed her, then let her go.

She sighed, then shook her head as she walked away. She stopped next to George and gave him a pat on the neck. "Have a good day, George."

Layne remained where he was, watching Silver walk past the barn and out of sight. He needed to tell her. He just wasn't sure how. Maybe Jackson would—

"Heeehaaaw!"

He snapped his gaze to the burro. "You really know how to hijack my train of thought, George."

At the burro's snort, Layne ambled toward him. "Hey, I do have a train of thought, and it's more than just about food, like yours." He rubbed George behind the ears and the burro pressed against his hand, emitting a contented grunt.

"Okay, so your thoughts also include affection. Now, let me get this feeder filled for you." He gave George a final pat on the back and headed for the barn.

After grabbing a hay bale, he carried it outside and cut it open by the porch. It wouldn't all fit in the feeder, but George wouldn't let any of it go to waste. He dumped the rope in the trash in the barn, then headed for the house again. He'd let Amanda know he would be working with her husband and then call Tanner to see what he needed.

After stepping into the warm house, he shucked off his jacket and dropped his hat on the side table in the entry. "Amanda?"

When no one answered, he headed down the hallway to the office. As he approached the doorway, he could hear Jackson on the phone. "Just stay put. I'll be right there."

Layne stepped into the office to find little TJ asleep in her port-a-crib and Jackson clipping his phone to his waist. "Everything okay?"

"Hey, you made it. No, but it's nothing major. Dani is stuck on the driveway. I need to get her pulled out. Since you're here, could you hang out in here and watch TJ for me? I don't want to wake her. She's been teething and not getting much sleep at night."

"And that means you haven't been sleeping much either."

Jackson sighed. "Neither me nor Dani. That's why she's stuck. She forgot about that double rut with the two humps and now she can't get out."

"I get it. My sister was so tired with her baby teething that once she parked her car under the carport at home and fell asleep in the car. The whole family spent hours trying to find her. No problem. Anything else I can do while I'm in here?"

Jackson glanced at a pile of paper on the desk. "No. I'll take care of things when I get back. It shouldn't take long. If you're bored, you can always watch the video feed on the security cameras. There's bound to be a rabbit or something."

"Or something, like George."

Jackson walked around the desk and past him. "Thanks. I owe you one."

"I'll add it to your tab."

Layne heard Jackson chuckle in the hallway and then the front door closed. He looked down at five-month-old TJ, whose cheeks were a little flushed. Poor girl. Good thing she wouldn't remember her first teeth coming in.

He moved into the room and took a seat behind the desk, pulling the pile of paperwork over to take a look. He knew exactly where Dani was stuck, and it was going to take more than a few minutes, so he might as well make himself useful.

Shuffling through the papers, it was clear there were a variety of issues to be resolved, so he started organizing the paperwork by project. He was about halfway done when movement caught the corner of his eye and he glanced at TJ again, but she hadn't moved. Looking up at the computer where the security footage played, he frowned. That was Silver. She was only a few feet from George and the hay feeder, and she spoke to a man he'd never seen before.

The man was shorter than her and much older, maybe mid-fifties with a substantial paunch, and slicked-back black hair that glistened in the sun. He wore a tan sport shirt which was open at the neck revealing a couple of gold chains, a corduroy blazer, khakis, and sunglasses.

Layne turned the volume up just a little to listen without waking TJ.

Silver threw her hands in the air. "You've got to be kidding me. Benedict, I told you we have a lot of work to do first."

That was Silver's boss, the owner of the company? Layne was not impressed.

"I told you not to call me that! Listen, if you want the fucking funding, you'll do this TV spot."

Silver held her hands out to her sides. "And then if none of it connects? We'll look like a laughingstock. Then how the hell will you get any grants?"

Benedict shrugged. "I won't look like an idiot. *You* will. That's what's so perfect about it. You can say there's a link, and the money flows in. If there isn't a link, I can still grab money because I'm the behind-the-scenes man. It's a win-win."

"You idiot. How many people will fund you if I'm proven wrong and I'm on the team?"

"I just won't mention you. Or if I have to, I'll replace you."

Silver's mouth opened and shut a couple of times, before any words came out. "You would take me off my own discovery?"

"In a minute. You bitches are a dime a dozen, all begging for a chance to dig in the dirt. You can be replaced like that." He snapped his fingers.

George looked over at the sound and moved toward Silver.

She didn't notice, completely focused on her boss. "And that's where you're wrong. That's because we do things the right way. We have sterling reputations. Those in the academic and funding communities know that we're thorough. You're not going to get grants without us. Who wants to risk hundreds of thousands of dollars on unknown scientists? And don't forget my following. Where else can you find a credible anthropologist who is also an ancient astronaut theorist?"

Silver shook her head. "No. I won't talk about the Thunderbird yet. We follow the protocols. If you want me on that TV spot to bring attention to the discovery, then fine. I'll do it, but I'll only discuss the caves, not the Thunderbird or any possible link to Sumerian culture."

The man strode right up to Silver and poked his finger in her shoulder.

Layne rose, ready to interfere, but as he stepped around the desk, he remembered TJ, who continued to sleep, though she'd moved a little. He couldn't leave her. It was just one example of why he had no interest in having his own children. They could pull a person in opposite directions.

He stepped back to keep an eye on Benedict just in time to see George nudge Silver for a pat, forcing her boss to take a step back.

She grinned. "Good job, George."

"You listen to me, bitch. You'll do that TV spot and you'll say what I tell you to say."

Layne curled his fingers into his palms, itching to lay the little man flat out.

Silver laughed even as she started rubbing George along his neck. "If I said what you told me to say, the funders would laugh you out of the state. You don't have a clue of the impact this can have."

"Oh, I know what impact it can have. It can make me rich, and you're not going to get in the way of that. You think you're so smart, but I hold all the money, so you will do as I say."

Silver shook her head. "Your short-sightedness is going to be your downfall. If you want me to do the spot, then we do it my way, or we don't do it."

"Fuck you, Silver."

"Those are my terms, take them or leave them."

"You cunt. You're going to regret this."

Layne saw red and started around the desk again, only to hold up as he passed the port-a-crib. Silently, he swore.

A loud bray came from the computer before Silver's voice floated to him. "See, even George thinks you're an idiot. That's pretty bad when you're looked down on by an ass. It's your choice, *Benedict*. I'll be in the lodge with Jade and Amber. Let me know what you decide."

Taking a deep breath, Layne returned to the desk and scanned the other cameras, looking for any sign of Jackson. He found Jackson's truck and Dani's car heading toward the house. He studied the landscape to see how close they were.

"That fucking cunt. Thinks she knows everything. She's nothing but a fuck hole."

Layne snapped his gaze back to the screen with Benedict and growled. That man needed to be taught a lesson.

George seemed to think so too, as he bared his teeth and gave another loud bray in Benedict's face.

"What the fuck do you know? Fuck! Now she has me talking to donkeys."

Layne watched Benedict give George a wide berth as he walked toward his car.

On the other screen, Jackson pulled up in front of the porch. Layne whispered. "Come on, Jackson. Move your ass."

Silver's boss pulled out his phone and started texting.

The front door of the house finally opened, and Layne moved silently to the doorway of the office.

As Jackson started down the hallway, Layne strode toward him. "I gotta go."

Jackson's eyes widened, but that's all Layne saw as he passed him. He stopped in the entryway and slammed his hat on his head before exiting, leaving a confused Dani in his wake.

CHAPTER 18

AT THE TOP of the porch steps, Layne scanned the parking area.

Benedict put the phone back in his pocket, then hit his key fob to unlock his car.

Striding down the steps, he yelled. "Hey, Dick!"

The man turned toward him. "Do I know you?"

Layne stopped five feet away because if he got any closer, he'd probably do something he'd regret. "You can't be talking to women like that on the Rocky Road Ranch. You shouldn't ever talk to them like that, but here, in particular, that's not allowed."

"Who the fuck are you?"

"Layne Dawson, foreman. This is a private enterprise with our own rules, and you just broke half of them."

Benedict scanned him from head to toe. "Obviously, you're just a hired hand. So let me make this clear. What I'm spending on those bitches to stay here for the month is paying your salary. So basically, you work for me, and since they work for me as well, I'll talk to them however I want."

Layne forced himself to remain where he was, no matter how much his fist ached to find the man's jaw. "Money doesn't talk here on the Rocky Road. People are treated with respect, and if you can't do that, then you can leave and never come back."

"Listen, cowboy. You obviously know very little about how the world works. Money is what makes things work. The owners of this ranch would not be happy if I took my business elsewhere."

"There is no other place."

"There's always another place."

Layne folded his arms over his chest. "Not with access to the dig site. It's surrounded on all sides by conservation land, and the closest lodging besides this ranch is a ten-mile hike over rocky terrain. So I suggest you follow the rules if you really want the money you think you'll get from the ladies' hard work."

Benedict squinted his eyes. "You think you have all the answers, don't you? You're way out of your league, cowboy. When news breaks about this Thunderbird thing, the Rocky Road will be begging to be a part of it. So if you want to keep your job, you better learn your place. I'm the one with the money, so I have the power to make or break you, just like I have power over those three bitches. Two of them know their place, but Silver needs a few more lessons. She far too full of herself."

Layne uncrossed his arms, his hands fisting of their own accord. "*Dr.* Collins is far more intelligent than you, so I suggest you listen to her. She can see the big picture, which you obviously can't."

The man scowled. "It sounds like she made you yet another fan. Oh, of course. You must be the man she's shacking up with. Listen, cowboy, you and anyone else can do her until the cows come home. I don't give a flying fuck, but she's my employee, so you better not get in the way of her work."

"I don't. I respect her. Maybe if you did, she'd be more accommodating."

The man snarled. "Respect her? What she needs is a good fuck in the ass and a—"

Layne took one step as his fist connected with the man's face, which sent Benedict Nagle spinning around before he crumpled to the ground.

No sound came from the prone man, but his chest rose and fell, a testament that he still lived. George came over to investigate, brayed loudly then turned his back, walking toward the barn.

Layne couldn't agree more.

Applause sounded from the porch, and he spun around.

Jackson stopped clapping and grabbed onto the front railing. "I've always admired your patience, but if you didn't shut his mouth, I was going to do it for all of our sakes."

He looked over his shoulder at the prone man and didn't feel an ounce of guilt. He never used his size and ability to bully anyone, but once in a blue moon, someone like Luke Hayden or this man needed to be taught a lesson. He turned back to Jackson. "I'm not sure it's going to help, and he'll probably bring charges against me."

"Good thing Sheriff Romero is an old friend of the family."

Layne shook his head. "I imagine that Dani will make me fill out one of those new incident reports."

Jackson nodded. "I already saved the video on the security camera. That will help as well."

"Thanks. You watched it all then?"

Jackson nodded.

"I suppose I should drive him to a walk-in clinic."

"I don't think he'll be walking anywhere for a while. Let's see what Amanda wants to do. She's the boss, and I doubt she'll want you anywhere near the man."

Layne headed for the porch. "Last I knew, Tanner was the boss."

Jackson opened the door. "Not of the guests, and that one is with the guests."

He'd rather talk to Tanner, but Jackson was right. Amanda was going to be furious. "You said you have that footage recorded?"

Jackson grinned, even as he started down the hall. "I'll send it to your phone. Amanda's out by the pool with Dad and Isaac. I'll be right there to back you up."

As Layne strode across the kitchen toward the sliding doors to the pool, he tried to think of another way he could have handled Silver's boss, but no matter how he looked at it, he couldn't see anything else he could have done.

A FEW HOURS LATER

Silver stood in front of the whiteboard they'd set up in the lodge and pointed to the map they'd drawn of the caves. "This was the place I was investigating, but there were anomalies here, here, and here."

"They could simply be a change in the earth's composition." Amber squinted at the map.

Jade held up a pair of glasses. "Will you put these on? There's no one here you need to impress."

Amber pouted. "I can see fine."

Sliver chuckled. "Yeah, when you're looking at something less than two feet away. Put them on. It's just us."

"Okay." Amber put on the pink eyeglasses and looked at the whiteboard. "Oh, there's an anomaly in the Clovis cave? I definitely want to check that out. It could be anything from ash to a buried treasure."

Silver rolled her eyes. "Now she finds it interesting. Amazing what a difference seeing makes."

Jade held up four fingers. "So we have four significant anomalies according to the GPR, but only three of us. Should we ask Dickhead for an assistant?"

Amber's eyes widened. "We've never been given an assistant. Do you really think he would approve that?"

"No." Silver put the green marker down on the tray at the bottom of the whiteboard. "Benedict wants maximum effort and income for little cost. I say we prioritize our top three and then whoever finishes first, can start on the fourth."

"What about Layne? Could he help? Do you think you could convince him?" Amber winked at her.

"No. He has to go back to working for the cattle side of the operation. Us getting him for a month was a very special accommodation."

Jade set her notebook on the coffee table. "Then who will we have? I really don't like the idea of not having a guide. We've never done that before."

Silver sat down in the winged back chair closest to her. "I asked Layne that last night. He said he thinks Amanda is going to suggest that Benedict hire someone not from Rocky Road. They are all booked up for the dude ranch side of things starting in mid-March, and she's going to need all the hands that Tanner can spare."

Jade nodded. "That makes sense. Then maybe we should skip the planning and get back up to Dawson Cave the rest of the week. There's bound to be some down time as we settle into our new quarters and find a new guide. We could plan more then."

"Good point. Has Benedict said where you and Amber will be staying?"

"Not long-term. He has us booked in at the Lucky Lasso

Saloon and Hotel. At least if the accommodations are poor, we can drown our sorrows in the bar." Jade waved her hand nonchalantly.

"Not to worry. I've been there with Layne. It's got an Old West theme from the 1800s, but it also has all the modern amenities, even a cute bartender." She looked directly at Amber.

Amber grinned. "There may just be some perks to living off the Rocky—"

The door to their lodge banged open and Benedict strode in, along with a rush of cold air. He had a bruise on his cheekbone that made his face look like a zombie.

"Silver, you're fired!"

She blinked. "What? Have you been drinking?"

"You heard me. I'm done with you, bitch. You're not worth the fucking trouble anymore. Pack your bags and get out. I'm not paying for your stay here any longer."

Jade stood. "You can't do that, Dick. We need Silver. This is her find."

He turned on her. "Shut it, or you can go too."

Silver rose. "Dick, what's got in your craw?"

He stepped up to her, his bad breath proving he hadn't been drinking. "I'll tell you what's got into me. Your God-damn boyfriend. I don't give a shit who you invite between your legs, but that dumb cowboy telling me how to act and attacking me is the last straw. You're fired."

She ignored the cold knot starting in her gut and set her hands on her hips. "Don't you think you should be firing Layne, instead of putting your whole operation at risk. Who will make the connection you need? Who will be the ancient astronaut theorist to bring the advertising dollars up?"

"Her and her." He pointed to Jade and Amber.

Amber shook her head. "I can't. I don't know anything about ancient astronaut theory."

"You'll learn. You're prettier anyway. The cameras will love you." He turned to Jade, who didn't say anything. "At least one bitch around here knows her place. Pack your bags, Silver. You're done."

She opened her mouth to reason with him, but he turned on his heel and headed for the door. Finally, she found her voice. "It's not going to work, Dick. Your money grab is going to fail without me."

He waved off her comment without looking back and slammed the door on his way out.

She stared at the closed door, trying to process the fact that she was fired from her own discovery, the one she'd waited her whole lifetime for. Her stomach cramped up, making it hard to breathe.

Jade touched her arm. "There has to be something we can do."

Amber joined them. "Yes. If we put our three heads together, we can figure this out."

All her research. All her compromises and fights with Dick. All the backbreaking work and uncomfortable lodgings and disappointments, just to finally find something earth-shattering, only to have it taken away in an instant. And why? "Layne."

Even as she said his name, her anger ignited. "I can handle Dick. I always handled Dick."

"Yes, you did." Amber's voice was quiet.

"I didn't need Layne stepping in. What gives him the right to hit my boss? Of all the asinine things he could have done. To physically assault Dick is the stupidest, pig-headed, most backward decision. How dare he?"

"Maybe because he cares about you?"

She ignored Jade's comment. "Like I didn't have to contend with enough male chauvinism from Dick, but now Layne thinks he's going to fix things for me that don't even need to be fixed?"

Amber touched her arm. "I'm sure he had a reason. You know how Dick is. Layne is a reasonable guy."

She turned on Amber. "Reasonable? Hitting my boss and getting me fired is reasonable?" Fury filled her. It felt good compared to the aching loss she felt deep in her gut that she didn't want to think about.

Jade's calm voice pierced her thoughts. "Maybe you should talk to Layne. Find out what happened. There are always two sides to every story."

"Right. I'll talk to Layne. But he's not going to like what I have to say." She stomped across the lodge and grabbed her fleece jacket, not even buttoning it as she stalked outside and across the yard toward the barn to find him. Walking inside, she noticed his horse in the stall, so she turned around and strode toward the clubhouse. No one was there either. "Where the hell is everyone?"

She walked back outside and took a deep breath, trying not to cry, holding onto her anger over the lump forming in her throat. This was Layne's fault completely. She'd done nothing wrong. She'd done everything right. *He* did this to her. Focusing on that thought, she started across the quad, back past the barn, and headed for the house.

As she passed the barn, her attention was caught by Dick's car in the distance, slowly leaving the ranch. "Asshole." Her fingers curled into her palms, just as the front door of the house opened and out stepped Layne.

He strode across the porch and jogged down the steps. "Have you seen George?"

"George? No, I haven't seen George. But I did see Dick. He came to the lodge to fire me!"

"What?" Layne strode toward her, and she backed up a step.

"He fired me because my 'boyfriend' attacked him. What the hell, Layne?"

He stopped twenty feet from her. "He fired you because I hit him? That makes no sense."

She advanced, pointing her finger at him. "No, what makes no sense is you hitting him. What were you thinking? He's my boss!"

"I hadn't planned to hit him, but the way he treated you and what he said about you made it impossible not to. He can't talk that way around you. Not around here."

She stopped in her tracks. "What do you mean the way he talked to me?"

"Your argument with him was on the security camera. I heard what he said to you. You don't deserve to be spoken to that way. No woman does."

"You spied on me? Then you decided how my boss should talk to me? You do realize he's spoken to all of us this way for the last six years, and guess what? We're just fine. He's an ass, but he provides the money that allows us to work. Did you really think because I now know you, I can't stand up for myself? Did it look like I needed a knight in shining armor to come to my rescue?"

"No, you put him in his place. I wasn't rescuing you. I let him know that he can't treat people like that on the Rocky Road. We have rules here. He broke them. I explained that he needed to follow them, and when he refused to modify his behavior, even going so far as to suggest what you needed, I made it clear with my fist. Sometimes that's the only thing people understand."

Her own hands curled into fists. "Well, guess what? Not only did your little lesson not work, but it hurt me. He's fired me. Now I can't even work on my own discovery. Something I worked for all my life. Something that was worth putting up with Dick for six long years. And you swoop in and take it all away."

"I didn't take it away, Dick did. But we'll get it back. I'm sure he can be convinced to rehire you."

She shook her head as the gut-wrenching loss started to overtake her rage, and tears began filling her eyes. She'd lost even more than her life's dream. "You don't get it. Dick will never take me back. I've lost everything now. I can't even stay in Four Peaks anymore."

He stepped closer, and she held her hands out to keep him away. "Don't. You did this. I was handling Dick just fine. You lost me everything."

"Silver, please. You don't have to leave. You can stay with me. Maybe we can find a—"

"Stop. Just stop. Don't you understand? You've destroyed me, everything I was and everything I hoped to be, gone. Leave me alone." As her new reality set in, the grief overwhelmed her, and she turned away. Even as she ran for the lodge, a place she couldn't even stay, her heart was breaking, over her dreams, her goals, and the man she'd come to love.

CHAPTER 19

LAYNE REMAINED WHERE HE STOOD, unable to move. His chest felt as if a bull was sitting on him, making it hard to breathe. And Silver's tears were like being gored by said bull, yet he was still alive. That she was hurt, devastated him, and that somehow it was his fault was too much to accept.

He wanted to comfort her, help her, but she blamed him. He couldn't wrap his head around that. He thought and felt that she loved him. Was he wrong?

"Hey, Layne. You okay?" Nash's voice came from behind him.

Slowly he turned around, to find the ranch hand leaning on a rake. "I don't know."

"That's understandable. Being dumped sucks. Trust me, I know." The man gave him a self-deprecating smile.

He shook his head. "But I didn't do anything wrong. I don't understand why this happened, but somehow my actions caused it. I've hurt her."

"Then you're one giant leap ahead of me."

Layne frowned. "What do you mean? You don't have anyone in your life."

Nash grinned. "Exactly. Women I like, like me well enough, but none feel strongly for me. I get pushed into the friend zone. But what I saw right there, that was emotional. That was passionate. For her to get that angry at you means she feels a lot for you."

"No, what it means is I destroyed everything she's ever worked for."

Nash shook his head. "That may be true, and you'll need to fix that part, but if that were all there was to it, she wouldn't be crying. She'd be telling you where to go and walking away. That's not what she did. She was angry, yes, but she was deeply hurt that it was you in particular who did this."

"Exactly how long were you watching us?"

"I'd just come from the back of the house and was headed to the barn to put this rake away, but you two were there and I didn't want to interrupt."

As much as he was probably an idiot for asking, he needed confirmation. "You really think that she feels something for me?"

Nash lifted his hat and reset it on his head. "Not just something...a lot."

Layne rubbed his mustache, trying to ignore how hard it was to breathe, his gut so tight he wasn't sure he could walk. "What I did was right. How can she not understand that?"

"From what I heard, I think she does, but by doing what was right, it sounds like you destroyed what was wrong, and wrong was working for her."

There was a weird logic to that. "The way you put it makes this whole problem make sense. Since when did you get so smart?"

Nash chuckled. "Don't give me that much credit. Anyone watching your argument with an objective view would see what was happening. You couldn't see it because you're in it." Nash's eyes narrowed. "Do you really have feelings for her? The man who just last month said he was perfectly happy with his bachelor life?"

At the doubt in Nash's face, he knew he wasn't ready to confess. "I have feelings for every woman I have a relationship with."

"Hmmm, okay. Well, I hope you were ready to get out of this one because fixing this mess would probably be impossible."

Layne felt the air leave his lungs completely at Nash's words.

"I best get this rake into the barn and head back out to Tanner. We're finishing the gate on the northeast enclosure. It's pretty cool that we have that grazing space now, thanks to Hannah. I'll see you later." With that, Nash strode across the parking area and into the barn.

Layne didn't move, Nash's words echoing in his head, until he finally gulped in air. He forced himself to take a few deep breaths in an attempt to clear his mind, but it didn't work. His thoughts spun in a vortex and his heart refused to slow down.

"Fixing this mess would probably be impossible."

The words were so final. They made it sound like he'd have to let go of Silver forever. But he couldn't. At the thought of going back to his bachelor life, bile rose in his throat. Every past relationship that ended, he'd been happy to go back to being alone. But he'd seen what it could be like with the right person, and he couldn't give up that life now.

He unclipped his phone and texted Jackson. *Can you stop by tonight? It's important.* He waited. Though it was less than a minute, it felt like an hour before he got a response.

You need to come in the ranch house right now. Amanda just got a call. That douche bag is pressing charges and Sheriff Romero is coming out to investigate.

"Shit." Could things get any worse?

The loud squeal of a burro came from behind the barn.

That wasn't normal. He ran for the barn. Turning the corner, he skidded to a halt just as a striped skunk in front of a toppled trash can lifted its tail and sprayed George.

The burro squealed again and turned around to run down the ATV road.

Unfortunately, when the skunk lifted its tail at George, it caught sight of Layne. Striped skunks could spray up to seven times in a row and the skunk was a large one.

He wasn't waiting around to find out what the skunk would do next. He ducked back around the corner of the barn and headed for the house, pissed that someone had left the green trash container outside overnight. They all knew to bring it in. Vegetable peelings lay scattered across the ground, which had to be the cause of the fight. If he were working as foreman, his real job, he'd have reminded someone to bring it in.

He strode across the parking area to the porch. He'd failed both Silver and George, and that didn't sit well with him at all. He would figure out how to fix both issues. He refused to accept defeat on either.

But first, he needed to keep himself out of jail.

———

THE FOLLOWING DAY.

Silver lay on her bed staring at the wood beams on the vaulted ceiling of the lodge. She couldn't think. She couldn't even feel. She'd barely been able to sleep, waking up from bad dreams every couple of hours. Her whole life had to turn into a nightmare for her to realize she loved Layne. It was too heartbreaking on every level.

A knock sounded on her door.

She couldn't even get up the energy to say anything. There were no words.

The door opened and Amber peeked her head in. "Silver? Are you awake?"

"No."

A chuckle followed that before the door opened. "She's awake."

"Good."

At the sound of Jade's voice, she glanced at the doorway where Amber held it open.

Jade walked in and sat on the bed. "We need to talk."

Amber came in and pulled the chair that was against the wall over to the bed and sat. "All of us, which means you, too."

She looked at her colleagues—no, her *friends* of six years, and just shook her head. She wouldn't see them again either. She'd truly had lost everything.

Jade scowled at her. "Yes, you *are* going to talk, because Amber and I have been strategizing and we need your input."

"I don't work for Asshole anymore, so whatever you decide has nothing to do with me."

"Oh, but it does." Amber smiled.

She didn't see herself smiling ever again.

Jade patted her leg. "Amber and I had a chat with Amanda. By the way, you can stay until the end of the month with us."

"I'm leaving for New Hampshire to visit a good friend. No idea what I'll do after that."

Jade shook her head. "We need you here with us because Amber and I just quit."

It took a moment for the statement to register, but when it did, she sat straight up. "You can't."

Amber nodded. "We can and we did. And boy was the Prick pissed. I can't tell you what a relief it was."

Silver looked to Jade. "But what will you do? You both need

jobs. And what about Dawson Cave? You deserve the credit even if I can't work on it."

Jade actually grinned, a very rare occurrence. "Now you see why we need you to strategize. Come out in the big room by the fire. It's freezing in here."

She hadn't noticed, but now that Jade said something, it was a bit cool. "Fine." She forced herself out of bed and followed Amber and Jade into the main room. Purposefully, she turned to the fire and held her hands out. The brain really did have control over the body because only now did she realize how chilled she was. Also, facing the fire meant not facing her friends.

"Want a cookie? These are chocolate with peanut butter chips." Amber's voice behind her sounded hopeful.

She sighed, knowing she needed to give them her attention no matter how much she wanted to wallow in the catastrophe that was her life. They hadn't done anything wrong. She turned around to find Amber holding the plate up. "Sure." She took one and bit into it, just to do something other than talk, then she sat on the arm of the chair near the fireplace.

"As I said, Amber and I spoke to Amanda, and we found out something very interesting."

She just looked at Jade as she took another bite, the sweet and salty waking up her tastebuds whether she wanted them awake or not.

Amber piped up. "The Prick is so screwed."

Jade nodded. "It's true. It turns out that the only access to Dawson Cave is through the Rocky Road Ranch, unless a team wants to hike ten miles over rough terrain."

She shrugged. "So? They can bring out tents, probably use some horses to carry stuff, and just camp out for weeks at a time. We've done that."

"Yes, we have, but that was because it was allowed."

Understanding wiggled its way through her brain. "You're saying the state doesn't allow camping on the four peaks and Rocky Road is the only real access. So?"

Amber jumped in. "So, the dude ranch is booked for the next two months! If any other researcher came out here, they'd have to wait. Even if the Prick were to get funding and hire more people, he'd be delayed by that long."

"That just delays the inevitable."

Jade pointed at her. "That's why we need you. We need to figure out how to take the discovery back within that two-month time frame."

"Take it back?"

"Yes. There has to be a way."

"I really don't see how. Benedict knows about the possibilities and will have people on site as soon as there's room at the Rocky Road, if he doesn't simply put his new people up in town and then pay Rocky Road for access."

Amber grinned. "Amanda said only guests have access."

As much as she didn't want to think, her brain started working, ideas turning. Still, she resisted. "Amanda knows how big this discovery could be for the ranch and for the town. I'm sure if the Asshole offers to pay her, she'll allow another team to travel through the ranch. She'd already agreed to allow us access after we left, so why not?"

Jade shook her head. "She won't. She got to see the security video of your argument with Dickhead. She says he's not allowed to step foot on the ranch, and she even has backing from the sheriff."

"The sheriff?"

Amber scooted forward on her couch. "Yes. The Prick pressed charges against Layne. Can you believe that?"

Despite her lethargy, worry wormed its way into her chest. "Will he go to jail?"

"Amanda didn't say. But she did show the video to the sheriff when he was here yesterday."

Shit, she'd been so upset, she didn't even know the sheriff had been there. "Shouldn't he have interviewed me or something?"

Amber shrugged. "Who knows how they do things in these parts. I gave up keeping track of every legal system in every place we work."

Jade cleared her throat. "Yes, but we aren't 'working' now, since we quit our jobs. I suggest we stay focused on how to take the discovery back. We know Dickhead has funding for at least a year. That means we have to find other funding."

Silver didn't see that happening. "Unless we can find something else to prove the alien connection or some other unique evidence, we won't be able to interest another funder."

"Then let's find something else." Jade snapped her fingers.

Silver cringed. "Please don't do that. That's what Benedict did when he told me he could replace me."

"I apologize. I know it's a long shot, but we still have a few days before we need to vacate the ranch. I already called over to the Lucky Lasso and reinstated our reservations. Turns out, they're not very busy unless it's Pioneer Days, whatever that is. I figured if we can't find something in a few days, we could stay a little longer. Dickhead still owes us our pay for this month."

Amber rose and started for the door. "I'll go ask Nash if he can bring us out to the site."

Silver held up her hand. "Whoa there. It's great that Amanda said we could stay, but that doesn't mean we can use her ranch hands."

Amber stopped and lifted her coat off a hook on the wall. "Yes, it does. The Prick paid for all services in advance for the full month. You know how much he likes to see what's left so he can hoard it. This time it bit him in the ass." She laughed and pulled on her down jacket before heading outside.

Silver looked to Jade for confirmation.

Jade silently nodded.

"You know this is a long shot, right?"

Jade nodded again.

"And that even if we find something earth-shattering, it could take months to secure funding."

"I know. But would you rather turn tail and run and let Dickhead win, or do you want to at least try to beat him at his own game? I always said I'd be better at presenting to funders than he is."

"I'd rather just lie on my bed and hate him."

"Dickhead or Layne?"

She widened her eyes at the question. "I don't hate Layne. I can't. As much as I hate the repercussions of his actions, he was just being Layne, protecting us from what he thought was a threat."

"Protecting you."

At Jade's observation, she had to concede. "Yes, but I have no doubt he would have done it for you and Amber as well. It's just how he's wired. Unfortunately, that short-circuited our livelihoods and our greatest discovery."

"Wow, you really care for him not to hate him."

She took a deep breath, gathering the courage to say it out loud. "Unfortunately, I fell in love with him. Now I have to try to fall *out* of love with him. No use loving a man who'll never leave Four Peaks."

"Not to mention he's destroyed your career."

"Yeah, that too. See why I'd prefer to wallow away the days on my bed until we leave?"

"I do. But you won't."

She managed the smallest of smiles at Jade's confidence in her. "No, I won't."

"SO WHAT DID THE SHERIFF SAY?" Jackson waved to the bartender.

Layne swallowed the last of the beer and set the bottle down on the bar at the Lucky Lasso Saloon. "He told Dick Nagle he'd look into it."

Jackson raised his brows. "No, I mean what did he say to you?"

"Honestly, he didn't seem to know what to say, but mumbled under his breath, something about pigs flying."

Jackson laughed.

It was a welcome sound as far as Layne was concerned. "He asked me why I did it. Then said he knew why. Then he told me not to do it again, but that if the man appeared on the Rocky Road, he'd be happy to assist me in removing him from the property."

"I'd be happy to help, too. Sounds like Sheriff Romero was having a hard time not siding with you. Do you have a court date?"

"Not yet. The sheriff said he'd release me on my own

recognizance, but since I was never taken into custody, I'm not sure how valid that is."

Jackson grinned. "Well, at least you have a lawyer in the family."

"I have one of everything in my family."

"You don't have an ancient alien theorist though. That *is* why you wanted to come out and talk, isn't it?"

He stroked the side of his mustache, not liking how obvious he was, but at the same time, thankful he had a good friend who knew when to give him hell and when to actually help. "Yeah. I need to fix this."

"You better fill me in on what you need to fix. Do you mean your relationship? I have to tell you, until Dani, I didn't have a lot of experience with relationships."

The bartender, Banner Jefferies, set two full beers down in front of them, grabbed up the empties and leaned on the bar to join the conversation. "Hey, my grandfather said Amanda booked him for mid-March. So is the dude ranch thing really happening?"

Jackson nodded. "It is. On the trial run, your dad's stories were one of the favorite night activities."

"Yeah, Grandpa knows the history of this town like he lived it." The young man with dark hair pulled back in a ponytail stood straighter. "I'm so glad those visitors liked him. That means the less times we have to listen to him." Banner laughed as he strode off to serve another customer down the long old-Western bar.

Layne took a swig before addressing Jackson's last comment. "The key to getting Silver back is getting her job back."

"Are you absolutely positive you want her back? Last you told me, it was just a temporary thing."

He knew exactly what Jackson was getting at. "Yes, I want her back. And yes, you were right. I love her."

Jackson smacked him on the back hard. The man didn't know his own strength. "How the mighty have fallen."

"Wise ass. Just help me with getting her job back."

"I don't imagine you can ask the guy you hit to rehire her."

Layne shook his head. "No. That's a dead end."

"Why would she work for such an asshole anyway?"

He'd asked himself the same question. "I believe it's because there are very few companies in America who hire people to do what she does. At least, that's what I gathered from our conversations."

"So maybe you can find her another company to work for?"

"It's not that easy, not that finding another company is easy either. She needs to be able to work on this cave." He lowered his voice. "She discovered that Thunderbird, and as you heard, it could be a game changer in her field. So she needs a company that will hire her to work on that specifically."

"Fuck, Layne. You're talking about the impossible. What company is going to want to—"

He waited for Jackson to finish, but instead his friend's expression changed and he didn't say anything. "What are you thinking?"

"I'm not sure. I was thinking about the ranch hiring her, but with Hannah and Brody leaving the area, managing a third enterprise wouldn't work."

"What do you mean?"

"I was thinking maybe the Rocky Road could have a third profit arm which would be the cave project, but the dude ranch is too new. We need all hands on deck. Already Amanda and Tanner are tossing employees back and forth like they're playing badminton."

"Badminton? It feels more like the speed of hockey to me."

Jackson chuckled. "Tell me about it. One day I'm working like a mule and the next I'm on the computer. And I'm a Dunn.

If I weren't building a house to go with our new barn, I could manage a new enterprise for you, but I'm stretched."

He appreciated the offer even as a glimmer of an idea hit him. "It doesn't have to be the Rocky Road. What if I started a company? Then I could hire her."

"I'm not so sure being her boss is such a good idea unless you've completely given up on your relationship. But yeah, if someone else in Four Peaks were to start a company up, then that could work. There'd have to be funding from somewhere. I know you're well-settled, but do you have that kind of capital?"

He had some, but not nearly enough. Then something Silver had said drifted through his memory. *It's tougher to get foundation funding. He always has to do backflips to get it because he's a for-profit company.* "What if I started a non-profit?"

"How would that help with funding? I thought non-profits use all their money for charity programs, like feeding the poor and housing the homeless."

"They do. But there are other types of non-profits, like those that support the arts or...or scientific discoveries." Even as he said the words, hope built in his gut.

"Really? So you could start a non-profit and get grants to fund Silver's discovery? Do you know how to do that?"

He chuckled. "Not a clue. But as you said, I have a lawyer in the family. I would need one of those. I remember that from when I served on the board of Pioneer Days for a few years. That's another non-profit."

"Damn. And here I thought it was just a town event." Jackson took a swig of beer.

Ideas flew fast and furious through Layne's head as he linked his experience with his goal. "I'll need a board of influential people. It would make sense to have a Dunn on it and maybe I could twist the Town Manager's arm."

"Be sure and ask Amanda's father. Since he's a state legislator and rich, he probably has pull if you have to raise money, especially from foundations."

He slapped Jackson on the back hard. "You're brilliant! We can definitely do this. Who else can we invite? I'll ask them all to the Rocky Road and see what they think."

"Hold on. If you want control of this organization, I suggest you have them meet at your house. First, they don't have to drive down our driveway, and second, it has less of a look of a for-profit business."

"Good point. Let's brainstorm other key players. If I'm going to ask my brother-in-law to do the paperwork for a start-up non-profit, I want to be sure I have the best possible board members to keep it going. Silver's discovery could take years to complete."

"And it would benefit the ranch and the town, maybe even the county and state like she said. Let me see if Banner has a piece of paper we can write on and a pen."

Layne lifted his phone. "What's wrong with typing?"

"Do you do that?"

He laughed, the feeling of possibilities running through his veins. "No. But you're younger than I am."

"I'll get Banner."

After obtaining a piece of cardboard from the box the cocktail napkins came in and a pen, they brainstormed a good twenty names. Layne examined it again, trying to decide it if they needed anyone else. He had one shot at this.

Jackson finished his beer and set the empty bottle on the bar. "So you think if you tell Silver what you're going to do, she'll forgive you?"

He rubbed the side of his mustache. "The thing is, the guy deserved it, so there's nothing to forgive."

Jackson raised his brows.

"Okay, maybe talking to her boss after seeing what an asshole he was, and hitting him may not have been the smartest move."

"Not to mention illegal." Jackson rose and laid his hand on Layne's shoulder. "I know it takes a damn lot to get you to use your fists. Hell, the whole town knows you're hard to provoke. Hopefully, Silver will be able to accept that. Tell me, knowing what you know about the outcome, would you do it again?"

"Confront him, yes. Hit him? No. His kind never change."

"You'd still confront him even knowing Silver would lose her job?"

"Yes, because no one should have to work under those conditions. Verbal abuse constitutes a hostile work environment."

Jackson shook his head. "Don't ever change."

"I've already changed. I've taken George under my care and have Silver living with me, if she'll return. I think that's enough for now."

Jackson grimaced. "Speaking of George, how's he doing?"

"He's better, but still not happy with me after the bath I gave him. He won't come near me. You'd think *I* was the skunk. He should be grateful I got that stench off him. I had to throw out my clothes."

"Did you give everyone hell for leaving the trash out?"

Layne grinned. "Nope, just Tanner."

"Tanner?"

"Sure. Since I've been working for his wife, it was his job to oversee the ranch hands."

Jackson laughed. "I wish I'd been there for that conversation. My brother does not like to be called out. No wonder he's been a grump lately."

"I'm back to working for him now. They have Nash bringing the ladies to the cave. So it's back to my responsibility to see that trash container is in the barn at the end of the day, and I'm happy to take it on."

Jackson glanced at his phone, which lit up from a text, the time appearing above it.

"You better get going. I'm sure Dani is wondering why we met tonight."

"Yes, she was. Do you want me to tell her about your idea? She's smart and might have some more ideas on the organization."

He started to shake his head, but stopped. He could use all the help he could get. "Yes, tell her. I'm going to tell the Dunns, too. If this is going to work, I'll need far more brain power than I have."

"And what about Silver?"

It only took a few seconds to recognize the wisdom of including her. "Definitely, and Amber and Jade. If I can lure them away from Dick Nagle, then we'd have a perfect group for going to funders."

"I don't envy you starting that conversation, but I'll gladly tell Dani. If I were you, I'd get your ducks in a row and make sure this non-profit thing is a real possibility first. They have three more days paid for on the ranch. You'll probably have a better chance with Silver if you can explain all you've done to keep her here instead of what you hope to do."

"That makes a lot of sense. I'm going home to make some calls. Could you fill in Amanda and Tanner too tonight? They understand the importance of Silver's discovery."

"I will. Dani could even call Hannah. She might be able to get the books set up. She's a whiz with numbers."

Layne swallowed the last of his beer and rose, waving to Banner. "I'm going to fill my family in tonight."

"About you and Silver or about your charity idea?"

He grimaced. "Both, eventually."

Jackson laughed as he started for the exit. "Good luck with that."

After paying his bill, Layne headed home himself. He didn't want to tell his family about Silver until he knew there would be a Silver in his life. He'd just make a few calls about his non-profit idea and see who would help him out. Jackson was right. If he could get some key players on board before talking to Silver and the ladies, they'd understand how serious he was.

He parked the truck in front of his house and stared at the windshield. This was what it felt like to have a goal and be driven to reach it. For the first time, he truly understood what Silver had been talking about. She had to have the patience of a saint to have waited six years to finally reach hers. He didn't even want to wait six hours.

And it had been taken away partly due to his actions. "I'm going to fix this. I swear, I will."

"AMBER, what did you do with the box of sample bags?" Silver rummaged through another trunk in the lodge that contained their smaller supplies.

"They're in the red trunk!"

Silver shook her head then closed the trunk to tell Amber she was wrong, when she noticed she was in the blue trunk. Why couldn't she focus? Moving to the red trunk, she found the small sample bags and stuffed them in her backpack.

For the last two days, they'd gone to the cave and looked for anything unusual. Finding nothing, they set to digging in the areas where the GPR had said there were anomalies. Jade got to hers first and found it was just a change in soil. Today, Jade would look into the fourth one, while she and Amber continued excavating their respective anomalies.

It was their final day working the cave. In her gut, she knew they wouldn't find anything, but her friends were hoping so much to find a way to take the site from Benedict Nagle Inc. that she didn't want to dampen their spirits. Besides, if she only had one more day to work on the discovery of her life, she wanted it to be productive and enlightening.

"Silver, did you pack the drawings I made last night? I can't find them." Jade dropped her backpack on the couch.

"I didn't. Did you bring them in your room?"

"I didn't think so, but I'll check."

She sat back on the couch next to Jade's backpack as Jade retreated to her bedroom. They were all a bit scattered, trying to do in a few days what should take a couple weeks normally. If only she hadn't gotten involved with Layne.

Even at that thought, she couldn't regret knowing him, just that he'd met Benedict. After processing what happened for a couple of days, she understood that Layne was just being Layne. And that was the problem. He didn't fit in her world with an asshole boss. And that was the only way she could do what she'd been driven to do since she was in college.

It just sucked. All of it. And she wasn't sure which was harder, recognizing that she and Layne could have never worked, or walking away from the discovery of her career.

Amber came out of her bedroom waving papers. "Jade, I found them!" She continued across the great room and into Jade's bedroom.

And then there were her friends, who now had no jobs because of her. She wanted to give up on all of it, but every time she lay down, the Thunderbird flew into her mind as if it were possessed. The first image to link two civilizations.

Unable to sit and wallow any longer, she rose and finished packing her backpack. "Are you guys almost ready? Nash will be banging on the door if we don't get over to the corral in five minutes."

She'd gotten to know Nash a little more over the last couple of days and she could see why Amber liked him...as a friend. He was like a brother with all the qualities that Layne had, just younger.

Amber ran back into her room.

Jade came out and grabbed up her backpack before walking to the door and pulling her coat off a hook.

"I'm ready." Amber came out of her room wearing her backpack.

Silver joined them and lifted Amber's coat from its hook. "You'll probably need this. It may be sunny, but it's cold."

"Sheesh." Taking off her pack, Amber pulled on her coat.

Silver threw on her own coat. "Let's get going. It's our last day, so we need to make the best of it." She opened the door and stopped.

"Um, Silver, are you going to let us out?"

Though she heard Jade's voice, she didn't move, her heart having closed her throat. Standing at the bottom of the porch steps was Layne. Next to him were Tanner and Amanda Dunn, along with Jackson. On the other side were Nash, Vic, Mr. Hardy from the hardware store, and Hannah, the wife of the youngest Dunn. Behind them were six other people she'd didn't know. Her gaze returned to Layne, her heartbeat sounding louder in her ears than a pick ax digging the dirt.

"Good morning, Silver." Layne lifted his hat just an inch in greeting, but his usual relaxed smile was conspicuously missing.

"Is that Layne?" Amber pushed past her. "Oh."

Jade came to stand beside her. "Is something wrong? I believe we still have today, right?"

Layne nodded. "Yes, you do. But first, I have something important to say to Silver that will concern you and Amber as well."

Silver forced herself to step forward, assuming he'd want to talk in private. She wished he wouldn't. It was hard enough knowing she'd never see him again without having a long good-bye. If only he could have waited until the end of the day.

He held his hand out for her to stop, so she did, not a little confused by why there were so many people there.

"Silver, I have come to tell you I'm sorry. I understand that my actions, while reasonable in my world, were not welcome in yours. As Nash pointed out to me, I tried to right a wrong, but wrong was working for you."

She raised her brows, surprised that he understood at least. "I accept your apology."

"You do? Thank you, but I know that my actions had a huge impact on your life."

She took a deep breath, not able to tell him it was okay. She could forgive him, but the ramifications were hard to swallow.

"All these people are here to ask for your help."

"My help? I'm leaving tonight."

Layne turned around to face the dozen or so people there, then turned back to face her. "My first request is that you don't leave. This is most important to me personally."

She started to shake her head, but again he raised his hand.

"Hear me out. The people here with me now are just a sample of the support we have for Third Rock Discoveries, the new non-profit we're forming, and we've already started to attract the funding needed to thoroughly explore Dawson Cave. Everyone from the Dunns, who will give you and your colleagues access to the conservation land, to Mr. Hardy, who has agreed to donate supplies, understands the significance of your find. They are all willing to help."

A man in the back spoke up. "Layne's got me working over-time on getting the legal status approved with the federal government."

Amanda chimed in. "My father has already started calling on favors from friends who sit on boards of private foundations. He's even committed to bringing support from the state."

Silver stared at Amanda, trying to understand what was happening.

Another man that looked suspiciously like the guy who

solved the town's computer problems spoke up. "I'm refurbishing a couple of extra computers for your new office."

"I already have your financial program ready for the money to roll in." Hannah grinned.

A man in a fancy western suede jacket and black jeans strode up next to Layne. "As the Town Manager of Four Peaks, I have secured lodging for the employees for the next year."

A young woman moved forward to stand on the other side of Layne. Silver recognized her as Stacey, the waitress who watched her podcasts. "Sheila and I are planning a fundraiser at Boots n' Brew. We have complete faith in you. We're just hoping you can sign a few things for the silent auction."

Silver nodded, though she couldn't really see very well as her eyes had filled with tears. The total sum of what was being offered finally coming into clear focus.

Layne walked up three steps until he was face-to-face with her. "There's many more. Everyone wants to help. We all want you to be a success." He turned his head left and right, looking at Jade and Amber. "We want all of *you* to be a success. All we ask is that you stay and complete the work you've started. You said it would impact not just this ranch, but the town and possibly the state. We're all behind you."

He took her hand. "And all I ask is that you let me love you through that time and beyond. Dr. Silver Collins, I ask you again. Will you stay?"

She blinked back her tears to focus on Layne's face. Why had she told him she didn't need a knight in shining armor when that's exactly what he was? He just wore a cowboy boots and hat instead of armor. She squeezed his hand in hers. "How could I not? You've given me everything I could have dreamed of, my life's work, and you."

Layne's lips lifted into a wide smile just moments before he took the last step and lifted her off her feet to twirl her around.

Her cowboy hat fell from her head, but she didn't care as he set her feet on the porch and they faced the group together.

Applause and cheers broke out below as her world and Layne's began their orbits around each other. Her heart filled, and she looked up at him. "I love you."

He smiled softly. "I love you, too. I didn't think my life could get any better, but you showed me what I was missing. Thank you for that."

She grinned. "You're welcome."

He threw his head back and laughed just before her arm was pulled away and she found herself in Jade's arms.

"You got a good one there."

No sooner had Jade let go then Amber pulled her in. "I'm so excited!"

Silver grinned. "Me too."

And it continued as people came up onto the porch and congratulated her and Layne on each other and/or on the new organization. She'd never stayed in one place long enough to have a community, so it was a completely new experience to have so much support. And after years of fighting for every dime and every new site, she was a bit at a loss. Of course, she knew it all stemmed from how well Layne was looked upon by everyone, but that they would extend their efforts on her behalf truly humbled her.

"Okay, everyone! I've got a chocolate chip pancake breakfast waiting in the clubhouse." Amanda waved people toward the quad.

"Don't have to ask me twice." Nash ran over to where Amanda stood.

Stacy stalked toward him. "I swear you have a bottomless stomach. How the heck do you stay so thin?"

"Hard work and good livin'." He grinned.

Vic bumped shoulders with Nash. "Liar."

"Hey, what would you know?"

Silver smiled at the banter as people moved *en masse* toward the clubhouse, Amber and Jade bringing up the rear.

Amber abruptly stopped. "Wait, we need Silver to celebrate."

Before Silver could answer, Jade hooked arms with Amber. "She'll come soon enough."

She smiled as her friends walked arm in arm to the celebration breakfast.

"Are you happy?" Layne stood across the porch from her, where the crowd had pulled him.

She strolled toward him. "I am, thanks to you."

He shook his head. "Only because I'd lost you everything. To be honest, I'm not even sure how this will all work out, but I'm hopeful."

She wrapped her arms around his neck. "In the last few days, I realized you were right. We shouldn't have had to deal with Benedict's abuse just to do a job we loved. But we had no choice. I think a small part of me felt denied the pleasure of hitting the man myself."

Layne wrapped his arms loosely about her waist. "I didn't realize how blood-thirsty you could be."

She cocked her head. "Six years can do that to a person. Are you sure you want me to stay? It could be even longer than that."

"I have no doubts at all. I've learned a lot from you, even that I can change if I want to."

"I don't want you to change. I love you just the way you are. If you can make accommodations so I can be part of your life, then I'm happy."

"Then I can move the rest of your belongings to my house tonight?"

"I'd like that." She smiled, far too happy to be in his arms again, and in his heart. She'd missed him more than she'd admitted even to herself.

His arms tightened about her. "I love you, Silver."

"I love you—" Layne's mouth claimed hers, kissing her as if they hadn't seen each other in three hundred years instead of three days. Her heart heated as the love in his kiss filled her.

Eventually, Layne released her lips. "We should probably head in to the breakfast Amanda prepared, especially if you still want to get up to the cave today."

She shook her head. "There's no longer a rush. If we can have access, even without funding, we can take our time and do it right." She released her arms from about his neck.

Layne let her go, but captured her hand. "Then maybe Tanner will let me have the day off and I can help you get settled in at the house."

She raised her brows. "You mean like help me test the king-sized bed in your bedroom?"

"Something like that." He grinned.

They started down the steps. "That would be lovely. It would also mean that Jade and Amber could get settled in at the Lucky Lasso Hotel and Saloon."

"That will only be temporary. The town manager used his discretionary budget to secure a house rental not far from where I live. It will be ready to move into within the month."

She stopped in her tracks. "That's what he meant by securing lodging?"

"Yes, but it's a small house. Only room enough for two people."

"Hmm, that was convenient."

Layne lost his smile. "I had to move forward hoping you would agree. I've never been so driven to accomplish something. To find a way to give you back what you had worked for all your life was on my mind every moment. It made me understand exactly how huge your loss was for you. If you didn't agree to my plan, I'm not sure what I would have done."

She touched his face with her fingers, still having a hard time believing he was real and he was hers. "We don't have to think about that. Now we can both work toward making Third Rock Discoveries a success."

He turned his face and kissed her hand before dropping a gentle kiss on her lips. "Do you like the name?"

She smiled. "It's perfect. It basically means Earth's Discoveries."

"Well, you did say you were the third rock from the cowboy, and this cowboy is very down to Earth."

She laughed and tugged him forward to the clubhouse. "It all makes sense—"

"Heeee-haaaw!"

She jumped before looking over her shoulder. "George! You scared me."

The burro stood staring at them.

Silver looked to Layne. "He's been doing that a lot the last few days. He yells at us, but doesn't come near. Do you think he's okay?"

"He's fine. He's just mad. He got sprayed by a skunk. It wasn't my fault, but I had to give him a bath with dish soap, hydrogen peroxide, and baking soda. He smells pretty now, but he wasn't happy. He's been mad at me ever since."

She let go of Layne's hand. "Then I think it's time you two made up."

Layne looked toward the clubhouse as if he planned to ignore the burro.

She was having none of that. "You need to be the bigger man. George doesn't understand what happened. He's just a child."

Layne finally turned around to face George. "I know. Hey, George. Are you ready to forgive me?"

George snorted.

Silver laughed. "Sounds like he enjoys holding a grudge. Come on, George. You have to admit you smell pretty good."

Layne glanced at her as if she'd lost her eyesight.

Upon closer inspection, she noticed all the red dirt on the gray burro as if he'd rolled in it. Obviously, George didn't like the smell of being clean. "He may be domesticated, but his wild instincts run deep."

Layne took a step toward George, who just watched him. "What do you say, buddy? Ready to forgive me? Silver did."

George just stared, but he didn't back away.

Layne took two more steps and stopped within arm's reach. "It's up to you, George."

She waited, holding her breath, wanting George to be friends with Layne again. For some reason, it felt like they needed that to make them all whole again.

George lifted his head, then stepped closer to Layne.

Layne scratched George behind his ears, the one place only Layne was allowed, and Silver sighed with relief. Then George leaned into Layne.

"Hey, don't be so pushy." Layne chuckled and held his hand out to her. "Come on. If I have to give him attention, you do, too."

She happily walked up to them and stroked George along his neck.

George gave a contented grunt, and she smiled. "Looks like all is forgiven."

"Until the next time I'm late on filling the hay feeder, he tangles with another skunk, or I look at him wrong." Layne gave George a final pat then stepped away.

She did the same. "I suppose we should get inside while there are still pancakes left."

He took her hand again, and they started forward. "They'll be pancakes left, don't worry. Be sure to eat plenty because we have a lot to do today to get you settled at home."

"Home. I like the sound of that."

"Me, too." Layne opened the glass door to the clubhouse, and she stepped inside. Everyone was talking, laughing, and eating. Big platters with stacks of chocolate chip pancakes were set about the tables. This was her new community. This was her new home.

Layne stepped beside her and wrapped his arm around her waist, letting her know he'd be by her side as they navigated their next steps together.

She looked up at him, too happy to voice her feelings, so thankful to have discovered this particular cowboy. In that moment, she silently promised him that she would always be his rock, no matter what.

Layne turned, noticed her looking at him, and lowered his lips to hers again.

Her heart filled with joy as he broke the kiss and gazed into her eyes. Then they turned and walked into their future together...complete with chocolate chip pancakes.

LAYNE GALLOPED BESIDE TANNER, anxious to have the day complete so he and Silver could enjoy a night out at Boots n' Brew. They had something to celebrate, thanks to Amanda. He'd been itching all afternoon to call Silver, but it was Amanda's news to tell.

As he and Tanner brought their horses to a stop before the barn, Nash, Silver, Jade, and Amber rode in, stopping by the corral where Vic met them to help with the horses.

He jumped down from Honor and immediately texted Amanda that they were all back.

Tanner dismounted and clapped a hand on his shoulder. "Are you texting my wife?"

"Sure am." He grinned.

Tanner shook his head. "I miss the days when this was a simple cattle ranch."

He shrugged off Tanner's hand. "No, you don't. Things are much more exciting around here now."

"What happened to you liking everything as it is?"

He laughed loudly. "I do. As it is now."

"Layne!" Silver dismounted quickly. "You're never going to believe what we found." She headed for him.

At her excitement, his own increased. He loved it when she was happy. It made their connection twice as real for him. "Is it an important find?"

She stopped halfway to him. "It's as big as you."

He laughed again and strode forward. "Tell me."

She held her hand out to her left. "Actually, Nash found it."

"Nash?" He looked to where Nash was helping Amber down from her horse. "Nash, what did you find?"

Amber spun around to face them. "He found where some of the Paleoamericans lived!"

Jade shook her head. "We don't know that for sure yet, but it does look promising."

Having reached Silver, he wrapped his arm about her waist. "That's excellent news. Where is this site?"

Silver looked to Nash. "Maybe you should explain."

Nash strode up, an ear-splitting grin on his face. "You know that huge boulder that rolled down and broke through the fence last year?"

Tanner joined them. "You mean the one where Lulabelle's calf got out."

"Exactly. I brought the ladies to look at the spot it came from and they found stuff in the dirt there."

Jade's single brow raised. "What he's really saying is we found two artifacts there with very little work, which means it could be something."

Layne looked at Silver. "Do you know which period?"

"Not yet. But I'm guessing between 11,000 and 8,000 BCE. So it would be from the oldest set of people, if I'm right."

Amber stepped up next to Jade. "I'm sure you are. Can you imagine if we could find all the sites where they lived from all the generations?"

"Whoa, not so fast." Silver put her hand out. "Even with this we have more than the three of us can handle."

Layne pulled her closer. "Maybe you could hire another person."

"I'd love to, but until we have funding, we're barely making it as it is."

"Maybe I can help with that problem." Amanda strode into their circle in her scrubs and stood next to Tanner. "I spoke to my father today. He took on the task of finding out what Mr. Nagle's grant required. As it turns out, it specifically calls for the current scientists to do the work. My father had lunch with the elder Mr. Sully and when Mr. Sully found out you three were no longer employed by Mr. Nagle, but now working for Third Rock Discoveries, he told Dad that Mr. Nagle's grant was null and void and would be pulled. So of course my father asked if they would like to fund TRD instead, and Mr. Sully said yes! It will take a couple of weeks, but it looks like you'll be getting all your funding back."

"Really?" Silver appeared stunned.

Layne squeezed her waist. "Really."

"OMG, we're going to be famous!" Amber squealed.

Jade smiled. "It looks like we have at least a year's work now and with this new discovery, we might be able to find more funding."

"New discovery?"

As Tanner filled in Amanda, Layne pulled Silver around to face him. "You, okay?"

She blinked and swallowed, but didn't say anything, just nodded.

"What is it?"

She looked around at everyone and her eyes began to water.

"Don't cry." He used his finger to gently wipe a tear from her cheek.

She smiled then looked at everyone, now silent and staring at her. "I'm humbled that you all have helped us so much. You didn't have to. We were just visitors, scientists, staying at your ranch, but if not for you, none of this, not the cave or the Thunderbird or the new site or the funding would have ever happened. It all would have remained hidden, possibly forever. It's this caring community that is bringing to life those who came before us and giving mankind a new understanding. That I, that *we*, could be a part of it is so humbling."

His heart swelled at Silver's words and he cupped her face in his hands. "Don't you see. You were the catalyst. Without you, we would not have looked or tried or mobilized." He hugged her to him, hating to see her cry, no matter the reason.

Jade cleared her throat. "Well, let's just say without each other, we wouldn't have been so successful."

"Exactly." Amber opened her arms wide. "It's time to celebrate."

"I suggest dinner and a bonfire." Nash looked to Tanner for approval.

Layne shook his head. "I think this calls for something bigger. Let's all go out to dinner at the Lucky Lasso and head over to Boots n' Brew."

Nash lifted his hat and reset it on his head. "Who's playing tonight?"

Amber elbowed him in the ribs. "Who cares? We're celebrating!"

Jade chimed in. "That sounds good to me. Amber, let's get back to the hotel and get changed."

"Yeah, I need to get the horses bedded down and home for a shower myself. I'll let Vic know in case she wants to join us. See you all at the Lucky Lasso." Nash tipped his hat before taking the reins of Amber's horse and his own and heading for the barn.

Amanda looked at Tanner. "You better hit the showers too. You smell like a horse."

Tanner grabbed her hand and started for the house. "Yes, but you love horses."

As everyone headed off in different directions, Layne remained where he was holding Silver. She lifted her head from his chest. "I thought you were looking forward to a night out, just the two of us."

"I don't know if you've noticed yet, but it's never just the two of us in this town. It's always us and anyone else nearby."

She smiled. "You're right. I hadn't thought of that. And in this instance, I'm thrilled to share our success with everyone who has been a part of it."

"So far." He gave her a sly smile.

"What do you mean, so far?"

"Just that I have faith that you will discover more, and that many more people will want to join you in your endeavor."

"You mean join *us*. We're a team now."

He wished it were warmer so he could feel all of her instead of her fleece coat, but that would have to wait for their shower. "Yes, us. All of us, but it was you that led us all to this moment. I thought I had the perfect life before I met you, but now I see it was missing that one thing every full life needs."

"What's that? Love?"

He lowered his head, his lips inches from hers and whispered. "No, someone who believes in aliens."

"Layne, you're—"

"A cowboy. I know. I'm your greatest discovery."

She smiled. "Also my largest and best and you can kiss me anytime."

He lowered his mouth to hers, unable and unwilling to refuse such an invitation from his amazing woman. Even as he enjoyed her familiar taste and her body pressed to his, he counted himself lucky to have had her drop into his life to stay.

She may believe in aliens, but he believed in her and that was all that mattered.

Once Upon a Haunted Haven

Disarming the Baron

Sci-fi Romance

The Eden Series

Cruise into Eden

Unexpected Eden

Eden Discovered

Eden Revealed

Avenging Eden

Beast of Eden

Bound by Eden

ABOUT THE AUTHOR

Lexi Post is a New York Times and USA Today best-selling author of romance inspired by the classics. She spent years in higher education taking and teaching courses about the classical literature she loved. From Edgar Allan Poe's short story "The Masque of the Red Death" to Tolstoy's *War and Peace*, she's read, studied, and taught wonderful classics.

But Lexi's first love is romance novels, so she married her two first loves, romance and the classics. Whether it's sizzling cowboys, dashing dukes, hot immortals, or hunks from out of this world, Lexi provides a sensuous experience with a "whole lotta story."

Lexi is living her own happily ever after with her husband and her two cats in Florida. She makes her own ice cream every weekend, loves bright colors, and you'll never see her without a hat.

Vist her website: https://www.lexipostbooks.com
Lexi Post Updates: http://bit.ly/LexiUpdate
Email Lexi: lexi@lexipostbooks.com

www.ingramcontent.com/pod-product-compliance
Lightning Source LLC
Chambersburg PA
CBHW030002010826
48973CB00007B/2131